CW01665910

# LOV
# NO BORDERS

A breathtaking and romantic historical saga

## GWEN KIRKWOOD

*Sinclair Family Saga Book 5*

JOFFE BOOKS

Revised edition 2023
Joffe Books, London
www.joffebooks.com

First published by Romaunce Books in
Great Britain in 2019

This paperback edition was first published in
Great Britain in 2023

© Gwen Kirkwood 2019, 2023

This book is a work of fiction. Names, characters, businesses, organizations, places and events are either the product of the author's imagination or are used fictitiously. Any resemblance to actual persons, living or dead, events or locales is entirely coincidental.
The spelling used is British English except where fidelity to the author's rendering of accent or dialect supersedes this.
The right of Gwen Kirkwood to be identified as author of this work has been asserted in accordance with the Copyright, Designs and Patents Act 1988.

Cover art by Jarmila Takač

ISBN: 978-1-80405-855-8

# CHAPTER ONE

A chance conversation with Lord Tannahill, a recent acquaintance, had alerted Adrian Fortescue to an astonishing possibility and offered him reason to ponder, and a chance to dream, however impossible those dreams might seem.

Adrian, known to his tenants and staff, as Lord Hanley, was the owner of the Silverbeck Estate, including all the farms for several miles around as well as the Silverbeck Hall and surrounding grounds and the whole of Silverbeck village. He commanded respect, more because he was a kind and honest individual, and a fair landlord, than because of his substantial wealth. Yet he was not a happy man. He had lost both his sons in the Great War but while his beloved wife had lived, they had shared their grief. Now he had no one to soothe his uncertainties about the future for he had no family to inherit, not even distant cousins. Yet this recent new friendship with Lord Tannahill had brought an unexpected glimmer of hope.

If anyone had told him he would seek counselling, much less confide the family's secrets with the modest wife of one of his own tenants he would have declared the idea absurd. He could not have said what prompted him to visit Moorend Farm and talk so frankly to Emma Sinclair, although he had learned to respect both Emma and her husband William, for their discretion and wisdom, as much as for their hard work and diligence as tenants. They had moved to Yorkshire from Scotland as a young couple with a baby son and taken on Moorend Farm when it was the most derelict and neglected place on the Silverbeck Estate. Over the years they had developed it into one of the best farms in the area with excellent cattle and horses which they bred and reared with pride, but it was not their success which led him to confide in Emma. He simply yearned to share his secret hopes with someone, and he knew instinctively that he could trust Emma Sinclair to be discreet. He considered that, being a woman, she might also understand Dorothea Whitelea's situation better than he did himself, especially since he knew the Sinclairs had had their own secrets to keep when they first arrived in Silverbeck as his tenants. It was only when Jamie, their eldest son, was thirteen years old that the truth about his birth had emerged. Ashamed when he was called a bastard by boys at school, he had run away to his Scottish grandparents in search of the truth.

Bob Rowbottom, the Silverbeck land agent, had heard the rumours and passed them on but neither he nor Lord Hanley had judged Emma and William for their human failings. Apparently one of the boys at school had overheard his elders gossiping and subsequently he had taunted Jamie Sinclair. There had been a serious fight between the boys at school when it was revealed that Jamie's parents had only been married the day before they arrived at Moorend, although Jamie was already several weeks old.

Adrian Fortescue, the man, was an ordinary human being, at heart. He had experienced joys and sorrows of his own. He understood a little of the shame Emma would have felt if she had arrived as a stranger and her secret had become common knowledge before they could earn the respect of the local people. He also sympathised with Jamie's shock and subsequent misery as well as his fear that he didn't really belong to the large and loving Sinclair family, even though that had proved to be misplaced for he was the youthful image of William Sinclair.

Whatever had happened in Emma Sinclair's past Lord Hanley knew she had a kind heart and was blessed with a wisdom beyond her years. It was for this reason he found himself at Moorend prepared to confide in her regarding a secret which clearly filled Dorothea Winkworth, or Whitelea, as she was now, with shame and humiliation. Yet it was this secret which had awakened his own hopes and dreams for the future. He couldn't blame any of his tenants for speculating about their futures as tenants of the Silverbeck Estate. Their daily lives depended on it — and on him. Everyone assumed, as he himself had believed, that he had no heir to carry on the estate after the deaths of Richard and Douglas, during the last year of the war.

The conversation between himself and Lord Tannahill had become more convivial, and their tongues liberated, by the brandies they had enjoyed. They had progressed to Christian names of Fordyce and Adrian. An exchange of confidences had followed after they had cast aside their habitual reserve. This was all the more surprising considering it was the first time Fordyce Redpath and his nephew, Rupert, had been to Silverbeck. While passing a group of family photographs in the hallway of Silverbeck Hall, Fordyce Redpath had remarked on the amazing resemblance between Richard and Douglas and the eight-year-old grandson of Fordyce's neighbour in Gloucestershire, Sir Thomas Winkworth. The name of Winkworth had caught Adrian's attention but in his merry state it did not register as clearly as it might have done.

When Fordyce's nephew entered later his attention, quite independently of his uncle's earlier interest, was also caught by the photographs of Lord Hanley's sons. There were several of Richard and Douglas as boys, and a more recent photograph of each of them in uniform. Rupert studied them curiously, drawing Lord Hanley's attention more acutely.

Later in the evening, when they were on their own again, and after more brandy than either was in the habit of drinking,

Fordyce remarked, 'They say we all have a double but I can't believe how closely my neighbour's grandson resembles your elder son, Adrian, even the way the boy sits his pony. We see him quite often because Sir Thomas Winkworth owns a small estate adjoining mine in Gloucestershire. He brings the boy to the hunt with him now that he's so proficient, or at least he did, but Winkworth's health has deteriorated recently. The resemblance is uncanny. Even Rupert noticed and I never think he is the most observant of young men.'

Adrian was silent for a moment, his mind a little hazy, and his words a trifle slurred.

'I remember Richard was engaged to a girl named Thea, yes Dorothea Winkworth. She came from Gloucestershire. Lady Hanley and I were very fond of her but we felt let down and disillusioned when she failed to keep in touch after Richard was killed. She had stayed with us several times but she didn't even return to Silverbeck for the memorial service. Shortly afterwards we heard she had married an old friend and neighbour by the name of Whitelea.

'Whitelea?' Fordyce sat up straight. 'Winkworth's grandson is named Ricky Whitelea. I recall Thea did make a hasty marriage,' Lord Tannahill reflected, but his mind was also a little unclear. 'I remember she gave birth to the boy barely seven months later, though rumours had it that her husband had been too badly injured during the war to sire a child. Whitelea was a decent man. He died eighteen months ago. His estate had to be sold. Thea and young Rick returned to live with Sir Thomas Winkworth. Although the boy is still quite young he is an excellent horseman. Thea used to ride to hounds too but we didn't see much of her after she married.'

The two men had gone on with their ramblings and eventually Fordyce convinced Lord Hanley so many coincidences were extraordinary.

'I think you should see the boy for yourself, Adrian. You are more than welcome to visit me at my home in Gloucestershire whenever you wish. I could arrange a meeting with the Winkworths.'

'I confess you and your nephew have aroused my interest,' Lord Hanley admitted. 'If Thea was expecting Richard's child it would explain why she did not return for the memorial service. My wife was so hurt at the time. We seemed to have lost so much, losing both our sons. I would certainly like to see the boy, but it would be better if Thea could be persuaded to visit here and bring him with her. Perhaps we could persuade her to attend a wedding which I am holding here at the Hall?'

'A wedding?' Fordyce echoed in surprise. 'Your own?'

'Good Lord, no.' Fordyce shook his head. 'I have persuaded William Sinclair, one of my best tenants, to allow me to hold the wedding reception here at Silverbeck Hall for his daughter, Marie. She is to marry Mark Blackford, whom you obviously know very well. I believe your nephew, Rupert, is to be best man. Both Marie and Mark have worked for me here at the Hall so it will give me great pleasure to give them, and the rest of my tenants, a day to remember.' He sighed. 'I admit I shall miss their youth and energy and their cheerful smiles. If dreams can come true and you have discovered I have a grandson it would be the greatest gift on God's good earth as far as I'm concerned.'

It had taken more than a personal invitation to a wedding at Silverbeck to persuade Dorothea to attend. Lord Tannahill had used all his powers of persuasion to induce the Winkworths to attend. In the end he had resorted to a frank talk with Dorothea's father in private. Sir Thomas Winkworth was far from well since a bad bout of bronchitis the previous winter so it was understandable that he had little notion to travel all the way to Yorkshire to the wedding of a young couple he barely knew and he sensed Dorothea was reluctant to visit Silverbeck again in spite of the warm invitations she had received from Lady Hanley after Richard's death. He had never understood her reasons for cutting herself off so completely. In desperation Lord Tannahill could see no other way and he put the case bluntly. He voiced his doubts that the late Thomas Whitelea could be the father of Dorothea's son and if he was not the boy's father, then who was? What had the boy to lose if it turned out that Lord Hanley was his grandfather? He might have much to gain. Lord Tannahill was considerate of people's feelings and he was alarmed when Winkworth clutched his chest and slumped into a chair, pale with shock. Eventually he recovered with the help of a drink of wine. Once he understood the reason behind the wedding invitation, he stuck to his decision to accept Lord Hanley's invitation to Silverbeck.

'It may be the last chance I shall have to travel again,' he told Dorothea, 'and I liked Lord and Lady Hanley on the two occasions we met before Richard was killed. You know I always felt we should have gone to his memorial service.'

'But Father it is such a long journey and you are not so fit since your last illness,' Dorothea protested.

'Fordyce Redpath has offered to drive us in his car. His nephew, Rupert, is best man at the wedding so he and his mother are travelling up a day earlier. Fordyce has bought a small second-hand car for Rupert to drive there.' Winkworth frowned. 'He said something about Rupert leaving the car for the bride and groom as a surprise wedding gift from him and his family. We shall not be the only guests staying at Silverbeck Hall. Apparently Mark Blackford, the groom, is some sort of relation to Lord Tannahill. He and Rupert were often here together during holidays from school and university. Rupert's mother will be returning home with us and leaving Rupert to travel by train with some of his friends who will be at the wedding.'

It had taken only one glance at Ricky Whitelea for Lord Hanley to realise the boy must be Richard's son. He looked exactly as Richard had been at the same age. He had the same wide smile and mischievous glint in his blue eyes. After the meal and formalities were over, Fiona Sinclair, youngest sister of the bride, had clasped the hand of her young niece, Marguerite, who was a flower girl. She had grasped the long skirts of her pretty bridesmaid's dress and they had chased her brother David and his new friend, Rick Whitelea, around the large garden, playing hide and seek or tag amidst a great deal of laughter. Rick had not been away to school yet so he had rarely played with anyone his own age and he enjoyed having new friends. He didn't want the day to end. He had been gentle and patient with Marguerite because her legs were too short to run as fast as his. He didn't want to go to bed that evening. He didn't want to go home the next day either. He pleaded with his Grandfather Winkworth and his mother to let him visit his new friends. Lord Hanley was delighted at this reaction. He invited Dorothea to prolong their visit. She refused. He sensed her agitation. She had been such an innocent, wide eyed young girl when Richard first brought her to Silverbeck. Happiness had shone in her dark eyes and she had the sweetest smile. Now she seemed reluctant to be in his company and she didn't meet his eyes when he addressed her. It made him unhappy to see her looking so anxious and tense.

Having seen the boy for himself Lord Hanley was convinced Rick Whitelea was Richard's son. Physically he was almost the image of the young Richard but he also had mannerisms which reminded him of Douglas and of his late wife, the way she had tilted her head to one side as though listening intently. How he wished she could have been here to share this discovery with him. How happy she would have been to know that a little bit of Richard still existed in the form of this sturdy small boy with his jolly laugh. She would have known how to put Dorothea at ease, how to draw out the truth and let Dorothea know how welcome she would be if she would come to visit them often.

# CHAPTER TWO

Lord Hanley was not sure how he could expect Emma Sinclair to help him but he found himself confiding in her anyway. She was a woman who owed nothing to education or lineage but she had an understanding of human nature and she was astute. When he tried to explain the situation she understood Dorothea's feelings at once, even while she sympathised with his yearning to get to know the little boy whom he was now convinced was his grandson. Emma didn't question his conviction about the child. She had already heard Mr and Mrs Rowbottom, as well as the Wrights from the Smiddy, voicing opinions on the amazing resemblance of the boy to the eldest son of Lord and Lady Hanley. They had spoken in wonder and without malice.

Also, Bob Rowbottom had called at Moorend, in his capacity of land agent two days after the wedding. He needed to discuss the possibility of them taking on the tenancy of Mountcliffe Farm for Alan, their second son. As usual these days he came into the kitchen with William for a cup of coffee and one of Emma's freshly baked scones.

'My wife and I gasped when we saw Miss Dorothea entering the church with her father and the child,' he said. 'We both realised immediately the boy must be Richard's son. He is the image of him. Joe Wright, the blacksmith, said the same thing.'

Emma suspected several of the other people who had lived in Silverbeck all their lives had probably made similar comments.

She faced their landlord uneasily. It was not her place to advise Lord Hanley on anything and especially something so personal, but he had asked for her opinion on how he should proceed with Thea when she didn't want to discuss the child, or anything else. Emma took a deep breath.

'I can understand that Mrs Whitelea will need time to accept that you feel only benevolence towards her and her child.' She shivered inwardly, remembering there had been nothing but malice towards herself from William's mother. Even William had never forgiven her bitter recriminations and spite. 'Perhaps, Lord Hanley, you could accept Lord Tannahill's invitations to visit him at his home? You would see Mrs Whitelea in her own surroundings. She might feel more confident, more secure, and more able to answer any questions you want to ask. I can understand her feelings. It takes time to — to believe in people's goodwill. So many are ready to condemn our mistakes. It is difficult to trust anyone if we already feel shame or guilt,' Emma suggested diffidently. She understood only too well how Mrs Dorothea Whitelea must feel. 'You did say her family were neighbours and attended the same local functions as Lord Tannahill?'

'Yes, it was at the hunt that Lord Tannahill's nephew first saw Rick. Rupert says he sits his pony well and clearly enjoys it. Richard was a splendid horseman.' There was a note of pride and longing in his tone.

'Then surely you should accept Lord Tannahill's invitation to visit? He does not strike me as the sort of man to issue an invitation unless he means it. If you were to meet the Winkworths at local functions perhaps you will be able to convince Mrs Whitelea she still has your respect and liking. She will need time to learn to trust you.' Lord Hanley looked at Emma doubtfully.

'She must know how I feel. We always made her welcome at Silverbeck Hall.'

'Maybe you did then, but consider how she must feel now the circumstances have changed so drastically, for her, as much as for you and Lady Hanley. She not only lost the man she loved, but she also lost the father of her child, if I understand the situation correctly?'

'I have no doubt Richard is the boy's father. If there is any shame then he must share the blame for it. He would never expect to die and leave Thea with his child.'

'Neither of them would have expected fate could be so cruel. It will take time and patience to convince Mrs Whitelea you truly want to get to know her for herself, as well as for her son. I-I can understand she will need reassurance. It may take several visits to convince her you do not blame her and she need not feel shame or guilt with you.'

'I see,' Lord Hanley said slowly. 'I am not a patient man, but I shall try. Thank you Emma. I knew you would understand.' Emma blushed. Their landlord never used the Christian names of any of his tenants, even less their wives. Despite his title and position she realised he was as human as any other man when he was troubled. He sighed heavily. 'You see things from a woman's point of view. I miss my wife so badly. She would have known how to handle the delicate subject of Rick's birth. You are too polite to say so but she would have said I am too eager. I want everything out in the open. I want to rejoice in the fact that I have a grandson. I want the world to know.'

'It may take some time to convince the boy's mother that you do not pity her, or worse, regard her with — with disapproval for her — her past,' Emma stammered, remembering her own humiliation. 'She clearly loves her young son. He is a happy child. We all saw that at the wedding.'

'If only we had known.' Lord Hanley sighed again. 'It was only a few months after Douglas's death that we heard Richard was missing and then the confirmation of his death too. There was no funeral for him but we held a memorial service in the church. Dorothea did not come. Then we heard she had married Whitelea, a man she had known all her life . . .' Lord Hanley could not hide the disappointment which they had felt. Emma felt it would take some time for real understanding and a true reconciliation on both sides.

* * *

Bob Rowbottom, the land agent, had had several meetings with William Sinclair to discuss taking over the tenancy of Mountcliffe but they had not reached a firm conclusion. It was the largest farm on the Silverbeck Estate and it was presently farmed by Gerry Wilkins, but for the past year, or more, rumours had circulated that he was giving up the tenancy, leaving his wife and grown up daughter and going to live in a cottage near the coast with Miss Cody, the daughter of the previous vicar. No one really believed Thora Wilkins would allow her husband to escape her selfish clutches. She regularly reminded people she was the wife of the largest tenant, while Irene Wilkins was as condescending as her mother. Gentle Miss Cody was popular with most of the people in the village, whatever transgressions she might be committing by communing with a married man.

'Is it really going to happen then?' William asked sceptically. 'The rumours have been circulating for more than a year, first one thing, then another. Alan and his lassie keep getting their hopes up, only to be disappointed when Gerry Wilkins changes his plans again. Has he actually given notice?'

'Yes he has. No going back this time. I have his notice in writing, though I don't think Thora knows that. He is due to quit at the end of September — shorter notice than usual but I needed to tie him down this time.'

'I can't believe Thora will let him get away with it. We all know she's the boss.'

'I believe he will have been to hell and back before he actually gets away from her,' Bob Rowbottom conceded with a shrug, 'but he is determined this time. Everybody knows about him and Miss Cody. Nobody seems to blame her, or Gerry. Thora is a cold fish if ever there was one and she's mean with everybody, especially the workers. At one point she tried to persuade me to let her keep on the tenancy herself but neither she nor Irene know one end of a cow from the other, even less how to care for animals or grow crops. I told her if she had had a son coming on, who had shown a real interest in farming, then Lord Hanley might have considered giving them a trial.'

'I don't suppose she gave you any praise for that,' William chuckled. 'According to the Wrights she barred poor old Gerry from the bedroom after Irene was born. She told him she had no intention of going through that again for any man.'

'Aye, I've heard that story myself. The Wrights hear all the gossip sooner or later with Joe being the blacksmith. Has he told you that Gerry has booked the auctioneers to hold the sale at Mountcliffe?'

'No! We hadna heard that! He'll be selling everything then?'

'So I believe. He says whoever is taking over the tenancy will have to bid for anything they want. He plans to buy a cottage for his wife and Irene near Penistone. She has a cousin living there. He told me he would like a divorce so he can make an honest woman of Miss Cody but Thora will not hear of it. He reckons he'll hold back any money settlement until she agrees.' Bob Rowbottom shrugged and raised his eyebrows. 'I do believe he has found his backbone at last. He should have stood up to Thora years ago. You don't know what a lucky man you are William Sinclair. Not many men have a wife like yours.'

'I know that,' William agreed with a smile.

'So, shall I tell Lord Hanley you're ready to sign the lease, you and your sons jointly? I believe he's been at Moorend a few times recently but he's not mentioned you reaching an agreement.'

'We havena discussed Mountcliffe. It was not me the laird came to see. It was Emma. He seems to have got himself into a state over the laddie who came to Marie and Mark's wedding. The wee fellow is the same age as Fiona. He seemed to enjoy running around with her and our David, and even wee Marguerite, Jamie and Rina's wee lassie. Fiona said he was very patient with her when her wee legs couldn't keep up.' William smiled, then sighed. He loved his children and his grandchildren but he was sorry that two of his family had returned to Scotland to live. Jamie and Marie seemed such a long way away. He didn't want Alan and Lynn to end up in Scotland as well.

'Aah, so Lord Hanley was looking for a wise word or two from your wife, eh? Well, I can't blame him. He's full of optimism about the lad one minute and down in the doldrums the next. I hope he can sort something out soon. My wife and I are convinced the boy is his grandson. It would explain why Miss Dorothea didn't come back to see them after Richard died. The problem might be proving the lad is Richard's — unless Miss Thea admits he is. She was a very decent, well brought up young woman. It will not have been easy for her.'

'No, I don't suppose it's easy for any woman in her situation. The war was responsible for a lot of heartbreak,' William reflected. 'Emma thinks Lord Hanley should go down to visit Lord Tannahill as often as he can and get to know her again to win her trust.'

'Mm, I suppose that's good advice. But to get back to Mountcliffe. One of our other tenants is interested and we have had an enquiry from a farmer on an estate near Doncaster who wants a farm to rent for his son. Both Lord Hanley and I would like Alan to take it on so long as he has your backing. We know the Tindalls are keen to help if they can, for Lynn's sake. They don't want their only granddaughter running off to Scotland to rent one of the farms on Mark Blackford's estate, even if he is your son-in-law now.'

'Neither do we,' William said drily. 'Alan's a good lad and a hard worker and we both think Lynn will make a good wife, but at the end of the day it's Emma and me who will be responsible if things don't work out at Mountcliffe and it's a big undertaking. Ideally I would like Alan to be responsible for the tenancy of all the lower ground at the same rent per acre as we pay here.' Bob Rowbottom opened his mouth to speak but William hurried on. 'Oh I know Mountcliffe is supposed to be the best farm on the estate but it doesn't produce any more than we do, here at Moorend. You have to admit Gerry had lost heart during the last few years. Some of the fields have been neglected. If he takes it on Alan will need to work hard to get them back into rotation and improve fertility. He'll have his hands full so I would like to take on the hundred and fifty acres of hill land myself, but at a lot less rent.'

'Aah,' Bob Rowbottom sighed. 'I knew you would want to strike a hard bargain.'

'A fair bargain. Gerry once told me he had never done much with the hill land because he's not interested in sheep and a lot of it is quite steep. Running a flock of sheep would increase the fertility in time and I believe Peter would take an interest. Then there's David. He is only twelve but he's almost as good as Jamie was at working the dogs. I don't want either of them going back to Scotland to farm. It would break Emma's heart if any more of our family went back. I believe it broke her own mother's heart when we came here.'

'Yes, I can understand that.' Bob Rowbottom scratched his head, then grinned. 'So what sort of rent have you in mind?'

'The same as we paid for Moorend when we first came here and a lease for five years until we get it improved.'

'Five years! You do drive a hard bargain, William. You understand I shall need to see what Lord Hanley says. He's the landlord and owns the land after all.'

'I know he does, but he listens to your opinion and I'm sure he would like to see it all farmed as well as it can be, even if the hill is rough and a bit wet in places. I'm sure I can improve it given time. We wouldn't put on breeding sheep to begin with because Alan will need all the lower ground, especially if both he and Peter are working the place, until Peter is ready for a farm of his own.'

'Mmm, speaking of Peter, what age is he now? I heard a rumour he was walking out with old Barclay's daughter.'

'Och, that's news to me.' William chuckled. 'He's only nineteen.'

'That's old enough to admire a pretty lass,' Bob Rowbottom grinned. 'It may not be long before you're pestering me for another farm to let.'

'All the more reason not to pay too much for Mountcliffe then if I'm to help all my sons into farms of their own,' William quipped swiftly.

'Ah, I should know better than try to make a good deal with a Scotsman!' the land agent said with an exaggerated sigh. 'I'll get away to the Hall now then and tell Lord Hanley the terms you would like for renting Mountcliffe.'

'All right,' William nodded. 'Let us know how we stand as soon as you can. There will be another wedding to arrange and a bit of bargaining to do with Gerry Wilkins over tenant's valuation no doubt.'

'Make sure you don't come face to face with his dragon of a wife then. Hey, and don't dismiss what I said about young Peter. I've heard that rumour from others besides the Wrights. She's a pretty lass and she's Barclay's only chick.'

'She's no more than a bairn if I remember her rightly,' William retorted irritably.

'She's sixteen going on twenty-six. She's a grand wee housekeeper. She's looked after her father since her mother died. She was barely fourteen but she left school straight away although I heard she was a bright lass at her lessons. Her father lets her help him with his accounts now and they always pay their rent on time.'

'Humph.' William grunted and Bob Rowbottom chuckled as he mounted his horse and rode away.

William had been fairly sure Gerry Wilkins would give up Mountcliffe eventually and he knew he should be honoured to be offered the tenancy on behalf of his sons, but he knew Bob Rowbottom would not have expected him to snap his hand off without discussing the conditions and trying to make a deal. It was not in William's Scottish nature to be subservient. Over the years they had developed a mutual respect for each other and a genuine liking of one man for the other. Equally important they both knew Lord Hanley was not a greedy landlord. He was a fair man and he appreciated the hard work most of his tenants put into making a living and paying their rents, but he did like to see the land well farmed and the animals cared for with diligence. As land agent Bob Rowbottom knew Lord Hanley admired William and Emma Sinclair because they had come to Moorend Farm as a young, newly married couple and at that time both the farm and the house were in a worse condition than any other on the estate. Now Moorend was one of the best and the Sinclairs had raised a family of hardworking sons and daughters any man could be proud of. The laird wanted to keep these hard working, well trained young people as his tenants. Already Jamie, the eldest Sinclair son, was settled in Scotland and his sister Marie had recently followed after her marriage to Mark Blackford.

* * *

It was customary at farm sales for the wife of the outgoing tenant to provide refreshments, usually helped by friends and neighbours. The actual day of the sale was always hectic both indoors and outside. Auctioneers and their clerks had to be fed as well as neighbours and other helpers who had set out machinery and carts and any other moveable equipment that was for sale. In the few days before the sale every pair of willing hands groomed and washed animals to present them at their best. Everyone who volunteered was welcomed to get the cattle into lots ready for the sale ring, and afterwards to guide them into pens and paddocks while they waited to be taken to their new homes. Usually any furniture from the farm house, which was not required by the owner or the new tenants, would be sold at the farm sale but Thora Wilkins had refused to allow either the auctioneers, Alan and Lynn, or anyone else to come into the house.

'Thora is making everything difficult,' Gerry Wilkins complained when Bob Rowbottom called to ask whether arrangements for the sale were under way. 'She has made a list of the things she wants taken to her new home but she refuses to let anybody in the house to see the rest. She and Irene have refused to provide refreshments or let the women into her kitchen to do it. She has booked a firm of caterers to come and she says they will bring all that's needed. God knows what that's going to cost me. I don't know how I've put up with such a woman all these years!' Bob Rowbottom bit back a smile. No one else knew how such a bluff, amiable man as Gerry had lived with Thora.

'Surely you will need some of the furniture yourself?' Bob Rowbottom suggested.

'No, we don't need much. Milly has more than she needs from her parents when they were at the vicarage. We have moved some of it to the cottage in Scarborough already.'

'If your wife and daughter are being so quarrelsome why don't you ask Harry Forbes to come a few days before the sale? He has bought a small cattle lorry. He could remove their furniture and take them to their new home? It will be short notice but it would give Alan Sinclair and his bride a chance to see round the house and buy what they want from you, before you move the rest into the barn for the sale?'

'That's not a bad idea! It will depend whether Thora will agree to leave before the sale though.'

'I should think she'll be glad to get away from the humiliation.'

'Aye, you could be right there. Maybe I'll tell her she'll have to arrange things herself, aye and pay for the move, if she doesn't want to leave when Harry Forbes can take them.' His eyes gleamed. 'That's what I'll do.'

Bob Rowbottom rode to Moorend next.

'Thora Wilkins is putting poor old Gerry through the mill to the last,' he said crossly as soon as he met William

Sinclair in the farmyard. 'She's refusing to make any of the food. It's what all the wives do to try and make the sale as successful as they can. She has ordered caterers to come and do it and Gerry will have to pay of course. When I left, he was going to see Harry Forbes to see if he would take Thora and Irene away with their furniture before the sale. If he arranges that, and if Alan and his bride want to buy any household stuff, they should be prepared to go and see Gerry at short notice. He has a good big dining table and a matching sideboard. They might be useful if Alan gets as many offspring as his father,' he chuckled. William grinned good-naturedly in response. He knew Bob Rowbottom secretly admired him and his large and happy family.

'Gerry says neither he nor Thora have room for big furniture where they'll be living. Miss Cody seems to have plenty of stuff from her parents so I reckon Gerry will be reasonable over the prices if Thora is out of the way. It would make things awkward if the auctioneers and clerks couldn't get access to the house. It's the custom to settle accounts in the farmhouse at a farm sale and most of the buyers are offered a feed when they go in to pay.'

Gerry Wilkins was surprised when Thora fell in with his plans, once she had had a night to think about it and talk it over with Irene. In fact she looked quite pleased with herself. The sale was fixed for Saturday the twenty fifth of September so Thora and Irene left Mountcliffe for the last time on Thursday morning. Once they had gone the atmosphere at the farm seemed almost light hearted, even though the men were busy clipping, cleaning and washing the cattle and the three pairs of horses. The machinery and tools had all been scrubbed and cleaned the week before and now they were laid out in numbered sale lots in the small paddock behind the house. Miss Cody baked bread and made a pot of soup each day at her cottage then brought it to the farmhouse to heat up on the range. She had cleaned out the mound of ashes and polished the doors with blacklead as soon as Thora had gone. She guessed Thora had deliberately left the place in a mess out of spite but she knew all about cleaning flues and she was undaunted. The old vicarage had had a range similar to the ones in most of the farmhouses. The men were grateful for hot soup and a bit of extra food with a short break in the middle of the day. Gerry told Milly everyone worked harder for the sustenance she provided. Thora had considered herself above such things as feeding workers, especially the ones who had come from neighbouring farms to lend a hand with the preparations. The regular Mountcliffe men had long since learned they could expect nothing from the snooty Mrs Wilkins or her daughter.

'I enjoy helping in my own small way,' Milly said shyly, 'but I'm glad I shall not need to cater for all the people you're expecting at the sale.'

'We want a good crowd so there will be plenty of folk to bid,' Gerry told her with a hearty laugh. 'I'd better make sure the caterers know they must bring plenty for everybody and I expect them to get here early to get set up tomorrow morning. Maybe I should try out the new-fangled telephone they've put outside the post office. It would save me riding over there. I know the shop has a phone at their end because I saw the number on the paper Thora left on the hall stand before she went. She said it was a widow and her daughter who are setting up a business. Thora probably intended phoning to check they were following her instructions. She seemed to like going over to that phone kiosk. I believe she thought she was the only one who knew how to use it so I hope I can manage it.'

'You will need some pennies to put in when the operator tells you. Take plenty, Gerry, in case you get cut off too soon, or something.' A small frown creased her smooth forehead. She wondered whether Thora really had meant to check on the caterers, especially now she would not be here herself. She tried to quell a premonition that something was wrong.

Alan and Lynn arrived to look over the house and see whether they wanted to offer for any of the furniture before it was put out for sale. They decided they would like to buy the dining room furniture and the carpet, as well as the kitchen table and chairs, so long as they could agree a fair price with Gerry Wilkins.

'All the stuff in the wash house will be to sell,' Miss Cody told them. 'I have my own tubs, rubbing board and mangle. Mrs Wilkins bought everything new for her cottage.'

'I'll bet she sent the bill to Gerry,' Alan said with a grimace.

'I'm afraid she did,' Miss Cody admitted. Gerry had been angry about that but she had soothed him down.

'We might as well have a look,' Lynn said. 'We shall need the everyday things more than a new carpet for the sitting room.'

'It is quite a good carpet in the sitting room and I'm sure Gerry will not want a lot for it because it's a lot of extra work lifting carpets for a sale. There is a greasy mark beside one of the chairs but I'm sure it could be lifted out with blotting paper and a hot iron.'

'We may as well take a look,' Alan agreed, seizing the chance to draw Lynn closer and give her a squeeze and a quick kiss the moment they were alone. They had both agreed they wanted a quiet wedding so it was all arranged for Tuesday morning. After the service and a luncheon for the close relations at the Tindal's place they would go away for two nights on their own and be back for the official term day on the thirtieth when they would take over the lease. They were both so happy to be getting married at last to care about a big wedding or a honeymoon. They knew they were fortunate to get a farm to rent, thanks to Alan's father.

Bob Rowbottom rode into the farmyard as Lynn and Alan emerged from the sitting room.

'I expect he wants to check everything is going according to plan for tomorrow,' Miss Cody said anxiously.

'I'm sure it will go well,' Alan said reassuringly. 'We have made a list of the things we would like to buy so long as Mr Wilkins doesn't ask too high a price.' Lynn handed over the list.

Miss Cody glanced at it and smiled.

'I would like to give you my two easy chairs as a wedding gift if you wouldn't be offended. I brought them with me from the vicarage. I have always loved them but they will match the sitting room carpet here and we haven't room for everything in our cottage in Scarborough. Gerry wants to take his favourite Berkeley chair and the three-piece suite in the sitting room. It was a present from his mother.'

They were interrupted when a flustered, angry looking, Gerry came rushing into the kitchen closely followed by Bob Rowbottom.

'She has cancelled the caterers! Now they can't do it at such short notice. What the hell am I going to do?' He flopped onto a kitchen chair and put his head in his hands. 'I shall be the biggest disgrace ever — a farm sale and nothing to eat. I must feed the auctioneers and their staff at least. How could she . . .'

'It's all because of me!' Miss Cody burst into tears. 'Thora wants to retaliate and prove I would never have made you a g-good farmer's w-wife. If only I had known yesterday . . . There's so little time . . .' Although Miss Cody was old enough to be Lynn's mother Lynn was a practical girl and she couldn't bear to see the gentle Miss Cody so upset. She moved to her side and put an arm around her heaving shoulders as she tried to control her tears.

'As Grandma Tindall says, "there's always a way". I'll help. I'll start baking cakes as soon as I get home. I'm sure Grandma will help too and I know she was churning butter today.'

'My mother will help too,' Alan said confidently, knowing his mother would never let anybody down, nor would she want to see Thora Wilkins reaping her revenge. 'Our Janet will bake pies or cakes if we ask her. She loves to bake and I know she'll come to help here tomorrow if you want her. Mother will probably bring Polly to help as well.'

'All the local wives usually help at a farm sale,' Bob Rowbottom said slowly. 'They would have come and brought food willingly if they had thought they were wanted.'

'Thora made it clear she didn't want any of them in her house.' Gerry grunted.

'It is such short notice,' Miss Cody said, trying to hold back tears. 'People may not have spare flour and yeast for the bread, or enough butter and sugar for cakes and pies.'

'I'll go across and ask Mr Nicol if he will make as many extra loaves and rolls as he can get in his ovens tonight' Gerry said. 'He knows I'll pay the bill before we leave. I can do the same from his grocery. Will flour, sugar and that margarine stuff do? I hear folks are using it to bake.'

'That would certainly save all the butter we can get for the sandwiches,' Miss Cody said hesitantly.

'Mrs Wright is Polly's Aunt. I'm sure she will make something. She'll certainly spread the word to everybody coming to the Smiddy, or passing by,' Alan said. 'Cheer up Miss Cody. I'll bet people will come and bring all sorts of food in the morning — just like in the bible with the loaves and fishes.' He patted the little woman's shoulder comfortingly. 'We still have a ham and a side of bacon hanging in the pantry at Moorend. I'm sure Mother will saw off a large piece of ham and boil it overnight in the wash boiler. That's what she does when the men come with the thrashing machine. That would make lots of sandwiches.'

'And maybe Mr Nicoll will have a cheese he could spare if you tell him the caterers have let you down,' Lynn suggested. 'Could you ask him Mr Wilkins?'

'The young folk are right,' Bob Rowbottom said admiringly as Miss Cody dried her tears on the bottom of her apron.

'Yes, that would be a big help,' she said brightening. 'I have made lots of jars of chutney. It would go with the cheese. I still have tomatoes in my greenhouse and lettuce. There's plenty of vegetables in the garden. I will go home now and get them prepared for a big pot of barley broth. That will help fill people up and warm them if the weather is cold.'

'Fine,' Bob Rowbottom nodded, 'my wife makes good lentil soup. I'll ask her to make a pot full and I'll bring it with me tomorrow morning. Alan's right, we'll have a feeding of the five thousand yet. I'll ride to the Tindalls now, Lynn. They live the furthest out and they will need a bit of warning. I'll call at Moorend and warn your folks too, Alan. Maybe I should call at the blacksmith's on my way through the village? Alan's right, the Wrights will have the news spread in no time.'

'We can't thank you enough Mr Rowbottom,' Gerry Wilkins said, his voice gruff with gratitude. 'You have always been an understanding land agent but nobody would expect you to help us out of this pickle. I hope somebody tells Thora her spiteful trick didn't work.'

'Oh Gerry, wait until we see how we get on tomorrow,' Miss Cody said nervously.

'I could help you make a list of the things we all need to do,' Lynn suggested, 'then we shall not all do the same thing. Just you wait and see, it will be the best sale people have ever attended.'

'You'll make this lad a grand wife, lass,' Gerry said. 'You can buy the furniture you have already chosen, but you can have anything else you want thrown in. We'll not bother putting any of it out for sale. You both deserve any help we can give you. Oh, except my double bed. We're taking that with us, aren't we Milly?' Miss Cody blushed and nodded. Alan and Lynn beamed at each other. They already considered themselves very lucky to be getting a farm to rent as well as one of the best houses on the estate, complete with a proper bathroom.

'We shall be very glad to accept your kindness, Mr Wilkins, thank you,' Lynn said. 'Grandad and Grandma Tindall are buying us a bed for a wedding present and you will be saving us a lot of money on all the useful everyday things.'

'Aye, we appreciate that Mr Wilkins,' Alan agreed, 'Whatever spare money we have we shall spend it on buying some of your best cows and we hope to get a pair of your horses. My father reckons they are well bred.' He grinned saucily, 'well for Shires that is. You know he's a Clydesdale man, but so long as they can work, Shires will suit me.'

* * *

In spite of the promises of help Gerry knew his Milly was worrying herself sick. He guessed she would be up half the night cooking and fretting. He needed to do something about it. Thora had always kept a live-in maid so he knew Milly would not stay with him at Mountcliffe overnight with Emily in the house, even though she was moving on to a new place on the first of October. He waited until the village was silent then he stole across to Milly's cottage. He persuaded her to drink some hot milk, well laced with brandy, then he took her to bed and made sure she slept. The following morning he was back across at Mountcliffe and ready to start the milking before either of his two men or Emily appeared. He was a happy man and wished he had met Milly when he was in his twenties. She was warm and loving and as different to Thora as it was possible to be.

Emma arrived at Mountcliffe early to bring the large boiled ham and two gallon cans of soup in the pony and trap, as well as a large basket of baking. Her daughter Janet had accompanied her to drive the trap back to Moorend in time for William or Alan to take the milk to the railway station. Miss Cody was just scurrying across to Mountcliffe from her cottage with two baskets full of provisions.

'Oh Mrs Sinclair, I'm so pleased to see you,' she said breathlessly. 'Emily promised to clean the range and get the fire going before she went to the milking but . . .'

'And I believe she has kept her word. I see the smoke rising and we're both here now, Miss Cody,' Emma said soothingly. 'Polly and Janet are coming to help when they finish the milking and get the essential chores done. They will give the men folk a good breakfast first, then William, Alan and Peter are coming to help sort out the cattle or send them in and out of the sale ring, or whatever Mr Wilkins wants done. I'm sure it will be a good sale.'

'You, and your family, are all being so good to us and I know what a busy life you have.'

'We hope you and Mr Wilkins will be very happy together. You both deserve it.' Miss Cody blushed and smiled as shyly as a young girl.

'I'm sure we shall be happy, even if we are living in sin,' she added wistfully.

'That may get sorted out sooner than you think,' Emma said calmly. 'We all know Thora liked to have plenty of money so she will probably be glad to agree to a divorce.'

'I do hope you're right. I don't care about money if Gerry and I can live together in peace.'

The morning had dawned bright and clear and it seemed that everyone in and around Silverbeck was up with the larks to get their own work done and cows back to the fields before they came to Mountcliffe. Mrs Wright arrived from the Smiddy, along with most of the farmers' wives who lived in and around the village. They brought baskets of cakes, pies, biscuits, scones, butter and homemade jam. Mr Nichol, the baker, had supplied all the loaves they would need. He had never liked Thora Wilkins and her whining, snooty ways so he had worked long into the night to make sure Miss Cody had enough bread to feed everyone who attended the sale. He would feel a small triumph himself if he could help make the day a success and thwart Thora's mean trick. The butcher shared his feelings and he sent four large steak pies. Two farmers' wives brought their paraffin stoves to help with heating the soup and boiling water for the tea. They all knew that reports of the sale would get back to Thora one way or another.

Miss Cody had reorganized the room Gerry used as his office so the auctioneers' clerks could work in there instead of the dining room when the buyers came in to pay for their purchases and take refreshments. Emma was surprised when Lord Hanley arrived with Bob Rowbottom. They had come in the laird's car and between them they were carrying the small milk churn which Bob Rowbottom had borrowed from

Emma yesterday evening. His wife had sent a large quantity of lentil soup which smelled delicious.

'My word that's really kind,' Emma said. 'Mrs Rowbottom must have spent her whole evening peeling vegetables and making soup to send us so much.'

'I grew the carrots and helped to peel the onions,' Bob Rowbottom offered with a grin. 'I reckon everybody in Silverbeck wants to see Gerry and Miss Cody make a success without Thora.'

'Did you really help peel the vegetables?' Emma asked incredulously and blushed because she had never visualised the land agent would be domesticated. 'We're truly grateful, aren't we Miss Cody?'

'We are. It is just as your son, Alan, predicted when he quoted the parable of the loaves and fishes. I should have had more faith myself. I had no idea everyone would be so kind and helpful when we were left in the lurch. We are all so fortunate to have enough food for ourselves when I think of all the miners' women and children who can barely afford one meal a day. The strike has gone on for five months now.'

'Some of the miners have gone back to work this past fortnight but I believe there are thousands still on strike,' Emma responded seriously. She had said several prayers for them all herself.

'Well for today we all want Gerry's sale to be a great success,' Mr Rowbottom said cheerfully, hoping to change the subject. 'Have you met Lord Hanley, Miss Cody?'

'I-I have seen you in the distance and at church, M'Lord,' Miss Cody stammered, blushing and looking as though she would like to disappear through the floor as Gerry came into the house. He had seen the laird's car arrive. He sensed Milly's embarrassment and went straight to her side and laid a comforting arm around her shoulders but that made her blush more than ever.

'I'm pleased you could come, Lord Hanley,' Gerry greeted him. 'I didn't know you had returned from your visit down south.'

'I returned yesterday evening,' Lord Hanley responded with a smile. 'You know Mr Rowbottom and I always attend the sales of our own tenants if we can. I'm sure you will have a successful day judging by the number of people arriving.'

'Aye.' Gerry shuddered and his arm tightened on Milly's shoulders. 'I thought the whole thing was going to be a disaster yesterday afternoon when I discovered Thora had — had left us in the lurch. I can't tell you — or any of these good Samaritans — how grateful Milly and I are for so much help and support, not to mention Mr Rowbottom here for spreading the word of our predicament.'

'Mr Rowbottom not only spread the word,' Emma said, 'He and his wife have made us a large cauldron of lentil soup.' Gerry's eyes widened as he looked across at the two men and Emma thought she glimpsed the shine of a tear as he expressed his gratitude.

* * *

Lord Hanley stayed throughout the sale. He ate in the dining room with the auctioneers and Bob Rowbottom. Emma thought he looked tired and a little down in spirits when he thought no one was watching. She knew he had been down to Gloucestershire to visit Lord Tannahill and both Marie and Mark had told her he didn't enjoy long drives alone. She understood why he was desperate to become reacquainted with Mrs Thea Whitelea and he must have stayed until the very last day to make the most of his visit, then driven all the way home yesterday to be here for the sale.

Towards the end of the day most of the farmers had left to get home for milking, including Emma's own menfolk, taking Polly, Janet, Fiona and David with them in the pony and trap. There were still a lot of dishes to clear and washing up to be done so William had agreed they would manage the milking at Moorend without her if she wanted to help Miss Cody with the clearing up. The auctioneers were still working in the office and had just had a fresh tray of tea and scones so Emma was alone in the dining room piling cups and plates onto a tray when Lord Hanley came in. He flung himself into an easy chair by the fire and sighed.

'I will give you a lift home in my car when you are finished here, Mrs Sinclair.' Emma opened her mouth to protest but he waved his hand at her. 'I saw William and your family leaving so I told them I would see you home with the various pans and other equipment you brought. I believe it will have been an exceptionally good sale. I suspect Thora Wilkins did Gerry a favour by clearing out. There's nothing puts people off more than a sour face and a sharp tongue. I'm afraid she had both.' He sighed heavily. Emma raised her eyebrows in surprise. She had never heard Lord Hanley criticise any of his tenants. She knew from Bob Rowbottom that there were qualities he despised but he never discussed his views with anyone else.

'You seem tired Lord Hanley. Shall I bring you a fresh pot of tea and a ham sandwich or a buttered scone?' she asked uncertainly.

'I am a little weary after the long drive yesterday,' he admitted. 'Unfortunately my visit was not a great success so it seemed a wasted journey.'

'I am so sorry to hear that. Was Mrs Whitelea not at home while you were there? I have heard Lord Tannahill usually manages to arrange things to his satisfaction. Rina, my daughter-in-law, knows him quite well. He bought some of her family's property in Scotland. He does seem a charming man as well as being influential.'

'I agree. He certainly made me very welcome and he has assured me I shall be welcome to visit at any time. He suggests I should make frequent visits, even if they are short ones. He thinks I shall have to be very patient with Thea. Lady Hanley would have told you I am not noted for my patience,' he added wryly.

'I think that applies to most men,' Emma said with a smile.

'Young Rick joined us twice for the hunt and I felt we had known each other since the day he was born. He talked so freely and with a child's honesty. Your youngest son and daughter seem to have made a great impression on him at Marie's wedding. He says he would like to go to school with other boys and girls — as they do. He is very confident on his pony, a little too daring in fact for my peace of mind. I suspect he needs a man's influence but I gather his Grandfather Winkworth has not been in good health for the past two years. His health was the reason Thea gave for being unable to join us at the hunt, or at an afternoon gathering which Lord Tannahill had arranged for some of his neighbours, but she did invite us to visit her father at home when he was able to leave his bed chamber. It is true he was finding it difficult to breathe. Lord Tannahill and I visited at the time Dorothea had stated but we were shown to her father's sitting room by the housekeeper. She said Mrs Whitelea had taken the opportunity to do some shopping while her father had company.'

'I suppose that might be true,' Emma said gently. 'She may not like to leave her father alone too long.'

'Mmm, I suppose so. It was the housekeeper who brought us tea. I can't help thinking Thea was staying out of the way until we had gone. Young Rick joined us the moment his tutor released him from his lessons.' Lord Hanley smiled reminiscently. 'At least he seemed pleased to see us. He reminds me so much of Richard. There is no doubt in my mind that he is my grandson.'

Emma was surprised at Lord Hanley talking to her so frankly. She was only the wife of another of his tenants after all. She wondered what he would have thought if he had seen her when she was a lowly kitchen maid at Bonnybrae. She shuddered. She tried not to dwell on the past. She decided Mr Rowbottom was probably right when he believed Lord Hanley was lonely since his wife's death. It must be hard to lose his wife and both of his sons. He didn't seem to have any close relations. That was probably the reason he had taken both Marie and Mark to his heart. He had enjoyed their youthful company and he had certainly been generous to both of them when they had worked for him and lived in his home.

A short time later Emma carried a tray of tea and refreshments into the dining room and found Lord Hanley asleep in the chair beside the fire. She set the tray on a small table near his chair and crept out.

# CHAPTER THREE

It seemed they had no sooner recovered from the buzz of the Mountcliffe sale than it was Alan and Lynn's wedding day. They had insisted on having a small wedding with only their families present but the Sinclair family alone made a small crowd. Marie and Mark drove down from Scotland, bringing four-year-old Marguerite with them. The little girl looked on her Aunt Marie like a second mother because Marie had spent so long at Bonnybrae while Rina was desperately ill, before the twins were born.

'It's so lovely to see you all,' Emma said, hugging Marie and then Marguerite who gave her a wide endearing smile, so like her mother's. 'Does Rina not mind you bringing Marguerite all this way without her?'

'No, she says she is pleased for her to get to know all her family. She thinks the Sinclair's are a warm and friendly family and she wants Marguerite to grow up knowing her Yorkshire aunts and uncles and her cousins.'

'We're just like any other family,' Emma said. 'You have all had your squabbles at one time or another.'

'I know we have,' Marie chuckled, 'but we're always there for each other if any of us are in trouble. You and Dad have set us a good example. Rina doesn't have any family of her own. You knew her brother died in the war, I think? She never hears from her mother since she went to live in France. She doesn't even have an address.'

'When you put it like that it is probably good for Marguerite to grow up knowing she has family here then.'

'She kept talking about seeing Rick on the way down. That was the little boy at our wedding who was so good at looking after her. I tried to explain he could not be here but she would still see Fiona and David.'

'Yes, Fiona is looking forward to seeing her. She loves children and thinks she would like to be a teacher. Meg and Ranald will be bringing Donald but he is not big enough to run around with them yet.'

'Jamie and Rina would love to have come and bring Liam and Reggie but you know how busy they are and Jamie doesn't like to leave Uncle Jim with all the work to do at Bonnybrae either.'

'We understand. Farmers can't drop everything for a wedding. How are you and Mark getting on, Marie? Are you happy up in Scotland?'

'We're fine, aren't we Mark?' Marie turned to her husband with a warm smile. He set down the suitcases he had brought in from the car and moved to her side. He put an arm around her shoulders.

'We certainly are. I don't know how I should have managed our small estate without Marie to keep me right.'

'That's not true, Mum, but Mark is kept busy, especially now he is getting customers wanting him to mend their cars and other machines. Our house is almost finished so we shall be busy moving into East Lowrie when we get back. It will be easier when we are near the village and he can build a workshop of his own nearby. I'm sure you'll like it, Mum. I do hope you and Dad will come up to Scotland and visit us?'

'We'll try but I think we shall be busier than ever now that Alan has got the tenancy of Mountcliffe. William is going to fence off the hill and run sheep there. He is teaching

David to work his two collie dogs. He thinks he has a natural instinct for it, like Jamie had.'

'The Tindalls will be pleased for them, aren't they?'

'Oh yes, and Lynn will make a good wife. She worked really hard to help Miss Cody at the sale.' Emma went on to tell her daughter all the news and how Thora Wilkins had cancelled the caterers and never told anyone.

'She would want the sale to be a disaster and to show Miss Cody in a poor light. As it turned out everyone was happy to help once Thora moved out. The sale was a great success. Alan bought ten cows.'

'There will be no rest for him and Lynn when they return from their brief honeymoon then,' Marie grinned.

'No they'll have plenty of work. They are going straight to Mountcliffe when they come back. Gerry Wilkins has arranged for him and Miss Cody to move to Scarborough the same day.'

'I think I will take Marguerite for a little walk to meet Fiona and David on their way home from school,' Mark said. 'It will do both of us good to stretch our legs after the long drive and it will give you peace to catch up on all the news.'

'Fiona will be delighted to see you both,' Emma said with a smile. She liked her new son-in-law more every time she saw him.

Fiona and David were having a rare day off school for the wedding so their friends were very envious. Marguerite danced up and down with excitement. Lynn had a brother but no sisters or cousins for a bridesmaid so, at ten years old, Fiona felt quite important. Marguerite followed her example and behaved beautifully but as soon as the luncheon was over she asked several times when Rick was coming to play with them. Emma was surprised that she remembered him until she thought about Jamie. He had remembered many things clearly when he was a small boy, even younger than his daughter was now, including where the gypsies lived. He had thought he could toddle off across the fields to see them by himself. She explained that Rick lived a long way away and they didn't know whether he would come back to visit.

* * *

Lord Hanley made another visit to Gloucestershire at the beginning of October but again he felt he had made no progress with Dorothea Whitelea. He returned feeling discouraged. He rode down to Moorend Farm hoping to find Emma Sinclair on her own for once. He knew William often enjoyed a visit to Wakefield on market days and usually met his cousin, Drew Kerr. Their Scottish ties had been a bond ever since William and Emma moved down to Yorkshire but their two families were even closer since William's daughter Meg had married Drew's son, Ranald. Both men were proud of Donald, their healthy young grandson.

Emma's maid, Polly, was in the kitchen but she showed him into the small sitting room where a fire was already lit to dispel the autumn chill.

'Mr Sinclair is at the market your lordship,' Polly mumbled uncomfortably. 'I could get Mistress Sinclair. She has gone to collect eggs from the hen houses in the paddock.'

'That will do very well, Polly, thank you. How is your aunt, Mrs Wright? The last time I was at the Smiddy to get my horse shod she had a very bad cold. Your uncle seemed worried.'

'She's nearly recovered, thank you, Sir. It's not often my aunt ails anything so we were a bit concerned. Mrs Sinclair let me go down to Silverbeck two afternoons to help her.'

Polly scurried away to get Emma and take over the egg collecting. Lord Hanley could be a charming man and he chose to put the woman at ease but Polly always felt awkward in the presence of gentry, or even with Bob Rowbottom, the land agent.

Emma hurried indoors but she stopped to tidy her hair and put on a clean apron before she joined Lord Hanley in the sitting room. She was glad she had lit the fire early.

Sometimes William brought Drew Kerr back with him if there was not much doing at the market or when either man had a particular horse or heifer on which to share their opinions.

Lord Hanley was standing with his back to the room staring pensively out of the window which looked down to the little burn, or beck as it was known locally, and beyond it down the valley towards Silverbeck village. He turned when she entered and greeted her pleasantly as always. She beckoned him to take a seat by the fire.

'Did you enjoy your visit to Gloucestershire, Lord Hanley?'

'I didn't have any more success than the last time,' he admitted disconsolately. 'Sir Thomas Winkworth is not in good health. In fact he seems unlikely to recover completely. Even so I think Thea is using him as an excuse to avoid me. She doesn't forbid Rick to join us at the hunt though, so long as Lord Tannahill invites him and promises to keep an eye on him.'

'That is a good sign then. You seem to get on very well with him?'

'Oh yes, even if I didn't believe he was my grandson, he's a fine boy, polite manners and full of questions on all kinds of things.' He sighed heavily. 'If only my wife had been here. She would have known how to put Thea at ease. As a woman yourself, Emma, can you offer any advice? I would ask Mrs Rowbottom but I doubt if she has your wisdom or your experience of life. You have raised a large family and made a good job of them all. You have also known the grief of losing two of them. Can you imagine how I feel?'

'I understand you would dearly like to know your grandson better, especially when he reminds you so much of your own son. I know you would like to help him in some way too, b-but I can also understand a little of how his mother must feel.' Emma flushed.

'Please, Emma, can you forget I'm your landlord for once,' Lord Hanley pleaded. 'Regard me as any other human being who needs your advice. Say what is in your heart and don't be embarrassed if you think I shall find it painful. Please? I need help if I'm ever to break through Thea's reserve.' He sounded so desperate Emma could not help feeling some sympathy.

'You must forgive me Lord Hanley if I try to see things from Mrs Whitelea's point of view rather than your own then?'

'Yes. Tell me plainly what is in your mind, anything which might help me win Thea's confidence. Do you think she feels shame because she has had a child sired by my son when he was not her husband?'

'Y-yes!' Emma said promptly. 'I-I'm sure she will feel that way, even if in her heart she is pleased to have his child as a reminder of their love. It will be more painful if seeing you reminds her of your son. She may have realised that you recognise Rick as your grandson because of his resemblance to his father.'

'I see . . . But how am I to break down the barrier she has erected so that I can tell her I do not blame her? In fact, I am delighted to know a part of Richard lives on through her.'

'I think you will need to earn her trust first. Reassure her that you only want to help her, as well as your grandson. She may be afraid you want to take him away from her . . .'

'Aah, I would never do that. It would be cruel to separate a child from his own mother and there is no doubt she loves him dearly. She is a good mother.'

'Then you must convince her of that. M-maybe you could begin by telling her you feel guilty on behalf of your son? He gave her the child. It was not his fault that he died before he could marry her, but it was not hers either,' Emma said diffidently. 'If — if you could convince her that you feel you owe her a debt on your son's behalf? Assure her that all you want is to make up to her for all the suffering she has had. After all she must have loved your son very much. She believed he intended to marry her?'

'Oh yes, there was no doubt about that. They were betrothed and planning to marry as soon as he could get leave, however short. His brother had already died fighting for his country and Richard didn't want to go back, but he had a strong sense of duty to his men,' Lord Hanley asserted. 'But Emma, I am beginning to see things from a different perspective. You see this from a woman's point of view.'

'Yes, I do, because it is always the women who bear the shame in such circumstances.'

'Then I must make Thea forget the disgrace she must have felt when she discovered she was expecting Richard's child. I must persuade her I am the one who feels shame for the part Richard played. I need to convince her I want to try to make amends if that is possible. I am sorry from the bottom of my heart she has had to bear this on her own even while I rejoice because she has a child who is a living part of Richard. You believe I should tell her I want to share the responsibility for Rick's future on behalf of his father?'

'Y-yes, something like that. Tell her what you have just said to me.' Emma bit her lip.

'If only Thea would give me a chance to talk to her. She is polite but she doesn't give me any opportunity to discuss anything. Lord Tannahill has invited me back for Christmas and he has promised to invite Thea and her father and Rick to join us at some time during the festive season. I am looking forward to it and to buying a gift for Rick, and perhaps for Thea too, but more than anything I long to clear the air with Thea so that we can be friends again. She is an intelligent young woman and we shared many stimulating discussions.'

'I expect she has erected defences against the world and not just you, Lord Hanley,' Emma said, remembering how defensive she had felt when Jamie was born and she had had to register his birth herself because she had no husband. She shuddered remembering her humiliation, the bitter resentment of Mrs Sinclair, William's mother; then her aunt's sneering scorn. But her mother had written her letters, always giving her a ray of hope that her child would be accepted into the Greig family, even though her parents did not know then who the father of her child could be. It was those letters, and later the letters from William, once he discovered where she was, that had given her strength and hope for the future. 'Perhaps you could write to Mrs Whitelea?' she said, coming out of her reverie. 'Surely she would read a letter? She would know then what is in your heart and that you only want to help. Assure her that you would never try to take Rick away from her. If she still will not talk with you I don't know what else I can suggest.'

'A letter? Of course! Why did I not think of that . . . ? Thank you my dear . . .' He broke off as the rattle of teacups sounded outside the door. Emma hastened to open it, thinking it was Polly with the tray of tea and cake she had asked her to bring when she returned from gathering the eggs, but it was her daughter, Janet.

'Are you ready for a drink of tea?' Janet asked cheerfully, setting the tray down on a small side table. Emma noticed with approval that Janet had brushed her curly dark hair and put on a clean white apron. She set out the teacups with calm efficiency.

'Shall I pour, mother, or shall I leave you to talk in peace?'

'We have done our talking, my dear,' Lord Hanley said, before Emma could reply. He felt more optimistic than he had for weeks. 'A cup of tea would be very welcome. Why don't you join us? Your mother is a woman of wisdom and she has given me some very good advice.' Janet smiled and raised her dark eyebrows, her green eyes dancing with amusement as she met her mother's gaze.

'I thought it was Polly bringing in the tea, dear. Bring another cup and saucer and join us' Emma said. 'I suppose your father is not back from the market yet?'

'No, he has not returned but Polly is giving Cliff and her brother, Tom, their tea in the kitchen before we start the milking. Fiona and David will be home from school soon.'

'Well there's no reason why you shouldn't join us if Polly is there,' Emma said with an encouraging smile. 'Will you have a buttered scone, Lord Hanley? Or would you prefer the cakes?' Emma asked.

'A buttered scone first please. Bob Rowbottom always speaks highly of your cakes and scones and your hospitality,' Lord Hanley told her. Emma noticed he looked more at peace with himself than when he first arrived. She would be glad if anything she had said could help him become friends with his grandson and the woman who should have been his daughter-in-law if fate had not been so cruel.

Janet returned with her own plate and cup and saucer.

'How old are you now young lady?' Lord Hanley asked. 'I think you must be at the age to learn to drive a car?'

'I was seventeen last February,' Janet said.

'Well then perhaps your parents would allow me to teach you to drive my car as I taught Marie.' He looked at Emma. 'Mr Thorpe, the headmaster at Silverbeck, tells me all your children are intelligent and quick to learn. Janet here looks as though she has inherited your calm and efficient nature too. What do you say Janet? Would you like to learn to drive so that you can act as my driver when I need one?'

'Oh, I-I don't know Lord Hanley. I mean I would love to learn to drive a car as Marie did but I work for my parents. I would need my father's permission.' She looked anxiously at Emma.

'I don't think your father would object to you learning to drive a car, Janet, but Lord Hanley, I hope you are not planning to steal away another of my daughters to work in your estate office?'

'No indeed. But it was young Mark Blackford who stole Marie away.' He sighed. 'Bob Rowbottom and I still miss her.' He turned to Janet. 'I don't expect to need a driver very often but I intend to go back down to Gloucestershire at Christmas. I would prefer to travel by train at that time of year but it would be more convenient if you were able to drive by then so that you could drop me and my luggage off at the station and pick me up when I return. I have tried to persuade Mr Rowbottom to have a go but he says he's too old to learn to drive a motor car. He is an excellent land agent so I didn't persist. I would not want to upset him.'

'I would love to be able to do that,' Janet said eagerly, 'but only if my parents agree.'

'I'm sure your father will give his permission, Janet' Emma said. She looked at Lord Hanley. 'William and I both realise the world is changing and it is not as peaceful as we had all expected after such a terrible war. So many things have changed and the miners' strike still drags on for most of them. I feel so sorry for the women and children struggling to feed themselves. Who knows what any of us are going to need?'

'There is certainly a lot of unrest' Lord Hanley agreed with a sigh. 'The government have imported thousands of tons of coal and I can't see how that can be good for the mine owners or their miners, not to mention the country and the hardship so many are still facing.'

'There seems to be a yearning for changes since the war finished,' Emma said.

'Yes, Lord Tannahill tells me they have installed coloured lights in London to direct the traffic in the Piccadilly area. A green light tells the cars when they can go. We don't have anything like that for you to worry about, Janet,' he said with a smile. 'Some developments are good. The radio is a wonderful invention and I am pleased to hear we are to have a British Broadcasting Corporation to choose suitable programmes instead of all that American jazz.' Emma exchanged glances with her daughter and smiled.

'I'm afraid some of the younger generation seem to like American music when they get the chance to hear it. William prefers his own Scottish tunes though.'

'Yes, I hear he plays the fiddle very well.'

'He has tried to teach each of our children but none of them are keen to learn.'

* * *

Some weeks passed before Emma saw Lord Hanley again but Bob Rowbottom had been at Mountcliffe several times to oversee the fencing off of the hill ground and the re-drawing of the map and sizes of adjoining fields.

'I can't have you taking good land and paying a pittance for it, William,' he chuckled.

'I dinna think Alan would let me get away with any of the good land anyway,' William said wryly, 'even if you weren't keeping a close eye on things. I'll have you know I'm paying a deal more than a pittance for this land. I don't know if it has ever been drained or limed in its life.'

'Well I admit you could be right about that. Gerry Wilkins was a good enough stock farmer, but he didn't like too much trouble. He hasn't done anything much with the Mountcliffe Hill since I became land agent. I would like to see you improve it.'

'I mean to try,' William said earnestly. 'If we can get it into good heart for sheep, and maybe do a bit of draining where that stretch of wet land lies then it would make a decent sheep farm for young David in a few years, especially if you add on that small farm between the eastern boundary and the village.'

'You mean Beckside? Joe Taylor's wee place?'

'Yes, that's the one. It has three decent meadows adjoining the hill and there's a few useful buildings. It's well sheltered too. I'm thinking ahead. If we get round to having ewes and lambs they will need some better pasture than the hill, and some shelter.'

'Well, well,' Bob Rowbottom stroked his chin thoughtfully. 'We are thinking about the future eh? That lad of yours is only eleven or twelve.'

'Maybe he is but he's shaping up to make a good shepherd and he can already work the dogs better than most men. Besides, when a man has several sons all wanting to farm I need to look ahead. I was the youngest in my family and the only one my father didn't put into a farm.' William couldn't hide the bitterness. 'I hope I shall do my best for all my children.'

'I'm sure you will if your wife has anything to do with it. I can't imagine her favouring one more than another. We'll wait and see how you get on improving the Mountcliffe Hill first. One step at a time. Joe Taylor at Beckside is a fit enough man at present but he's in his sixties and I heard his wife was not keeping well. They only had one daughter and she married a builder. They moved down to Birmingham.' He frowned. 'I'll need to choose the right time to mention all this to Lord Hanley. I don't know what's got into him these days. I have never known him to be moody and he seems in such low spirits. Even when Lady Hanley died he was never as bad as he is now. He seemed on top of the world after he had been to see your wife but for the last three weeks it's like walking on eggshells.'

William told Emma what the land agent had said when they were in bed that evening. They were always careful not to gossip in front of Polly in case she passed things onto the Wrights, who were her aunt and uncle. Everyone knew the blacksmith and his wife enjoyed a good gossip.

'What did he want when he came to see you while I was at the market that day?' William asked. 'It's since then the laird has been tetchy according to Bob Rowbottom and I've never known him to criticise Lord Hanley before.'

'You know Lord Hanley is desperate to claim the boy, Rick, as his grandson, ever since he saw him at Marie and Mark's wedding and realised how much he resembles his own son. He wanted a woman's advice on how to get Mrs Whitelea to confide in him, or at least talk to him. How could I advise our landlord on anything, and especially on such a delicate matter as the boy's parentage? I did suggest he might write her a letter. I didn't know what else to say. Maybe he doesn't like her reply, or maybe she has ignored his letter too.'

'I suppose even landowners and titled gentlemen can't have it all their own way,' William said with a sigh and turned to give Emma a goodnight kiss. 'I'm a lucky man,' he whispered, drawing her closer into his arms.

# CHAPTER FOUR

A few days later Polly was hanging the washing in the garden when she came hurrying into the house.

'Lord Hanley has just ridden into the yard,' she panted. 'Shall I set a tea tray?'

'Oh dear,' Emma muttered warily, remembering Bob Rowbottom had told William how irritable he had been. He had not started Janet with the promised driving lessons yet. Had he come to reproach her over something she had suggested? 'Don't set a tray yet, Polly. He may not be coming to the house, or he may not stay. I'll call you if he wants anything.' She patted her hair into place and smoothed down her apron which was clean and white that morning. She was always a bit nervous in the presence of the gentry but she felt worse today. She hoped she would not burst into tears if Lord Hanley was angry with her. He knocked firmly on the door a lot sooner than she had expected. He had seen Cliff Barnes in the yard and he knew the big man was kind to animals and especially horses, even if he was a bit simple minded. He gave Cliff a shilling and asked him to take his horse to the stable, then he bounded up the steps to the house.

Emma feared he was going to seize her and dance her around the kitchen for a moment, and indeed he had been tempted. He controlled himself, however, and greeted her warmly, his smile wide, his eyes shining.

'Your advice worked, Emma. You're a wonderful woman. . . .'

'It d-did? M-Mrs Whitelea? Did you write to her?'

'I wrote to her as soon as I got home. I had begun to despair when time passed and she didn't reply.' He pushed a hand through his hair making it stand on end like any schoolboy. 'Then the day before yesterday I received a brief note asking me to look out for a personal reply. Thea had been wary about replying in case my secretary opened the letters before passing them on. I sent her a telegram assuring her I had no secretary and I open all personal mail myself. This morning I received a long letter.'

'Oh! I-I'm so glad Mrs Whitelea has responded.'

'More than responded, she has been frank and open — almost as though it was a relief to explain the circumstances surrounding Rick's birth. You were right Emma, Thea has suffered shame and guilt. She admits it prevented her from keeping in touch with us.'

'Maybe it was easier to write things in a letter than to explain face to face,' Emma nodded.

'You are right. She has confirmed that Rick is Richard's son, my grandson! How happy my wife would have been to know that, whatever the circumstances.' He sighed. 'She would have understood. Thea says the night before Richard had to return to his regiment he was dreadfully low in spirits. He seemed to dread returning but he said he had a duty to his men. She says it was almost as though some sixth sense told him he would not come back and she gave him all the love and reassurance she could because she loved him with all her heart. Before they parted Richard promised to try to get a forty-eight-hour pass. If she would meet him in London they would get a special licence to marry. The celebrations could wait until he was home for good. I don't think Thea will mind me telling you this. I explained that you were the one person who seemed to understand and that you had suggested a letter might be an easier way to communicate frankly. In spite of her shame at the prospect of being an unmarried mother, she says she can never regret Rick's birth because she is thankful to have a part of Richard still. "He is the only man I shall ever love," she wrote.'

'It must have been dreadfully hard, learning of his death,' Emma murmured with feeling.

'It was dreadful for us as his parents so it would be worse for Thea, poor child. In her letter she says she wants me to know the night she spent with Richard is the only night she has slept with any man at any time and it is easier to tell me in a letter.'

'Yes, I can understand that,' Emma said, but she felt uncomfortable that Lord Hanley was sharing such confidences with her.

'Apparently Thomas Whitelea was a very kind man and they were almost like brother and sister as children. They shared the same tutor until he went away to school. They went hunting together and to the same functions. He guessed her secret and offered to marry her to save her from bringing shame to her parents, especially when her mother was already gravely ill. He had been severely injured during the war and he told her candidly he could only ever give her his name because he could never sire children. Thea says he suffered a lot of pain due to shrapnel lodged in his groin. He had lost a lot of blood and the doctors were unable to remove it all. She says some days, when it was almost unbearable he said he wished they had left him to die. Poor fellow. I believe Thea has told me all this because she wants me to have no doubts that Richard is the boy's father but I have no doubts anyway since I saw him.'

'Mrs Whitelea will want you to understand he was there for her when she most needed a friend,' Emma said, remembering the old postman and how grateful she had been for the slightest kindness before Jamie was born, but she felt uncomfortable and shocked that someone in Lord Hanley's position was telling her so much about the private lives of two people who were strangers to her.

'Yes Whitelea was a very good friend. I wish I could have had the opportunity to tell him so myself. Thea says horses had been the love of his life but he could never ride for more than half an hour at a time due to the pain, and his small estate had already been badly neglected during his absence. She says her mother guessed she was expecting a child and that it must be Richard's. They used her illness as an excuse for a quiet wedding and Mrs Winkworth gave them both her blessing. It was Thomas Whitelea's suggestion that they name the boy Richard Thomas Fortescue Whitelea.'

'That was good of him to give the child your son's name, including his surname.'

'Something Lord Tannahill said makes me wonder if his death was really an accident or if the pain had become too much to bear. Apparently he was drowned while sailing on a river boat on the Mississippi. He wrote Thea a letter advising her to sell the estate if he did not return. She did as he said and paid off any debts, then invested the remaining money for Rick's education. They live with her father now but Winkworth is not in good health himself, as I believe I told you.' He frowned and stared into the leaping flames of the fire as Emma added two small logs.

'Would you like a cup of tea and some shortbread Lord Hanley?' Emma asked, hoping he had finished talking about personal matters.

'No thank you, Emma not today. I have taken up enough of your time and you must wonder why I am telling you so much about our affairs.'

'I-I am honoured that you trust me, Lord Hanley.'

'I needed to confide in someone and I know you will understand and be discreet. I have not been easy company these past few weeks. I feel jubilant since Thea's letter arrived. I know I have you to thank for the candour which now exists between Thea and myself. Unfortunately Thea's troubles are not over. Lord Tannahill tells me the Winkworth's are not a wealthy family. He believes Thea's father has advised her to sell the estate when he dies. If that happens I shall try very hard to persuade her to come and live with me at Silverbeck Hall and let me help with Rick's education, but there will be a lot of gossip from those who knew Richard and see Rick's resemblance to him, whatever his surname.'

'I'm sure Rick will be accepted for himself. He already has a charming personality and lovely manners for a young boy. He was very kind, and patient, with my young granddaughter, Marguerite. She asked for him when she came down for Alan and Lynn's wedding.'

'Yes, after Marie's wedding he enjoyed playing with Fiona and David so much he said he wished he could go to school with them. If he and Thea come to live with me it may be good for him to get to know the local people and attend the local school, at least until he is older and ready for boarding school. I had a word with Mr Thorpe, the headmaster but he is planning to retire next year, or at least semi-retire. His son is going to take over. I understand young Thorpe is extremely good at mathematics and science but he has always wanted to teach so he will be an asset.'

'I didn't know that. Mr Thorpe has taught all our children so far.' Emma sighed. 'All things have to change I suppose.'

'I'm afraid they do, but sometimes it is for the better. I am glad the miners' strike has ended, at long last.'

'Yes, six months is a long time. William's relatives, the Kerrs, live on the outskirts of a mining village and he says some are not too happy about the settlement because the miners will have to work an eight-hour shift instead of seven.'

'Yes, so I believe, but at least the negotiations will be with the local owners. I know some of the landowners are greedy, but the family which owns most of the mining in this area seem to consider its workers as far as possible, given so much disagreement amongst both owners and miners. Did you know there is coal beneath our feet, and most of the Silverbeck Estate?'

'No! I didn't know that. Do the underground tunnels run beneath us then?'

'No. I'm told the coal seam is not deep enough to make it worth the investment that would be needed to extract the coal safely.'

'I think I am pleased to hear that.' Emma longed to get on with her work in the kitchen but she felt unable to rise until Lord Hanley made the first move. Almost as though he had read her mind he stood up. As she followed suit he laid a hand on her arm.

'I know I may have shared confidences I should perhaps have kept to myself but I really want you to understand how difficult it may be for Thea if she and Rick eventually come to live at Silverbeck. You have a great influence on your family, and on the Wrights' niece, Polly, as well as other people in the village. You and William have earned a great deal of respect in the area. If Thea and young Rick can be persuaded to live with me will you try to smooth their path a little? Some people revel in malicious gossip.' Emma chewed her lower lip but she met his gaze.

'I-I will certainly try to squash any gossip I hear, b-but it is unlikely that Mrs Whitelea will be in the company of ordinary people like us.'

'If Rick attends the village school Thea will probably be seen driving him to the school and home again. We have always supported the local tradesmen and the stores, the butcher, the baker and so on. I don't want Thea to feel isolated or ill at ease. Will you help her if you can, Emma? Please?'

'I will do my best,' Emma promised, wondering how she could possibly help a member of the gentry. 'Miss Cody's friendship with Gerry Wilkins attracted a lot of gossip at first,' she said thoughtfully, 'but you saw how everyone rallied round to help them when they needed it. They all wished Miss Cody well in her new life. I'm sure your grandson and his mother will be made welcome if they come to live at Silverbeck Hall. There must be many people who lost fiancés or husbands during the war. Some people will understand and sympathise.'

Later that evening, in the privacy of their bedchamber William remarked on Lord Hanley's lengthy visit.

'Even Cliff noticed he had been with you a long time.'

'I expect Cliff was more worried in case he didn't get his tea,' Emma said summoning a laugh. They all knew of Cliff's colossal appetite.

'But he was in the house with you a long time? Was he still as irritable as Bob Rowbottom said?'

'No, as a matter of fact he was jubilant because he had received a letter from Mrs Dorothea Whitelea.' Emma had decided she would not tell anyone, even William, of the details regarding Thea's relationships, either with Richard Fortescue, or with the man she had married. It was not her business and she knew the woman would be embarrassed if she knew how much of her private life had been discussed.

'Why would that change his moods so much?'

'Mrs Whitelea admitted that Rick Whitelea is the son of Richard Fortescue. Now that has been confirmed, Lord Hanley feels he has been given a purpose in living because he has a grandson to inherit. He is pinning his hopes on him and his mother coming to live at Silverbeck Hall now.'

'I thought she lived with her own father? Why did he want to talk to you about it?' Emma heard the touchiness in William's tone. Ever since they married William was inclined to be a bit possessive. Most of the time she didn't mind because she knew it was a sign he cared about her.

'She does live with her father at present but he is not in good health. Lord Tannahill had told Lord Hanley he thinks the Winkworth Estate will have to be sold when Thea's father dies. I suppose it's easy for two wealthy widowed lords to think they can decide the fate of a woman and child,' she said crossly. 'I'm afraid Mr Rowbottom and the rest of us may have to put up with some irrational moods if Mrs Whitelea decides to stay in Gloucestershire.'

'You may be right about that, Emma, but I still don't understand why Lord Hanley should confide in you, or what you can do about it? Did he just talk? Did you make him tea?'

'Oh William,' Emma was tired but she turned towards him and stroked his face. 'I think the man is lonely. He wanted to share his good news and he wants us to squash any gossip and try to make Rick and his mother feel welcome if they do come to live up here.' She sighed heavily. 'Ever since Jamie ran away to Scotland, after those horrid boys called him a bastard, everyone has speculated about our own past. Lord Hanley thinks I shall understand how Mrs Whitelea will feel. Anyway,' she said changing the subject firmly, 'he took Janet for her first driving lesson this afternoon and she says he's taking her again tomorrow. He had asked her if she could ride a pony.'

'Of course she can. Marie taught her all the things Lord Hanley taught her whenever she brought the pony here. Janet really loved learning to ride, just as she loved learning to milk. She loves all animals.'

'I know, but she couldn't tell Lord Hanley Marie had taught her to ride on his wife's pony. He will see whether she is good enough tomorrow. He says it will exercise the pony and save him driving here to collect her.'

'Mmm, I hope he doesn't try to get Janet to work in the estate office,' William muttered.

'I'm sure he will not manage that,' Emma said soothingly. 'Did you read Jamie's last letter about wee Marguerite? She's got a wee pony of her own now and he says she is already enjoying riding it. Marie or Rina take her out most days.'

'All right, all right,' William said gruffly, drawing her into his arms with all his old masterful determination. 'I know you are changing the subject away from Lord Hanley. That suits me so long as I know it's only me my wife loves.' He laid a cheek against her long dark hair and allowed his hand to wander over Emma's soft curves. As always the flame of passion flared between them. At times like this Emma felt like a young girl again, forgetting she was forty-five and supposed to be a mature woman with wisdom.

The following afternoon Janet disappeared into the hayloft as soon as she saw Lord Hanley's car arriving in the farmyard. William raised his eyebrows in surprise and followed her into the stable but she had disappeared up the ladder into the loft. He stood on the lower rungs and poked his head through the trap door.

'Hey Janet, surely you're not hiding up here to avoid Lord Hanley, lassie?' he called.

'Oh Dad, I can't possibly go with him,' Janet wailed. 'I didn't think he would come again. I nearly ran into a gate post, then I slammed my foot on one of the pedals so hard he almost hit his head on the windscreen.'

'Well everybody needs time to learn if it's something new,' William said encouragingly. 'To tell the truth I'm amazed at someone in Lord Hanley's position taking time to teach a bairn of one of his tenants. It's a good opportunity for you . . .'

'I-I know but — but I c-can't . . .'

'He wouldna have come again if he thought you were hopeless.'

'He-he's just being kind but I'm not like Marie. I'll never be able to drive a motor.'

'All right. I'll tell him you don't feel like going today,' William said.

'Or any other day,' Janet called urgently.

A few minutes later it was Lord Hanley's head which appeared through the trap door of the loft. He paused until his eyes grew accustomed to the gloom and he spied Janet cringing in a corner.

'Hello Janet, are you ready for our next lesson?' he called cheerfully, pretending he had not spoken to William.

'I-I-I can't possibly drive again. I-I might have k-killed you.'

'But you didn't, and if you had it would have been my own fault. You were doing so well I didn't give you enough warning that we were going to turn through that narrow gateway. I should have told you to swerve out a bit before you turned in. Anyway, we're going to drive around the estate today. It's time we were off though if I'm to have you back for the milking. Come on. We'll dust ourselves down and get going.' His tone was firm but kindly. He didn't wait for an argument. Quivering inside Janet followed him down the loft ladder. He was surveying the stable.

The work horses were out and only Peggy, the milk pony, was munching contentedly on her hay.

'Your father tells me you have an empty stall now that your brother has taken his favourite work horse with him to Mountcliffe.'

'Yes, we've had Daisy since she was a foal. Alan and I both loved her,' Janet said warmly.

'Your father tells me there will be a stall for May if you ride her home. If we get on now there will be time to see how you handle her. I think you will enjoy riding her. She is a sweet-tempered mare.' Before Janet had time to realise his intention he was holding open the door of his car and ushering her into the driving seat. If it had been anyone else but her father's landlord Janet would have refused for she could be stubborn. As it was, she obeyed meekly but she was trembling inside and she turned to him pleadingly as he got into the passenger seat.

'I-I really d-don't think I c-can do this, Lord Hanley.' He guessed the tears were not far away. 'I-I could have killed you . . .' She shuddered. She had dreamed about him hitting the windscreen. He smiled at her.

'But you didn't and I was not in the least bit worried.' He took a deep breath, frowning a little. 'Janet I am going to tell you a little story, something I never even told my dear wife, but I think you are like your mother so you will not broadcast it to the world?'

'Of course I wouldn't, not if it is a secret.' He nodded.

'Well then, when I got my first car I went to Leeds to collect it. I had never driven a car in my life. The garage proprietor gave me brief instructions and explained about the pedals and signalling my intentions when I wanted to turn. I set off very confidently. The garage was in a quiet part with lots of space around about it and at first I did all right but to get onto the road for home I needed to go along one of the main city streets. There were a few cars and several horses pulling their carts or carriages but I kept close to my side of the road. All went well until I met a lorry. It was a big lorry, like the army have. There was a high stone wall on my left-hand side and I was so intent on not running into the side of the lorry that I scraped the offside of my new car along the wall.'

'Oh dear! How awful,' Janet gasped, her eyes wide. 'Were you hurt?'

'Only my pride,' Lord Hanley admitted with a boyish grin which seemed to make him look years younger, Janet thought.

'What did you do?'

'I found a place to turn and took it back to the garage. The man and his son chuckled gleefully. I believe they had expected something like that to happen, but they agreed to repair the car as good as new, and they did. I asked them to deliver it next time so that I could practice where there was no traffic. So you see that is why I was so anxious to teach both you and Marie to handle the car and understand everything about driving it before we go near any traffic at the railway station. Mark Blackwood, your brother-in-law, is an excellent driver and confident without being arrogant. I don't know where he learned to drive but he seems to have a natural affinity with cars and engines.'

'Yes, Marie says he would spend hours studying anything new or experimenting with ways of making engines go better. They have moved into their new house on the edge of the village of East Lowrie and Mark is building a workshop now, fairly near the blacksmith's smiddy. He thinks they may be able to help each other sometimes when Mark needs machinery parts welded. They are coming down for another visit before Christmas if the weather is good so I expect he will tell you all about it.'

'They're coming again so soon?'

'Well Mark did promise he would bring Marie to visit at least once a year as soon as he had saved up to buy a car of his own. Your friend, Lord Tannahill, and his nephew were extraordinarily generous. They gave Mark a second-hand car as a wedding present so now he has no excuse for not bringing Marie to see us. We all miss her.'

'I expect Lord Tannahill guessed Mark would really appreciate such a gift and he is well able to maintain and repair it if needed.'

'We are all grateful to them. It means we shall see Marie more than we could have expected. Jamie's wee girl, Marguerite, will be coming with them too. We all love her with her big smile and laughing eyes. Marie says she often talks about us all and looks forward to her next visit to Granny and Papa. Rina encourages her. She has no family of her own and she believes it is good for Marguerite to experience a warm and loving family.'

'I do agree with her,' Lord Hanley said a little wistfully.

The lesson was going well. Lord Hanley was a patient teacher and he enjoyed all young company. Towards the end he directed Janet to turn left into the same narrow gateway as the day before but this time he told her in good time what they were going to do. 'Now make sure there is nothing behind then draw out a bit and turn in. That way you are not turning in at such an acute angle.' She obeyed his instructions, albeit slowly, then turned to him with a triumphant and grateful smile when they were safely onto the drive to Silverbeck Hall. He grinned at her like a victorious schoolboy.

'I assumed you know what acute and obtuse angles mean Janet?'

'Oh yes, of course. Mr Thorpe tried to make sure we were all proficient in English and mathematics. He made the other subjects interesting too so most of us were keen to know more about other countries and history and we all loved to hear about nature.'

'Mmm, I am very pleased to hear that,' Lord Hanley said thoughtfully. 'Now we will park here and see how you get on riding May. Her real name is May Blossom because she was foaled in May when the hedges were white with blossom, but it soon became shortened to May because it is easier to say and to call her from her paddock.'

William was relieved and delighted to see Janet riding jauntily into the farmyard in time for a cup of tea before milking started. She rarely allowed anything to beat her so he was pleased the driving lesson must have gone well. Recently he had resented the amount of time their landlord seemed to want to spend with his wife but perhaps Emma and Bob Rowbottom were right when they thought he was lonely. He had always imagined titled gentlemen would have lots of friends and plenty of money to indulge in pastimes, but in his heart he knew no amount of money could compensate for losing a wife and family as Lord Hanley had done. As far as he knew he had not taken the same interest in the families of any of his other tenants so maybe this was his way of repaying any help Emma had given him.

'William! You were miles away,' Emma chuckled. 'I asked if you wanted a piece of gingerbread.'

'Oh, oh yes please. I was thinking about Lord Hanley. Janet has returned from her driving lesson and looks well pleased with herself. She'll be in soon to tell you about it. I'm beginning to think I should buy a second-hand van and learn to drive myself. I can't have my daughters beating me to modern ways. A van would save many a cold wet journey to the station in the trap with the milk.'

'There's no reason why you shouldn't when I think of my brother Joe being able to drive all these years. You could ask Mark to help you choose a van when he and Marie come at the end of November. He would probably give you a lesson or two if you asked him.'

'Mmm, I might do that. He would know more about engines than I would.'

'Lynn seems to have got quite a few customers coming to Mountcliffe every morning to buy fresh milk. They all say they would have done it years ago but Thora Wilkins wouldn't let them near the place. She is making quite a lot of butter with the surplus and Mr Nichol buys whatever she has to spare to sell to his customers. It is the same with her eggs. Alan says they are going to set more eggs for hatching come the spring.'

'Aye Lynn is making Alan a good wife,' William agreed. 'Neither of them are afraid of hard work but I expect when he builds up his cow numbers a bit more he will need to take the surplus milk to the station the same as everybody else. There aren't enough folks in the village to buy it all.'

'No-o, I suppose not,' Emma said thoughtfully, 'and it will make a difference if they get a bairn or two. Children take a lot of time and energy.'

As Janet gained more confidence Lord Hanley told her she was making an excellent driver and he would take her into Wakefield soon to see how she coped with more traffic. His praise helped her confidence. She had asked her mother to keep the driving lessons a secret when she wrote to Marie or to Jamie and Rina.

'I want it to be a surprise to Marie when she comes down to visit.'

'In that case I had better not mention it to Maggie. She seems to see Rina and Jamie every day and Joe takes her to see Marie at least once a week so she would be sure to tell them all.'

'They all think I'm still a child so I want to show them,' Janet said with determination. Emma laughed.

'They will know you're no longer a child lassie when they see you again. You're a proper young woman now.' She sighed. 'You seem to have grown up so quickly.'

'Aye y'are a young lady, Miss Janet,' Polly chipped in with a grin. 'Aunt Ivy was telling me the last time you took the milk pony to be shod there were two young men admiring you and they asked Uncle Joe who you were and where you live.' Janet frowned at her but Polly chuckled. She had been a maid at Moorend since she was fourteen when the Sinclair's first arrived with Jamie, a baby of a few weeks old at the time. She had known and cared for them all since they were born through the various stages of life.

'Who were these two young men, Polly?' Emma asked curiously. She could tell from Janet's flushed cheeks that she had been aware of them.

'Uncle Joe said one of them is Brian Shaw from Thorley Grange. That's about four or five miles away in the direction of the Kerrs so Meg or her husband might know them. Their own blacksmith has retired. He's like Uncle Joe, he doesn't have a son or a nephew to take over. The other fellow was his cousin — Leonard Shaw. Uncle Joe was not sure where he comes from but he seemed to know about horses.'

Later, when they were alone in the kitchen, Polly told Janet the two young men were planning to come to the Silverbeck dances in the hope of getting to know her, but Janet blushed shyly and turned the idea aside, although she and Peter both enjoyed dancing and they usually went to the local dances. She knew Peter had a strong liking for Helen Barclay and always managed two dances with her, but she was only sixteen and her friend always saw her home.

'I don't think I shall be going to the next dance,' she muttered. 'Marie and Mark might be here then.'

'Course they'll not be here by then. Anyway, Uncle Joe says they seem nice young men.'

* * *

Janet made good progress with the driving and a few days before Marie and Mark were due to arrive Lord Hanley instructed her to drive to the outskirts of Wakefield to see how she coped with the traffic.

'I think you will manage well, Janet. That will give us time to drive to the station once or twice before you need to drop me off there when I go to Gloucestershire for the Christmas holidays.' Janet smiled. She knew how much he was looking forward to seeing young Rick Whitelea again.

As soon as Mark drew the car to a halt in the yard at Moorend Marguerite scrambled out and ran to greet Emma, calling, 'Granny! Granny we're here!' She flung herself into Emma's waiting arms.

'How like your mother ye are lassie, with your big smile and sparkling dark eyes.'

'Can I sleep with Fiona? Can I go to meet her and David walking from school?'

'Of course ye can ma bairn, but it's not quite time for them to finish their lessons yet. You will be going to school yourself after the summer.' Emma always found herself falling back to her Scottish accent when she was feeling emotional and they all found Marguerite the most warm and loveable child.

'I know. Uncle Joe wants me to go to Locheagle School because he went there when he was a wee boy. He said you went there too. How did you walk so far, and why didn't you go to school where Fiona goes?' Her childish brow wrinkled at such a puzzle. Emma laughed.

'Uncle Joe lived at Locheagle then, and so did I. We didn't have far to walk to school because we lived in a cottage in the village with Uncle Richard and Uncle David and our mother and father.'

'Oh. Like I live with Liam and Reggie? And my mummy and daddy?'

'Yes, that's right. I expect you will all go to school at East Lowrie like Auntie Maggie and Uncle Jim.'

'That's what Aunt Maggie says. It's an awful long way to walk,' she added with a worried frown.

'Maybe when you are good at riding your pony you will be able to ride your pony to East Lowrie and put it in Uncle Mark's stable until you are ready to ride home again.'

'Yes, that's what Mummy says, but I have to get really good first, and I have to learn how to put on the saddle and bridle properly and learn how to groom Patsy's coat so that it always looks shiny. Auntie Marie says I can walk to her house from the school to have my lunch with her if I want to and if it snows and gets too deep I can stay with her and Uncle Mark.'

'It sounds as though you have got it all planned young lady,' Emma said with a smile. 'I think you will enjoy school and learning how to read and write and count.'

'I can write my name and my address at Bonnybrae Farm. Uncle Jim showed me how to do it, and Mummy showed me how to write my numbers and count to a hundred. That's an awful lot, isn't it Granny? We have a lot of chickens but we don't have as many as a hundred.' Emma smiled.

'You would have a lot of eggs to sell if you had a hundred chickens,' she said, 'but Uncle Jim and your daddy have more than a hundred sheep.'

'But sheep don't lay eggs every day so that's all right.'

Marie came across and hugged Emma warmly.

'This rascal has chattered all the way here,' she said. 'I thought she would be exhausted.'

'I expect it's excitement but I am pleased she remembers us and wants to come.'

'Oh she remembers all right. She would come every weekend if she could . . .' She broke off as Lord Hanley's car drew into the yard and pulled up neatly beside where William was greeting Mark. Marie's eyes widened when Janet got out of the driving seat with a big grin. 'You're learning to drive, little Sis!' Lord Hanley hurried round the car, smiling widely.

'She is, and she is doing exceedingly well, as you did yourself my dear.' He opened his arms wide and to Emma's astonishment he embraced Marie in a warm hug, before shaking hands with Mark.

'It's lovely to see you both. I hope you will come to the Hall and have lunch with me, or dinner if that would be more convenient. Can you squeeze your parents and Janet in the car and bring them too?'

'Oh I think so. Janet is too slender to take up much space,' Mark said with a smile.

'I know you will be visiting the Kerrs, and there will be other things to take up your time, so shall we say Wednesday evening then I have got my booking reserved?' He regarded Emma, his eyebrows raised in question. She glanced at William but he seemed as bemused as she was herself by their landlord's familiarity and hospitality towards his family. He shrugged, then nodded agreement, clearly astonished.

# CHAPTER FIVE

Lord Hanley had made two visits to Gloucester since Christmas, both at Thea's invitation this time and with her home as his base.

'He feels she is beginning to feel at ease with him again,' Bob Rowbottom told Emma and William. 'He is more like his old self now, and he is full of the boy, Rick and his doings. Of course he will never be the happy and contented man he was when Lady Hanley was alive, but that's understandable.'

'I am pleased to hear Mrs Whitelea understands his desire to get to know his grandson,' Emma said. 'After all Rick is his only relative.'

'He still seems to spend a good deal of time with Lord Tannahill and his nephew, Rupert, riding round their estate,' Bob Rowbottom said.

Although Lord Tannahill's daughter, Lady Sylvia Redpath, would be a wealthy young woman one day it was Rupert who would inherit the estate and his uncle was keen that he should learn the business of estate management thoroughly so that he was never dependent solely on managers. Sylvia enjoyed riding with them and on days when she was to accompany them Lord Hanley usually brought Rick along too. Neither of the youngsters ever seemed to tire of riding and Sylvia was always pleasant and friendly towards their young neighbour.

'I am going away to a school for young ladies after the summer,' she told Rick on one of their rides. 'Don't you ever wish you could go to school, and meet new friends?'

'We-ell, sometimes I would like a tutor who is more interesting than Mr Soames,' Rick admitted, 'but best of all I would like to go to school with my new friends in Yorkshire. Their names are Fiona and David Sinclair and they have a little cousin called Marguerite, but she doesn't go to school yet. Grandfather Fortescue knows them all. They don't have to live at their school. They go every morning and come home every night to their parents. I would like that.'

'I see,' Sylvia said with a frown. 'Do you wish you could live in Yorkshire with your new grandfather?'

'I would like that if Mother came too. Grandfather Winkworth says I am the man of the family now so I must always look after my mother because he is too old now and he's not very well.'

'I see. I can't remember my mother very well because she died when I was five but I never wanted to go away to school and leave Daddy. He's the best father in the world, but I shall be fourteen in the summer and Daddy says there are a lot of things a young lady needs to learn and he can't teach me, because he is a man.' She giggled a little. 'He says it would be selfish of him to keep me always at his side. He has promised I can come home again though if I hate living away but he hopes I shall make new friends and invite them to come and stay with us, like Rupert used to invite Mark Blackford, who is still his best friend, even though he is married and lives in Scotland.'

'I know Mark,' Rick said eagerly. 'Mother and I went to his wedding to Marie Sinclair and we stayed with Grandfather Fortescue. It was great fun. I didn't want to come home but Mother said Grandfather Winkworth would be missing us.'

'Come along you two,' Lord Tannahill called. 'We're going in for tea and cakes before Lord Hanley and Rick ride back home. You seem to be having a serious conversation.'

'I was telling Rick that I shall be going away to live at school after the summer,' Sylvia said, 'but I shall always be back here for the holidays. I know nearly as much about the estate as Rupert does, don't I Daddy?'

* * *

It was the middle of May when the telegram arrived for Lord Hanley, just a fortnight after he had returned from his last visit to Gloucestershire. It brought the news of Sir Thomas Winkworth's death. Although he had suffered with his chest for some years in the end his death was sudden. The doctor said his illness, and resulting difficulty in breathing, had been a strain on his heart. Lord Hanley made immediate preparations to travel down to Gloucestershire again, this time on the train so he asked Janet to drive him to the station and said he would write when he expected to return. It was Thea who had sent the telegram so he knew he would be welcome at the funeral. He was thankful they had healed the breach between them before this second major upheaval in her young life. He intended to give her all the support he could so he was a little surprised to hear that Lord Tannahill had already offered his help, including buying the estate at a fair price and giving her the option to continue living in the house if she wished. It was the day following the funeral before the two men had the opportunity for a proper conversation.

'Fordyce I thought you understood it is my intention to offer Thea and Rick a home with me at Silverbeck Hall and to make Rick heir to my estate,' Lord Hanley said in injured tones.

'Yes, of course I know that, Adrian,' Lord Tannahill said patiently, 'but you must have realised what a proud and independent young woman Thea is. I'm sure you would not want her to be anything else. This way she has a choice. If she decides to move to Yorkshire to make her home, and Rick's, at Silverbeck, you will know she has chosen to do so because that is what she wants, and not because she has no other option.'

'We-ell yes, I hadn't thought of that. I do understand it is no great advantage to you to have her living in the house once you take over the estate, but what if she decides that is where she wants to stay?'

'I think you have to allow her to make her choice. My advice is to go home and give her time. She will have a lot to do winding up her father's affairs. I have already advised her to take the best deal she can get if someone offers a higher price than I have offered, but she knows the estate is run down and has been neglected in recent years. Whatever she decides it will take a few months to sort out her own affairs and the remaining staff will need to look for work elsewhere. There are always accounts to settle.'

'Mmm, I understand what you are saying. I intended staying with her until her affairs were settled, but perhaps you are right. I don't want to force myself on her, or smother her with my presence.'

'I don't think you will need to worry. If Rick has anything to do with the choice I'm sure he will want to live with you. He is ready for a man's influence and his Grandfather Winkworth has not had the energy to keep him company for some time now.'

So it was that Lord Hanley sent a telegram to Bob Rowbottom informing him he would be back sooner than planned and asking him to go to Moorend to ask Janet to meet him from the train the following afternoon.

'It doesn't sound as though things are turning out the way he expected,' Bob Rowbottom said gloomily to William, 'but I thought he would realise you couldn't pack up an estate and move house and home all in a couple of weeks.'

'Emma is sure he has set his heart on having Mrs Whitelea and the boy to live with him.'

'Then I dread to think what he will be like if things don't turn out the way he expects,' Bob Rowbottom muttered. 'He went through a bad patch at the time of the Mountcliffe sale, when he was waiting for a reply from Mrs Whitelea. In all the years I've been with him I've never known him to get so down in spirits, or irritable and impatient.'

'I expect Lady Hanley soothed him and took his mind off things when she was alive.'

'You could be right I suppose. Does your wife always calm you down, William, when things are not going as you expect?' he asked with a grin.

'I hadn't thought about it but I suppose she does. We comfort each other when there's trouble with any of the family. I know Emma was really upset when Jamie ran away and she was disappointed when Marie went to live in Scotland. We both miss her but we like Mark and they seem to be happy together so we have a lot to be thankful for.'

'Maybe there's something to be said for having a large family,' Bob Rowbottom reflected. 'You still have four at home to take up your attention, and Alan is just down the road.'

'You're right,' William grinned. 'I hope you'll remember two of them are laddies and likely to want farms some day?'

'Only two?' Bob Rowbottom raised an eyebrow. 'From what I've seen recently your lass, Janet, would be as good a farmer as any of the young men around here.'

'She enjoys the life and working with animals it's true, but farming's a hard life for anybody — there's ploughing to do and manure to cart and spread and . . .'

'She could always employ a man like Cliff Barnes for the heavy work, as you do . . .'

'Aye but the likes o' Cliff would be no use for skilled jobs like ploughing. My father used to say a good farmer should be able to show a man how to do every job on the place and if he can't men soon lose respect and think you're dependent on them.'

'Your father was a wise man and right in many ways. He certainly seemed to make a good job of teaching you how to farm anyway, I'll grant him that, but what makes you think Janet couldn't tackle the skilled jobs? She has learned to drive a car already which is more than you or I have done.'

'Aye, the lassies have beaten me to that but have you heard I've bought a van? I'm learning to drive now. Mark helped me decide which one to buy when he and Marie came to stay. Ploughing is a different thing. Apart from skill it's hard work plodding behind a pair of horses all day, keeping the furrow straight and even . . .'

'I know it is but Janet can do that already.' Bob Rowbottom smiled craftily. 'You should be proud of her.'

'Janet canna plough.' William often fell back to his Scottish accent when he argued or got indignant'.

'I'd like to bet you a pound note she can but I know I would win,' Bob Rowbottom chuckled. 'I wondered if you knew. I saw her myself. She was in the field next to the Common. I had ridden over to see how the gypsies had left things when they moved on. I was surprised to see Janet behind the plough. I sat on my horse and watched from the other side of the hedge. She had taken Peter his dinner I think and while he ate and had a rest she took over the plough.'

'But Peter likes the horses to have a rest while he eats his lunch. He usually . . .'

'I know he considers his animals but Janet had ridden to the field on your young Clydesdale mare. Peter changed her with each of his horses in turn so Janet could have a go at the ploughing and both the horses had a rest and a nosebag in turn. As far as I could see she managed as well as Peter himself.'

'Well, well,' William muttered in disbelief. 'They never breathed a word to me. Ploughing is not Peter's favourite job but he makes a reasonable attempt. He's not as good as Alan so maybe he welcomed Janet taking a turn. Did she keep a straight furrow?'

'I couldn't tell the difference so it couldn't have been bad.'

'Mmm, Peter will make a better shepherd and dog handler than Alan ever would.'

'None of us can be good at everything,' Bob Rowbottom reflected. 'You're a lucky man William Sinclair. All of your family are hard workers and they're not afraid to tackle a new job.'

Later that evening William asked Emma if she knew Peter had been teaching Janet how to plough.

'They didn't say so,' Emma said, 'but I saw them discussing something and I guessed when Peter had left his dinner behind that Janet would be joining him at the field. I didn't know she could manage two horses and a plough though. Did she make a mess of it?'

'No, not according to Bob Rowbottom anyway. Neither of them mentioned anything to me though.'

'Well don't be angry, William. Women have attempted all sorts of jobs since the war and men were glad of their efforts then.'

* * *

As things turned out Lord Hanley did not have too many months to wait before Thea had sold her father's estate and cleared his affairs. She came to stay at Silverbeck Hall for three weeks before making up her mind whether she and Rick should move to Yorkshire to make their home permanently with Rick's grandfather.

'I feel cut adrift, without roots,' she told Bob Rowbottom's wife, Mary, when she asked if Thea and Rick were enjoying their stay at Silverbeck. They had met by chance one afternoon in the farm office while the men were out inspecting a cottage in the village which had been damaged by fire. 'I don't feel I belong anywhere at present but Adrian is eager for us to stay here and Rick is keen to come. He wants to go to the village school with the Sinclair children.'

'We all think Lord Hanley has been lonely since his wife died,' Mary Rowbottom said gently. 'He has been overjoyed since he discovered he has a grandson. He told Bob, my husband, how grateful he is that you were able to give Richard some joy, however brief, before he died fighting for his country. We are all convinced he will make Rick his heir whether you move to Yorkshire or not. Bob thinks most of the tenants feel more reassured now they know there will be another generation to carry on.'

Later Mary Rowbottom mentioned their meeting to her husband.

'Thea is just the same pleasant young woman she was when she used to stay as Richard's fiancé. She has no pretensions, and not a trace of snobbery. I'm sure the village people will soon accept her and Rick if they do come to live here. I think most people will sympathise rather than condemn. A lot of them must remember Richard and his brother when they were young.'

Lord Hanley saw his solicitor even before Rick moved to Silverbeck Hall, and with Thea's consent his name was legally changed to Richard Thomas Fortescue. He started school as Rick Fortescue and in the way of children he was accepted as one of them, especially since he was already friends with David and Fiona Sinclair. It took Emma a little while to accept Lord Hanley's grandson as any other ordinary friend of her own children but it was his decision to ride his pony down from Silverbeck Hall to Moorend, then walk with Fiona and David to school.

'Mother wanted to drive me to school in Grandfather's car,' he explained to William when he asked politely if he could leave his pony at Moorend. 'I prefer to go to school with David and Fiona. I have never had other children for friends before.' He had a sparkle in his blue eyes and a mischievous smile which was hard to resist. Almost every day he came into the kitchen at Moorend after school with Fiona and David and enjoyed his tea with everyone else before saddling his pony and trotting off back to the Hall. Sometimes when there was a new calf to see he went with Janet to take a look and his greatest joy was seeing the new Clydesdale foal with its gangly legs and determination to stand and suckle its mother.

Gradually he became like any other member of the Sinclair brood. Sometimes he, with David and Fiona, would call in at Mountcliffe on their way through the village to see Lynn and Alan if a new brood of chicks had hatched, or when a sow had a litter of young pigs. He loved all the animals as much as Fiona and David did. Sometimes he was reluctant to saddle his pony and leave Moorend if there were interesting things to see or do. Thea realised she had never seen him so happy and content with life and she was thankful. He was eager to learn his lessons now and he benefitted from competition with other children. Even when winter came he insisted on riding to Moorend and walking to school with David and Fiona instead of stabling his pony at Mountcliffe, as Alan had suggested, so that he would not have so far to walk.

As ever there were a few people who were envious of the Sinclairs because they were tenants of two good farms and some suggested they were befriending Lord Hanley's grandson to curry more favour with their landlord. In fact, Emma and William were surprised by Lord Hanley's readiness to allow Rick to attend the village school and to visit Moorend so freely. He and Fiona were the same age and so in the same class so there was a bit of friendly rivalry over who was best at certain subjects.

'Lord Hanley believes the lad will pick up a lot of useful knowledge if he spends time with your children around the farm,' Bob Rowbottom told William one morning after Emma had voiced her concerns at Rick lingering until dusk before he rode home. 'He told us he had begged Janet to teach him to milk so she had given him a go on one of the elderly cows and she said he had done well. I don't know whether your daughter would agree with that,' he chuckled.

'He did do surprisingly well to say it was the first time he had sat under a cow,' William said. 'I was at the milking myself but we hadn't realised it was getting dark outside. I wouldna like the laddie to get into trouble or to have an accident on his way home.'

'He's a good rider,' Bob Rowbottom declared. 'You'd think he was born to the saddle but Richard and his brother were good horsemen, and so is Lord Hanley. Maybe it's bred in him, though he tells me it was Mr Whitelea who bought him his first pony and taught him to ride. Even so I understand your concern. A dog or a fox, even a rabbit, could startle the pony and cause him to be thrown from the saddle. I will have a quiet word with Mistress Thea. It's no use me telling his grandfather. He's so delighted to have the boy living with him he would climb up a moonbeam to snatch the moon if Rick asked for it.'

'He seems to get on well with all the children at school now they have got used to his speech being a bit different to theirs. All of ours have had a bit of teasing at one time or another when they use words they have picked up from Emma or me.' William grinned. 'I don't think it bothers Master Rick one bit.'

'It bothers him more if your lassie beats him at mathematics,' Bob Rowbottom laughed. 'I hear the schoolmaster's son is teaching the older classes now and Fiona and Rick have both moved into his class for most of their lessons.'

'Yes, they have him for English, mathematics and science anyway, history and geography too I think,' Emma said. 'The vicar still comes into school to teach a few of them Latin and both Fiona and Rick are finding it quite difficult. They would rather go outside to the school garden as David does. Mr Thorpe takes them for that himself. He makes them work hard at the weeding but they don't seem to mind. He told them they would thank him someday when they were growing their own vegetables. He thinks Fiona is like Marie and she ought to be a teacher. Apparently she likes helping the younger ones with their lessons. Whenever Marguerite comes to stay Fiona plays school with her and they get out the blackboard which Thomas made. They're always doing sums and letters. Marguerite is a bright wee thing and she seems to enjoy Fiona's company.'

'I expect she enjoys having her grandparents to spoil her even more,' Bob Rowbottom grinned. 'I almost forgot, I came to tell you a bit of news. I'm getting a young man to train as a land agent so he can take over when I retire . . .'

'Retire? Ye're surely not thinking o'retiring for some years yet, are ye?' William asked in consternation. 'I'm only just getting used to your Yorkshire dealings and sayings. I shall need to get my other two laddies into farms before we can let ye go.'

'Better to deal with the devil you already know, eh?' Bob Rowbottom said with a twinkle in his eye. 'I'm not thinking of retiring yet. Marie was all the help I needed, and Mark proved useful too, as well as being a good chauffeur at the time I needed one. He was picking things up fast as we went around the farms but I reckon his heart will always be more in engines than in his estate.

'Aye, I believe ye're right there but he and Marie seem to make a good partnership and they're certainly happy together.'

'I'm pleased for both of them, but we missed them. This young man's name is Michael Watt but he prefers Mike. He comes from Lancashire so he should be fairly hardy and used to mixed farming. There was one applicant from Norfolk but he was more familiar with big fields, big farms and big crops, and not so much livestock. His father is a land agent and his elder brother is hoping to carry on in his shoes, but he says a lot of the farms have been badly neglected since the war. They couldn't get tenants for some of them. He reckons quite a few new tenants have moved down from Scotland.'

'Are ye suggesting we should move to Norfolk to get a better deal?' William asked, half joking. Before Bob Rowbottom could reply Emma spoke up.

'Move to Norfolk? Not on your life William Sinclair! I never want to pull up my roots again. We were young and strong when we came to Moorend. We're too old for another move and our bairns are scattered enough already.'

'I ken that, Emmie,' William soothed, putting an arm around her shoulders and drawing her closer, with a grin at Bob Rowbottom. 'Ye needna worry lassie. I've no desire to move further south either. How about you make Bob Rowbottom a good cup of tea and a bite to eat so we keep the right side o' him?' He winked at the land agent. Emma always offered him refreshment anyway these days. He seemed at ease in her comfortable kitchen.

Time moved on. David was fourteen in 1929 and eager to finish with school and start work at Moorend as his brothers had done. There was plenty for him to do as Peter usually spent some of his time helping Alan and Lynn at Mountcliffe and now that Lynn was expecting their first child she would be glad of David's help with her hens and ducks and feeding the young pigs. Fiona being three years younger would continue at Silverbeck School but Emma was surprised when Lord Hanley continued to send his Rick there too. Long before they were fourteen both Fiona and Rick had surpassed the rest of the children in the school. The friendly rivalry between them spurred them on. Neither of them liked to be beaten. Rick was more advanced in mathematics while Fiona usually surpassed him in English and Latin. Mr Thorpe Senior was not in the best of health and he knew the time had come for him to give up completely. He cared deeply about all his pupils and he decided to visit Moorend Farm to talk to Emma and William about Fiona's future. He told them he and his son would like to keep her at the school as a pupil teacher, working with the younger children, as she did already in an unofficial capacity.

'It would be a pity to allow so much talent to go to waste,' he declared. 'She has a good knowledge of all the basic subjects, but we believe she is well advanced in English, mathematics and science. She would be paid a small wage but if she wants to progress, perhaps with a view to attending a teacher training college, she could attend evening classes to pass the required examination. Harry has volunteered to help her with further studies. We are both convinced she will make an excellent teacher. The Rev Simms says he has found her a pleasure to teach. He would like to continue tutoring Fiona in Latin for a small fee, payable in eggs and butter,' Mr Thorpe added with a smile, 'if that would suit you. We all believe Fiona should attend a teacher training college eventually if you are agreeable. I believe there are scholarships to help with the expense now. That would need to be checked of course. As a fully trained teacher she could earn a decent wage for life, although I expect some man will seize the chance to make her his wife, knowing how skilled your daughters are in household tasks, Mrs Sinclair. My son and I have not mentioned any of this to Fiona in case you disagree, but I'm sure you must know she enjoys learning and she has patience and a natural way of encouraging the younger children to enjoy their lessons. Not everyone possesses such a gift.'

'Mr Thorpe I believe you are determined to make one of my daughters into a teacher,' William said with a chuckle. 'I remember it was Marie you thought should be a teacher until Lord Hanley persuaded her to leave school and care for his wife.'

'Yes, Marie would have made an excellent teacher too but she seems to have made a fine choice in life. She looked beautiful and very happy on her wedding day.' He sighed. 'It made me feel an old man attending the wedding of one of my pupils. All your children are intelligent but they have worked hard too, even the boys. I believe that is due to the example set by yourself and your wife. I hear Janet has learned to drive already. I saw her in Lord Hanley's car. Is he hoping to commandeer her for his estate office too?'

'Oh no,' Emma said emphatically. 'He has got a trainee land agent to assist now. I expect he will teach him to drive eventually. Janet chauffeurs him when he needs a lift to the station, but she has no interest in working in the estate office.'

'I can believe that,' Mr Thorpe chuckled. 'The first day she attended school Janet made it clear that her animals meant more to her than anything else. Although she always paid great attention to her lessons she was always ready to go home at the end of the day to make sure they had survived without her. I remember your eldest daughter, Meg, was the same, but they both loved poetry and nature study. How is Meg by the way?'

'She still enjoys helping her husband with the animals but she and Ranald have a son and wee girl now so they come first.'

'I am pleased she is happy. Knowledge is never wasted whatever work they choose'.

'We have never insisted any of them must work here at Moorend,' William said. 'We were disappointed when Jamie ran away to Scotland of course but he seems to be doing well. Worst of all was losing our son, John after he was gassed during the war. Nothing could be worse than that so we feel they must decide what they want to do with their lives.'

'I am pleased to hear you feel that way,' Mr Thorpe nodded. 'Lord Hanley is sending Richard to a private school after the summer, and from there he hopes the boy will go to university but I hear he is very keen to ride around the estate with Mr Rowbottom, the land agent.'

'Yes, he is, but they're never too young to learn about the land and the management of the estate,' William said. 'I don't think anyone will be surprised if he inherits Silverbeck Estate someday so it will be better if he understands how things should be done.'

'I'm sure you're right,' Mr Thorpe agreed. 'But please give my suggestion for Fiona some thought and let me know what you decide. Harry would welcome her help with the younger children now that I am giving up completely.'

'We will discuss it with Fiona,' Emma said. 'We shall support her whatever she decides to do, isn't that so William?'

'Yes. We thank you for taking time to call, Mr Thorpe.'

'It is a pleasure,' the old teacher replied with a smile. 'Give my regards to Marie. I see her sometimes when she is down visiting you. She always walked to school with your little granddaughter to meet Fiona and Rick. Is her husband still interested in motor cars or is he too busy with the estate?'

'Oh he has built himself a garage now and he repairs motors and engines from miles around. He still has the Strathlinn Estate of course but he says Marie is more efficient at running that than he is. They work well together. Mark couldn't stop reading and talking about that young American Captain who flew an aeroplane all the way from New York to Paris. He is sure we shall all be taking to the air before long.'

'Ah I remember reading about that. Captain Charles Lindberg was his name I think?'

'Yes, that's right. Mark was even more impressed when a woman flew from Newfoundland to Wales the following year. I believe he would have travelled down to see her land if he had not been so busy.'

'I expect they have children of their own now to care for.' He was sorry he had asked when he saw Emma's eyes cloud.

'N-No, Marie and Mark have not been blessed with children.'

Emma sank onto the old rocking chair when William showed Mr Thorpe out. It was six years now since Marie and Mark's wedding but they had no children. Marie adored Marguerite and the twins, but even they were not the same as having children of her own, at least not to Emma, whose life revolved around her family. Marguerite and the twins now rode to East Lowrie School each day on their ponies and turned them out to graze in the paddock with Mark and Fiona's. All three children ran eagerly from school at midday to eat their lunch with Marie, and Mark too when he was at home. The school was at the same end of the village as the Blacksmiths where Marie and Mark had chosen to build their new home. Emma was convinced Marie must long for a child of her own but if there were problems she had not confided in her mother. Emma was thankful Mark and Marie were able to share their work and interests and they certainly seemed happily married. Mark always said he could never have managed the estate without Marie's help and without her he would have sold it and left the country.

Emma was grateful because Mark had kept his word to bring Marie home to Yorkshire at least once a year and because Lord Tannahill and his family had given them a generous wedding gift of a motor car they had come to

Moorend at least twice each year so far. Emma chewed her lower lip. Every time they returned to Scotland they tried to persuade her and William to return with them to see their new home, visit their Scottish relations, and see their childhood haunts. They had named their house Marsinford, a combination of their own names. Although he was laird of the Stavondale Estate, Mark was adamant he did not want any confusion with Stavondale Tower, which now belonged to Lord Tannahill along with the Home Farm.

It had been Marie's suggestion that Mr Mason, the East Lowrie blacksmith, should take on an apprentice rather than give up the Smiddy. The surrounding farmers were relieved they would not need to walk their horses several miles to another blacksmith to be shod but Mrs Emily Mason was most grateful of all because it meant she could stay in the house where she and her late sister had been born. Also, her nephew, Angus Brownlea, could make his home with them and train to be a blacksmith like his grandfather. It was Angus who had made a pair of high wrought iron gates and carefully constructed a design to incorporate the name Marsinford House. The boy was also making good progress at shoeing the horses which came to the Smiddy so he was overjoyed when his uncle offered to show him how to make the more intricate curves which were part of the design he had drawn for the gates, but which were proving more difficult than he had anticipated.

'Eh laddie, 'tis a pleasure to help a youngster as keen as you are. Ye remind me of my own apprentice days. Your grandfather taught me everything I know, as well as giving me his blessing when I wanted to marry your aunt Emily. It's bred in ye to be a good blacksmith. If it hadna been for you and our young laird I would have given up by now. Ye've made your aunt the happiest woman in East Lowrie. She and your mother were born in the Smiddy House and she hopes to end her days here.'

Mark proudly hung the gates between the pillars of the high wall which now surrounded the house and extensive garden. Both Angus and his uncle grinned with pleasure when Marie expressed her sincere praise.

'You have given our new home the finishing touch. The gates look splendid,' she told them. Many of the customers who came to the Smiddy also praised the gates on the young laird's new house and two farmers ordered a name on a sign-post for their own farms. Angus enjoyed this artistic work for testing his skills and he agreed to do it in his own time after finishing his day's work for his uncle. Since the Masons had no children of their own Emily was jubilant that her nephew had settled so well and she couldn't praise Marie and Mark enough for making things possible for them.

# CHAPTER SIX

Bob Rowbottom and his wife had only one daughter and she was married and lived in Ireland so he was uncertain how he could help his twenty-four-year-old trainee land agent settle into a new area. He had come as a stranger to this part of Yorkshire himself but he had been newly married and happy to have his young wife to himself. Lord Hanley and his wife had been young then too and they held a yearly dinner for the tenants and several other people from the area and introduced himself and Mary to everyone.

Lord Hanley had allocated Mike Watt a cottage within the boundary of the Hall's private grounds. He had instructed one of the odd job men to whitewash the walls inside and out and to paint the woodwork to ensure it would be clean and fresh. Bob wondered if that had been Thea Whitelea's suggestion. A new carpet square for one room and a woven jute floor covering for the kitchen cum living room had duly arrived and Rick's mother had taken it upon herself to provide some of the essential furniture from the spare rooms and attics at the Hall, making sure Mike had a bed and a chest upstairs, a kitchen table with a couple of chairs and a dresser, plus two comfortable armchairs, an oil lamp and several candle sticks.

Bob Rowbottom guessed Thea was missing Rick now that he was boarding away at school during the week. Even at weekends he spent most of his time riding around the estate either with him and Mike, or with his grandfather. He was developing a genuine interest in the way the estate was run, and in getting to know the tenants and what they needed in the way of repairs or improvements. Although he was only fourteen he was shrewd enough to see which tenants appreciated whatever their landlord did for them and which ones did little or nothing to help themselves. He never failed to call in at Moorend to see his friend David Sinclair. He still found Fiona as challenging and competitive as she had been while they were at school together and he admitted he owed much of his present success at his new school to her. This was not strictly true. It was Harry Thorpe who had instilled in him a thirst for knowledge and he now excelled at mathematics and physics. Although Lord Hanley employed an excellent cook at the Hall, Rick still delighted in sampling Emma's cakes in the Moorend kitchen. He had no objection to eating with Cliff Barnes or Tom Nichol the live-in workers. In comparison Bob Rowbottom felt it must be a lonely life for Mike, alone in his cottage. He remarked on this to his wife.

'You must invite him to have a meal with us on Sunday,' Mary suggested promptly. 'I have a couple of rugs and a stool he can have for his cottage if he wants them, and some spare cutlery and plates.'

'All right I'll ask him to come for Sunday dinner. He told me his mother had packed a chest with bedding and spare clothes and towels. His father was a Colonel in the army I think, and his family don't seem to be short of money as far as I can gather. They employ a cook and a cleaning woman as well as a gardener. His father has opened a bank account for him to draw on until he gets his first pay and he has advised him to pay a woman to come in and clean the cottage, do his washing and perhaps cook him a meal now and then. He asked if I could recommend anyone.'

'His father must realise he needs to set a good example if he is to go round advising and inspecting the tenants, but he'll not get to know many of the village folks while he's living out at the Hall that's for sure,' Mary said sympathetically.

'I know, but Lord Hanley thought it would be more convenient for him being nearer the estate office and there's stabling for six horses so there's room beside Thea's and his own, Rick's and Lady Hanley's elderly mare. Thea seems to enjoy riding round with Lord Hanley. It has given him a new lease of life. He's got his sense of humour back. I suspect his discovery of a grandson has also prompted him to bring in Mike as a trainee ready for when Rick takes over and we take a back seat'.

'Do you call Mrs Whitelea Thea to her face?' Mary Rowbottom asked curiously. She knew her husband was always deferential even though he and Lord Hanley got on so well together.

'Yes. Lord Hanley asked me to use her Christian name and she agreed. Didn't I tell you he has had Rick's name changed to Fortescue, officially. His solicitor arranged it. He wanted Thea to use the same name because it was what would have happened if Richard had not been killed so soon.

'What did she say?'

'She is keeping the name Whitelea. She says she was grateful for it at the time and it would feel like denying he ever existed.'

'Mmm I expect Lord Hanley hoped to avoid people asking awkward questions as Rick grows older,' Mary reflected.

'I expect people will get used to it in time. I think they have done all the gossiping in Silverbeck and now they have accepted Rick for the pleasant, well-mannered lad that he is.'

'I'm glad to hear that, for his own sake. But getting back to your new assistant. Couldn't you introduce Mike to some of the Silverbeck tenants who have sons his age?'

'I suppose I could. Maybe I should take him to Moorend and introduce him to the Sinclairs. They are the friendliest and most hospitable family I know. William Sinclair is the best example of a good tenant too. It's true he likes a good bargain, but it would be experience for Mike learning how to negotiate with the tenants. The ones who are always making demands and never expect an increase in rent take more controlling. William Sinclair always agrees to a fair deal and he's a good farmer.'

'Mmm, it seems there's more to being a land agent than I supposed,' his wife said with a smile. 'I thought you just rode around on your horse all day or drank coffee in the estate office.' Bob grinned back at her.

'If only life was that easy. I look forward to the day we can retire and move to Ireland to be near our lass, especially now we have a couple of grandchildren.'

'That will not be for a few years yet,' Mary said with a sigh, 'but we have been lucky when you think of Lord Hanley losing both his sons, and then his wife.'

* * *

At the first opportunity Bob took his protégé to Moorend and introduced him to William Sinclair along with a bit of banter.

'Well laddie ye'd better come in and meet the family and find out for yourself that Scotsmen are not as bad as this Yorkshire rogue makes us out to be,' William said with a wink at Bob Rowbottom. 'It's teatime anyway. We always have a drink and a bite to eat before we start the milking so ye're welcome to join us.'

Bob Rowbottom duly introduced Mike to Emma who immediately pulled out a chair and sat him next to Peter'.

'Peter is not always here at this time of day,' she said. 'He and Alan work together at Mountcliffe, especially now Alan's wife is getting near her time.' Mike sent an enquiring glance at Bob.

'We have not been to Mountcliffe yet,' Bob told him. 'But Mr Sinclair here is always on the lookout for a tenancy for one of his sons.' He winked at William, 'So you'd better beware.'

'Well it seems they all want to farm,' William agreed. 'David here has been left school a year now. We have given him plenty of hard work but he still wants to farm, isn't that right, laddie?'

'Aye, it is,' David grinned mischievously. 'I'm the youngest so I'm waiting for Dad to retire so I can take over here at Moorend.'

'Aah, so that's why ye're wanting me to teach ye to plough, is it?' William quirked an eyebrow at his youngest son, as Fiona burst into the kitchen.

'Well hello, lass,' Bob Rowbottom greeted her with a smile. 'Mike this is the youngest of the Sinclair chicks, and she's as bonny as the rest of them.' He eyed her black wind-blown curls and rosy cheeks. 'What are you doing with yourself, Fiona? Are you missing Rick now he's moved to a school the other side of Wakefield?'

'Fiona is a pupil teacher at Silverbeck School,' Emma said with pride. 'She got an excellent leaving certificate so young Mr Thorpe has volunteered to be her mentor. He is encouraging her to take examinations at the evening classes in Wakefield so that she can apply to go to teacher training college and become a fully qualified teacher.' Fiona blushed and rolled her eyes at her mother's report.

'Well you couldn't have a better coach from what I've heard of Harry Thorpe. I believe he's something of a genius with mathematics, and logic, whatever that means.'

'It's nice to meet you Mr Watt, but if you'll excuse us,' Peter said pushing back his chair, 'Janet and I had better get away to the milking. Tom and Cliff will have brought the cows in by now.'

'Before you go, Peter, I wondered if you and Janet would introduce Mike to some of the other young folks at the Silverbeck dances. He's a stranger to this area.'

'Of course,' Peter agreed with a grin. 'There's a dance most weeks in the hall near the church. It's quite a walk from the Hall though. Would you ride down to the village? I could ask Alan if you can stable your horse in the stable at

Mountcliffe. It's the farm in the middle of the village so you wouldn't have far to walk from there. In fact if you want to come this Saturday we could meet you at Mountcliffe and all go in together, couldn't we Jan?'

'Of course,' Janet smiled, 'But I shall tread on your toes if you call me Jan,' she winked at Mike. 'My name is Janet.'

'All right, I shall remember that,' Mike said smiling back at her. He looked at Peter, 'And thanks for the offer.'

'Drink up then lad,' Bob advised him. 'These folks need to get to work, but we'll make a quick call at Mountcliffe to introduce you to Alan Sinclair. I expect he will be at the milking too but we'll not hold him back,' he said with a nod to William.

'Knowing Alan he'll not let you. In fact he'll be more likely to hand ye a stool and a pail and set ye both on to help.'

'Not for me these days,' Bob grinned. 'How about you, Mike? Can you milk a cow?'

'Oh yes. Father insisted I should work on a farm for at least a year before I went down south to college. I had a go at everything. I enjoyed it but my family doesn't own enough land for a farm so I settled for being a land agent. At least it lets me get outside in the fresh air.' William nodded in approval.

Janet loved dancing. Although she couldn't play the fiddle, like her father she had inherited William's sense of rhythm, and she was light on her feet, so she was never without a partner. She knew all the young folks in the village, as did Peter. Most of them had attended the village school around the same time, but when it was a well-known band people came from surrounding villages too, some walking miles, some in groups by pony and cart, a few riding their own horses, which they turned into a small paddock which was situated behind the Smiddy and belonged to the Wrights.

As Janet and Peter were walking down the village street to the hall with Mike Watt, Janet was surprised to see the two young men she had met at the Smiddy. She remembered the one with the limp was Brian Shaw and she guessed it was his cousin who had persuaded him to come to the dance. Certainly she had never seen him here before. They all arrived at the doors of the hall together.

'Aah, Miss Janet Sinclair I believe,' Leonard Shaw greeted them confidently and held out his hand to Janet. 'Mr Wright, blacksmith, told us you come to the dances regularly. We intended to come before this but I have been away. We hoped we should see you here, didn't we Cos?'

'I er y-yes,' Brian said. His eyes moved questioningly to her companions.

'This is Brian Shaw from Thorley Grange. This is my brother, Peter Sinclair,' Janet introduced them, 'and this is Mike Watt. He is new to the district and he is working for Lord Hanley as a land agent.' Brian was first to extend a welcoming hand and a warm smile and for some reason Janet felt pleased about that. 'I am pleased to meet you, Mike. This is my cousin, Leonard Shaw. He is staying with us for a few weeks, but his home is in Lancashire where he breeds horses.' Leonard didn't seem particularly pleased to meet another young man and Janet suspected he was more interested in eyeing up the girls.

'I'm a Lancashire lad too,' Mike said with a grin. 'Are we likely to have another War of the Roses?'

'Not with only two of you,' Janet laughed. 'We should soon overcome you.'

'Indeed we would,' Brian agreed. 'You had better be on your best behaviour for once Leonard or Miss Sinclair will be despatching you back home again.'

The village hall was already fairly full and the band was tuning up. Mike Watt immediately turned to Janet to ask for the first dance. He gave her a rueful smile.

'I promise not to pester you all evening but I need to get my bearings and hope Peter will introduce me to some of the other young ladies.'

'Oh we shall both introduce you to our friends and the locals are all friendly.' Leonard Shaw was scowling at Mike but seconds later he was asking another girl to dance. 'Mr

Leonard Shaw is as big a stranger to this village as you are, Mike, but I see he's not waiting for any introductions.'

'No, I'd say he seems confident of his charms,' Mike grinned.

'Exactly.' Janet rarely made hasty judgments but there was something about Leonard Shaw which irritated her. She got the impression that he was far too sure of himself and she guessed he did not hesitate to use people to get what he wanted. Her glance moved to his cousin, already seated and watching the dancing. Brian had probably only come to the dance to please his cousin.

As usual Janet was in demand but she made sure she introduced Mike to several of the other girls she knew. The next two dances were very energetic and Janet seized the chance to take a seat next to Brian Shaw while she recovered her breath.

'Am I right in thinking you are here to please your cousin and supposedly keep him company?' she asked ironically, her brows arching. She knew his cousin had not been near him since they entered the hall even though Brian didn't know anyone else.

'We-ell, as you can guess dancing is not my favourite pastime these days, but we have not seen Leonard for some time. My parents thought it was the least I could do to accompany him since he wanted to come.'

'I think you are more tolerant than I would be. Anyway, we shall have a waltz coming up any time now after the lively dances we have just had. Will you dance with me?' She saw the dismay in his eyes and knew he was about to make some excuse. 'No, don't refuse. I know it's not the accepted thing for a girl to ask the man to dance so please don't humiliate me.'

'May I have the next dance, Miss Sinclair?' Janet looked up to see the confident smile of Leonard Shaw.

'I'm sorry but I'm already spoken for,' she said and turned her head so that only Brian could see the unspoken message in her green eyes. Don't let me down!

'Brian doesn't dance — not since his accident,' Leonard announced holding out his hand, but Janet turned away, feeling for Brian's hand which lay between them on the bench. His fingers fastened firmly round hers as he stood up, pulling her with him.

'I hope you will not regret this, Janet Sinclair.'

'Almost everyone gets up for the waltz so even if we only walk or shuffle round no one will notice us.'

'I suspect Leonard will,' he grinned. 'He's not used to a pretty girl turning him down, especially for me.' Janet felt very comfortable held so firmly and there was no doubt Brian Shaw must have been a very good dancer before the accident which left him with a limp. As the dance ended her eyes were shining with pleasure as she looked up at him.

'Your limp is much better than it was the first time I saw you at the Smiddy and you certainly know how to dance. I enjoyed that.'

'Really? I have to confess I would never have asked anyone here for a dance, but I enjoyed it too.'

'Then I shall make it my mission for tonight to say I am booked for all the waltzes, oh and any other slow dances? Is that all right with you?'

'It is more than all right for me, but are you sure? We heard from Mr Wright that you are always in demand at the dances.'

'I never suggest anything I don't want to do. Anyway I don't like to see anyone sitting out all evening, especially when you don't even know anyone to have a decent conversation with.' She looked across at Mike, now dancing with the pretty daughter of one of the other Silverbeck tenants, while Peter was partnering Helen Barclay for the second time.

'I see my brother, Peter, is still keen on his present partner, Helen Barclay. Her father is also a Silverbeck tenant. She is only sixteen and Peter is twenty-five at the end of this year but he is really keen on her. Even so he would have made a point of coming to speak to you if he saw you on your own all evening.'

'I don't think the gap in their ages would make any difference if they love each other,' Brian reflected. 'She doesn't look like a giggly teenager.'

'No, she's a lovely girl and Mr Rowbottom says she's very capable. Her mother died when she was fourteen so she left school to keep house for her father. I shall be very happy if I end up with Helen for a sister-in-law. We're very lucky so far — all our family have married lovely people.'

'You're fortunate to have such a close family. I am an only one. I think that is why my parents have always encouraged Leonard to visit us so often, though to be honest I have never minded my own company or been lonely, but then I went to boarding school when I was ten.'

'Did your cousin go to the same school with you?'

'No, he didn't want to live away from home. He has an elder sister and a younger one and I think women seem to have doted on him all his life.'

'I get the impression your cousin is a selfish young man. Oh dear,' Janet clapped a hand to her mouth and her green eyes looked at him in horror. 'I shouldn't have said that. I know you didn't ask for my opinion. Will you forgive me? I'm not usually so outspoken, or so critical.' Brian looked at her and a slow smile began to spread over his face, softening the angular planes of his high cheek bones. His dark eyes gleamed with humour.

'Do you know I have never known a girl before who didn't consider my cousin to be the most desirable man in the room. When I consider it, I believe you may be right. He is inclined to arrange things to suit himself. I don't think even my parents ever see through his manipulations.'

They fell to discussing their families and their respective farms and the work they did.

'Your cattle are all pedigree?' Janet exclaimed eagerly. 'I would love our herd to be pedigree. I can remember all our cows from when they were born, and which bull was their sire. My father is not interested in keeping the pedigrees yet. He and Drew Kerr both enjoy going to the market and doing a wee bit of wheeling and dealing. I think they encourage each other to see who can make the most profit. Since my brother Alan married, he has taken on the tenancy of Mountcliffe and my father uses that as an excuse for looking for heifers at a bargain price. I suggested that we could make our own herd pedigree and he could buy his bargains for Alan, but so far he has not been persuaded, although he often asks me about the breeding of our own heifers when they come into the herd for milking and he likes to know which bulls are passing on the better qualities and conformation. His excuse is that I shall get married one day and leave him with the records to keep but I have no intention of getting married. I would hate to leave all the animals I have helped to rear since the day they were born. I could never live in a town.'

'I expect your father prefers Ayrshires, him being a Scotsman?' Brian asked. 'Ours are all Dairy Shorthorns.'

'We still have a few Shorthorn cows descended from the ones my parents took over when they came to Yorkshire. They are more placid than the Ayrshires in my opinion.'

'Yes so I have heard. Would you . . . ?'

'Perhaps you will favour me with this dance Miss Janet Sinclair?'

'What?' Janet turned her head impatiently and saw Leonard Shaw smiling down confidently at her. 'Oh, no, sorry. This is another waltz. I have promised all the waltzes to Brian this evening. Anyway, we were enjoying an interesting conversation when you interrupted.' Brian tried hard not to smile but he had his tongue in his cheek and he didn't meet his cousin's startled gaze. He sensed Leonard's annoyance at being refused again but for once he didn't care how his cousin felt. He was delighting in Janet's company. Indeed, he found he was enjoying the whole evening far more than he had dreamed possible. He stood up and drew Janet confidently into his arms as the music began to play again.

'It will be good for Leonard to meet with a little opposition for once,' he murmured, close to Janet's ear. She smiled up at him and saw his dark eyes were bright with mischief.

'I do agree, but it was true I was enjoying our discussion. So, few men think women understand about animals and farming. Peter has been teaching me how to plough but Dad doesn't know yet. I admit it would be hard work if I had to do it all day but at least I can make a straight furrow.'

'I shall be surprised if there is anything you can't do once you set your mind to it, Janet. You put me to shame. I would never have had the courage to get up and dance if you had not persuaded me this evening. I would like to repay you for your time and patience because I know you rarely sit out for a single dance. The blacksmith's wife told us that. Will you allow me to take you out for a meal one evening soon? I know of a nice place in Wakefield. Would next Friday evening suit you? Please say yes?'

Janet began to laugh. 'And shall we both ride there together on your horse?' she asked merrily. 'Or did you want me to go on the train and meet you there?' she asked uncertainly when she saw he was in earnest.

'I would never ask you to do that! My father will be happy to lend me his car. My parents will be delighted to hear I have enjoyed this evening. They are always on at me to go out more now I'm recovering from the accident. I think that's why they keep inviting Leonard to stay.'

'All right. I have never been out just for a meal, except for things like weddings. It will be a new experience for me. Er . . . it will only be the two of us? I mean you will not be bringing your cousin too?' she asked diffidently. 'I think I have offended him by refusing to partner him. He ought to be pleased to see you are not spending the whole evening alone waiting for the dance to end.'

'Don't worry about Leonard. It will do him good to see that not every girl in the room is eager to get his attention.' He chuckled suddenly. 'He will be in a bad humour for a day or two when he realises he is not invited to join us for the evening.' His brown eyes twinkled. 'He can find his own pretty girl to take out for the evening. He only ever thinks of going to dances.'

'Even though he knows you don't usually enjoy them?'

'He doesn't consider that. Come to think of it maybe he is a bit spoiled and egotistic when I see him as he must look through your eyes. Your brother is keeping an eye on us. I suppose he sees you home, does he?'

'We usually go home together but I know he would rather take Helen home.' She grinned. 'He hasn't plucked up courage yet to ask her father's permission if he can walk out with her. I suppose you couldn't blame her father if he is wary of Peter's intentions when he is so much older. As far as I know he has never shown an interest in any other girl, but Mr Barclay will not know that.'

Brian didn't say anything for a moment or two but his mind was busy. If he and Janet enjoyed an evening together next Friday perhaps he could suggest they make up a foursome with Peter and Helen, so long as he could borrow the car again. It might be a way of getting to know Janet's family. He wondered how her father would react to his daughter being friendly with a cripple — a farmer who would never again be fit to do a day's ploughing. He had just begun to learn to plough when he had the accident. He was pleased to know Janet was as interested in animals as he was himself, especially cattle. He knew he was a good stockman and that more than made up for many of the jobs he could no longer do on their own farm. His limp had improved considerably in the past few months but he knew his injured leg would never be as strong as it had been.

'Maybe your brother and Helen could make up a foursome one evening. That might allay her father's fears.'

'That's a great idea! I would never have thought of that. I'll suggest it to Peter.'

# CHAPTER SEVEN

Fiona longed to go to the dances too but William refused to give his permission until she was seventeen. Even then he said she would have to persuade David to take her and see her home, but David showed no interest in dancing or girls. He spent all his spare time training his beloved collie, which naturally earned their father's approval.

The rest of the family teased Fiona, telling her their father was extra protective because she was the baby of the family. This was true, although neither William nor Emma would ever admit they were not looking forward to all their children leaving the nest. Alan lived near and Meg was not a great distance away but Emma knew it was not the same as being under the same roof. It still made her heart ache when she thought of Jamie and Marie both living so far away back in Scotland and she often thought of her own parents and how sad they must have felt when she and William moved away to live in Yorkshire. At least she was more fortunate than they had been because Mark kept his promise to bring Marie back to visit regularly and they always brought wee Marguerite with them. She knew William adored their eldest grandchild as much as she did and she was thankful that Jamie and Rina were happy to let her visit when they could not bring her themselves.

Meanwhile Fiona worked hard at her evening classes and Harry Thorpe was always prepared to help her. He seemed even more proud of her excellent results than her own family. They expected she would do well and teased her about being the brains of the family, although she knew they were proud of her underneath the banter. Her success was due to her enjoyment of learning, but she also wanted to repay Harry. She was determined not to let him down when he gave her so much time and encouragement. She was enjoying being a pupil teacher but it made her keener to become a properly qualified teacher.

'Sometimes I almost wish you were not doing so well with your examinations, Fiona,' Harry said one day, surprising her. 'You will have sufficient qualifications now to apply for teacher training college after the summer and we shall miss you terribly when you go away.'

'I'm not looking forward to living away from Silverbeck and everyone I know,' Fiona confessed, 'but I do want to be a good teacher.'

'You already are a good teacher. It's a gift. You have a way of encouraging even the most reluctant children to learn, but I know getting your qualifications will make a big difference to your future prospects. I keep telling myself I must not be selfish and I should encourage you to go to college.' He sighed. 'We shall all miss you though, especially now my parents are growing frailer. My father is beginning to find even his gardening too much these days, although he has always loved to get outdoors with his pupils. Mother worries him too. She seems to live in the past more and more as the months go by.' He sighed again. Fiona knew Mrs Thorpe sometimes wandered into the village and forgot where she was going. Harry had rented a small cottage of his own some distance away when he was working at another job but since he returned to take over the village school he had moved back into the schoolhouse. Fiona sensed he sometimes found it a strain, especially when his mother forgot he was a man of twenty-six and no longer her little boy.

Janet was more nervous and excited than she had expected when Friday arrived. She told Emma she would be going out for the evening as soon as they had finished the milking.

'Is that a hint you want to gobble up your meal and have a bath? Is there a dance tonight?'

'No,' Janet found herself blushing. 'A young man called Brian Shaw is coming to take me out for a meal. He is borrowing his father's car.'

'Oh, I see . . .'

'Oh Mum,' Janet smiled wryly. 'Don't look like that. He is perfectly respectable. He was at the dance to keep his cousin company last week because neither of them knew anyone from Silverbeck. Brian has a lame leg so he was sitting at the side on his own but his cousin didn't seem to care.' Emma smiled. She could tell Janet had been annoyed with the cousin, whoever he was. 'I had met them a while ago at the Smiddy so I missed a dance to go and chat for a bit. We got talking about cattle. They have a pedigree herd of Dairy Shorthorns . . .'

'Aah, now I understand. That topic would suit you fine.'

'Yes it did. He was every interesting. Anyway I persuaded him to get up to try a waltz. He got on quite well, then he asked me up for the last waltz and thanked me for making his evening more pleasant than he had anticipated. He said he would like to take me out for a meal to repay my kindness.'

'That sounds decent of him. I hope you enjoy it. Will his cousin be there too?'

'I hope not!' Janet said heatedly. 'I reckon he's one of those selfish wretches who only thinks about himself. I think Brian understood that I wouldn't go if he was there too.'

'Didn't he mind you being so outspoken about his relations?' Emma asked in amusement. Janet was usually one of the most tolerant and patient of her children but when she felt strongly about things she showed her father's flash of temper, although she had not inherited his ginger hair.

'I don't think he was offended, in fact he seemed to agree with me when he considered his cousin's behaviour.

We shall not be late home by the way so there's no need for you to worry. Peter has met him.'

This was the first of several Friday or Saturday evening outings when Brian took Janet for a meal or to see a film. They went to the dances if they were held at Silverbeck but Leonard Shaw always came to them too which rather spoiled it for Janet. He had never asked her to dance again which was a relief, especially as she had plenty of partners without him and most of them understood when she saved the waltzes and slower dances for Brian. She thought it strange that Leonard often seemed to be staying at Thorley Grange, although he was supposed to work for his father in Lancashire where their main business seemed to be breeding and training horses. The best went forward for racing with the rest being sold as hunters or working ponies.

Twice Brian had suggested to Peter that he would be happy to make a foursome if Helen Barclay's father would give permission for her to join them. Helen was delighted with the idea and eventually Peter plucked up courage to call on Mr Barclay and ask if he would allow Helen to go with him, Janet and Brian. Mr Barclay seemed reassured when Brian drove into the yard in his father's car with Janet beside him. Peter jumped out to greet him and hold the door open for Helen to get in.

'You must all come in for a night cap and a chat when you return,' Mr Barclay said pleasantly. 'I would like to hear a bit more about your brother and his sheep dogs, Peter. I could do with a good working dog myself.'

Janet liked Helen even more as they got to know each other and Mr Barclay would have had to be blind not to see the happy serenity which seemed to surround his daughter like a warm cloak. He began to enjoy Peter's company himself as they got to know each other better. Consequently Peter was grateful to Brian for his help in their blossoming friendship. He and Helen always took time to chat with Brian for a while, if Janet was dancing, and gradually other friends stopped to join them. They found Brian interesting and easy company. Mike Watt seemed equally pleased to find a new friend in Brian because it was taking time to become accepted by the Silverbeck locals and discover which of them he might encounter as Lord Hanley's tenants.

'I am quite happy to come to the Silverbeck dances now I am getting to know everyone,' Brian assured Janet one evening when they were deciding what to do the following Saturday.

'You know I love the local dances but it makes me happier now I know you don't mind coming too,' Janet said.

'My only regret is that I don't get to see you home myself,' he said with a grin and chuckled when Janet blushed. He had found her delightfully innocent the first time he had kissed her goodnight. Even at the end of the dances he usually found an opportunity to evade his impatient cousin so he could be alone with her for a goodnight kiss.

The evening Brian invited Janet to accompany him to a tenants' dinner and meet his parents for the first time she was a bundle of nerves but Emma was delighted for her.

'We must go into Wakefield and choose some material to make you a lovely dress for the evening. You must choose a style that you like too. I remember the first tenants' dinner I attended with your father when we first came to Moorend. I was nervous but Lady Hanley and Mrs Rowbottom soon put me at ease and the Tindalls were so friendly and down to earth. We have been friends with Lynn's grandparents ever since.'

The first time Emma had gone to Wakefield on her own she had met Miss Grace Hill and her sister who owned the haberdashery shop. The two ladies were getting old now but they were reluctant to give up their business. Over the years Emma had become good friends with them and she still supplied them and a small group of their friends with her butter and fresh eggs every week. She used to take it on the train but the demand had increased and now Janet usually drove her to Wakefield in the van to save her carrying so much weight. So both Emma and Janet received a warm welcome when they explained they wanted material and a pattern to make Janet a dress for an evening dinner.

'I don't want anything with frills and flounces,' Janet said when Miss Hill went to fetch a pile of pattern books. She scrutinised Janet for a moment over her steel spectacles, then replaced the large book with another. She smiled.

'You do not need anything fussy I can see. You are tall and slender. Something elegant, I think.'

'I agree,' her sister said promptly. 'Do you go to dances dear?'

'Yes, I love dancing. But this is not a dance,' Janet said anxiously. 'It is a tenants' dinner.' Brian had told her he never liked wearing his evening suit and bow tie, but he would need to do so to please his parents.

'Mmm, definitely elegant then, and long enough to reach the ankles,' Miss Hill said. 'There is a very simple pattern here, with long sleeves, but the material would need to drape easily. Or here is a dress which would be very versatile. It is true the bodice is cut fairly low with a square neckline and broad straps instead of sleeves, but it has a demure little jacket to go over the top with a row of tiny covered buttons from the neatly fitting waist to the neck with a small stand-up collar which would make it ideal for a sober dinner party. At a later date you could exchange the jacket for a light stole or cape and wear it for a dance.'

'I like that idea,' Janet said immediately. 'Do you agree, Mam? Would it be difficult to make? Will you have time?'

'I shall if you and Fiona do all the baking this week,' Emma said with a laugh.

'The dress itself is fairly simple with mainly long seams,' Miss Mary Hill mused. She had trained as a tailor in her young day. 'What makes it so elegant is the cut. It is cut on the bias and will flatter your slim figure, and you move so gracefully. I could cut it out for you while you are doing the rest of your shopping if that would help, Emma?'

'Oh it would help a lot,' Emma said gratefully. 'I would hate to make a mistake with the cutting.'

'Then we should choose a material,' her sister said promptly. 'I believe there are some lovely remnants in the chest which was delivered from our Leeds supplier earlier this week.'

'Yes, you're right, my dear sister,' Miss Mary said happily. She had loved making clothes all her life and especially when they pleased her customers but her eyesight was getting poor these days. 'I recall there was a lovely deep pink crepe which would suit Janet's dark hair so beautifully.'

'Yes, so there was. I will bring it through.' She bustled away to the storeroom. They heard her call through, 'There is this lovely lemon brocade too. It reminds me of the sunshine. Would you like to see it too, Janet?'

'Yes please,' Janet said with a smile. 'Ooh, that's beautiful,' she exclaimed as soon as Miss Hill opened up the lemon material'.

'Mmm,' Emma agreed. 'That will really suit your fair skin, Janet, as well as your green eyes and dark curls.'

* * *

Janet had offered to drive herself to the dinner in her father's van to save Brian the double journey of collecting her and bringing her home again, especially when she guessed his parents would be needing the car too, but Brian insisted he would come for her. He was disappointed and a little annoyed with his parents. He had visualised this evening as an opportunity for his mother to invite Janet to stay overnight so they could begin to get to know her. He had met most of Janet's family several times and they always welcomed him into their home with warmth and kindliness. He knew Mike Watt had found the same friendly welcome too and he realised it was a natural part of their usual hospitality. He had also learned that Lord Hanley and Mr Rowbottom were equally at home at Moorend, as was their laird's grandson, Rick, whenever he was not at school.

Brian knew his own mother was hospitable by nature so he had expected that she and his father would be eager to meet Janet, especially since she was the only girl in whom he had ever shown a serious interest. In his heart he knew that his feelings went deeper than friendship so it was important to him that his parents should know and like the girl he hoped would become his wife, although he sensed he might not find it easy to tempt Janet away from her beloved cows and a warm and loving family. He needed his parents' approval as well as their help and support to welcome her into his own family circle. He was dismayed that his suggestions of introducing her to his parents had all been met with vague or evasive refusals from his mother.

Brian was usually tolerant and patient, pleasant and easy going by nature, but he had inherited the thread of steely determination which had made his father a more successful man than his younger stepbrother, Leonard's father. He was determined to take Janet to the tenants' dinner and to introduce her to both his mother and his father. When he told them he intended inviting Janet as his partner his mother had declared the invitation was only for the four of them and Leonard was already expecting to attend. Leonard's continued presence in his home was beginning to irk Brian and over this he was determined to have his way. So it was more by design than chance when he ran into their landlord down by the small wood where their own young stock were grazing for the summer. He knew Sir Anthony Rogan fairly well by now. He had been surprised when their landlord had made several visits to see him while he was in hospital after his accident. He had seemed genuinely concerned, even speaking to the surgeon and urging him to do his very best to repair Brian's shattered young limb so that he could ride again and continue his life as a farmer. They had enjoyed several long discussions on various topics. When Sir Anthony greeted him with apparent pleasure while out for his early morning ride Brian lost no time in asking if he could be permitted to bring a friend as his own dinner guest at the tenants dinner.

'Would that be a lady friend then young Brian?' Sir Anthony asked with a twinkle in his eye.

'It would.' Brian flushed slightly. 'She doesn't know it yet but she is the girl I hope to marry and I would like to take the opportunity of introducing her to my parents at the tenants' dinner, so long as it would not be inconvenient to your arrangements,' he added hastily.

'It will be no trouble at all, young sir. I am delighted to hear you are doing so well and enjoying a social life again. I noticed in church that your limp has improved considerably in recent weeks. Perhaps young love has magic cures that none of us knew about, eh?' he chuckled. 'I look forward to seeing you at the dinner.' He touched his hat and continued on his ride.

Brian sensed his mother was a little irritated because he had made his own arrangements, but his father readily agreed he could drop them off at Thorley Manor early then take the car to collect Janet.

Leonard immediately went off on some ploy of his own and Dan Shaw watched him go with a slight frown as he turned to speak to his wife.

'We have to remember, Emily, Brian is twenty-five and a man now. We have to let him make his own decisions, even his own mistakes if necessary.' He held up his hand before his wife could interrupt and he lowered his voice. 'I have always thought Brian a good judge of both men and beasts. Maybe you shouldn't pay quite so much attention to Leonard's tittle tattle about the girl.'

'But he was with Brian when they met her at that dance and he said she's just a gold digger and she clung to him all evening. He says her parents are Scottish and they have a huge family and are always out to make money from a quick deal.'

'Has it ever occurred to you, dear, that Leonard might be a mite jealous? I heard them arguing when they came home that evening. Brian was teasing Leonard because the girl had twice refused to dance with him. Apparently she kept him company instead because he couldn't join in the dancing.'

'Leonard is an excellent dancer I believe. He has no need to be jealous . . .'

'Can we be sure about that? There's more to life than dancing. I'm beginning to think he's become a selfish brat. He ought to be helping his father a lot more instead of idling his time away here. I had a letter from Bert earlier this week and he was saying they have had a good crop of foals this year but he's beginning to find it too much to break them all in on his own, let alone train them to the standard he likes. I know Leonard's reason for coming here so often was supposed to be as company for Brian while he was recovering after his accident, but he has been getting on with his own life as normal for a year now. It's not as though Leonard helps Brian with any work.' Emily chewed her lower lip in silence, looking anxious because she knew Dan was a shrewd man and usually right in his judgment in spite of his easy-going manner. 'Eh lass, don't worry about the young folk,' he said gently. 'Enjoy a good natter, as you women usually do at these affairs.'

'We women!' Emily exclaimed half laughing, half indignant. 'It's you men who do all the gossiping. I wonder what Leonard is doing over there with the place names? He must have forgotten to look at the plan near the door to see where we're seated.'

'He usually sits beside Brian. He'll not know many other folk here.'

'Brian will be sitting beside his guest. He was determined to bring her. I have never known him be serious about a girlfriend before.'

'He's no longer a boy and it is what you wanted. You were saying the other day how much you longed for grandchildren while we're still young enough to enjoy them.'

When Brian entered the kitchen at Moorend, as he did automatically since he was always made welcome, he halted in the doorway and gasped.

'Oh Janet, you look lovely, absolutely lovely,' he breathed in awe. Peter laughed aloud at his stunned expression.

'Does that mean she usually looks like Cinderella?' he chortled.

'You know it doesn't. She is always lovely but I have never seen her in evening dress before and with her hair styled on top of her head.'

'Do you think I'm overdressed for a tenants' dinner?' Janet asked uncertainly.

'Oh no. All the women will be dressed, but I shall be the proudest man there.'

'Ye're quite a handsome laddie yourself in your finery,' William said, his eyes twinkling. 'Away ye go, the pair o' ye and enjoy the evening.'

'Borrow my fur cape, Janet. It might be cold on the way home later.'

'Thanks Mam.' Janet leaned forward and kissed her mother's cheek. 'And thanks for making me such a lovely dress.'

'Your mother made your dress?' Brian asked in astonishment as he helped Janet carefully into the car. 'She must be very clever with a needle.'

'She is. She taught all of us to sew but none of us are as good as she is, except maybe Fiona.'

Most of the other guests had already arrived by the time Brian drew up at Thorley Manor. As they ascended the steps into the wide hallway Janet gasped in astonishment at the sight of the young couple who were entering in front of them.

'Meg? Megan . . . ?' she called softly, unwilling to draw attention, but Meg turned her head and gasped in surprise.

'What are you doing here?' they said in unison, then dissolved into quiet laughter before hugging each other warmly.

'Brian this is my eldest sister Megan. She is Mrs Ranald Kerr now.' Ranald turned at the sound of his name.

'Janet! My word you look good enough to eat,' he chuckled. 'Why are you here?'

'I am with Brian.' She introduced the two men. 'Brian's family are tenants. This is not your landlord, is it?'

'Sir Anthony is our landlord since last year, or one of them anyway. You know Mother and Father moved to a small farm so Meggie and I could move into the main farm after Belle was born. It belongs to Sir Anthony Rogan. Tonight's invitation was really for my parents but Mother said she preferred to look after our two rascals and it was time we had a night out — so here we are.'

'Brian was studying the seating plan. 'What a pity,' he said. 'We're seated on opposite sides of the room. It would have been good to be closer.'

'Never mind,' Ranald said with a twinkle in his blue eyes. 'Now that we have met you must both come to visit us at home and have a meal with us?'

'Oh yes, please do,' Megan agreed eagerly. 'We would love to get to know you properly, Brian. Everyone is taking their seats. We had better go. I will phone you, Janet, and arrange an evening soon if that's all right with you, Brian?'

'I shall look forward to that,' Brian said with a warm smile. 'We may see you later though. Everyone moves through to the large sitting room until our names are called to pay the rent.'

'It is alphabetical order I believe so we should be fairly early in the queue,' Ranald said. 'We shall probably leave soon after to let my parents get home to bed.'

The tables were arranged in a U shape so Janet followed Brian to their places at the far end of one side.

'Damn! That can't be right!' Brian muttered in annoyance'.

'What's wrong, Brian?' Janet asked anxiously. 'These are our place names.'

'Yes, I know but we were supposed to be at the very end. Instead I shall be sitting next to old Lady Rogan, Sir Anthony's mother. Someone must have squeezed her in next to us.'

'Is that so bad?' Janet asked innocently.

'Normally no. She's a nice enough old lady but she's quite deaf and she talks all the time and monopolises the persons sitting next to her — and that's me tonight!' He reached for Janet's hand beneath the white damask tablecloth and squeezed her fingers gently. 'Will you forgive me if I can't pay you much attention? This has rather spoiled our evening.'

'Don't worry,' Janet whispered back. 'We shall be alone on the drive home.' He smiled tenderly at her. As he looked up, he saw his parents and Leonard directly across the room at the end of the other line of tables. There appeared to be a vacant place at the end next to Leonard. Brian thought it had probably been for him originally. He frowned. Lady Rogan was definitely not seated next to him on the table plan for tonight. He saw Leonard give a mocking sneer, then he pretended to lick his finger and give himself a stripe on his shoulder. It was a sign he used to make whenever he had scored a point over Brian when they were younger. Brian had no idea what he meant tonight so he shrugged and turned to Janet.

'You and your sister are very much alike,' he said. 'The same lovely dark hair and tall slender figures.'

'Thank you. I always admired Meg when I was younger. My sister Marie has Dad's hair colour but she's very pretty. Jamie, my eldest brother, and David have the Sinclair auburn colouring too.'

Another man took his place beside Janet and Brian introduced him as Jim Bennet. He looked a bit older than Brian but he had a pleasant smile.

'Is your wife not with you tonight, Jim?' Brian asked.

'No. She decided not to risk it. Our second baby is due in a fortnight and the first one arrived early. Large meals don't agree with her either at present. I arrived early and told Sir Anthony she wouldn't be here. I see they have removed her place name but left the cutlery.'

'I think someone has made last minute changes,' Brian told him with a wry smile. 'Old Lady Rogan has been added beside me but we're a set of cutlery short now I take a proper look.'

'I'll pass you these,' Jim said.

'You can change places with me too if you like?' Brian suggested, tongue in cheek.

'No thanks. I'd barely get peace to eat my meal for Lady Rogan's chatter and I'm looking forward to a good feed.' He grinned at Janet. 'Besides I'd rather talk to your pretty partner. It makes a change to see you without your cousin tagging along.'

'Oh, Leonard is here tonight. He's over the other side with my parents. I asked Sir Anthony if I could bring Janet as my guest and he agreed so long as I introduce her to him this evening.' He turned to Janet. 'I forgot to tell you he is acquainted with your father's landlord, Lord Hanley I think he said.'

'That's right,' Janet nodded. 'I suppose most of the landowners know each other.' An old lady with a walking stick arrived at the end of their table and Brian stood to draw out her chair and help her into her seat. That was the last chance he had to speak more than the odd sentence to Janet but she understood and they exchanged a wry smile now and then. Fortunately Jim Bennet seemed happy to converse with her on various subjects and he introduced her to the middle aged farmer who was now seated next to him in what would have been his wife's place. Jim knew the Kerrs so he was delighted when he learned she and Megan were sisters.

'I saw them come in. There they are seated over at the other side,' he said. 'Now I know why you seemed vaguely familiar. You're like each other. Gillian, my wife, will be disappointed not to meet you. She knows Megan fairly well. I think they meet when they're shopping and our children are about the same ages.' After that conversation flowed freely between them while Brian did his best to entertain the old lady on his other side. They were waiting for the main course to be cleared away when Jim Bennet mentioned Leonard.

'Brian's cousin seems to spend more time at Thorley Grange than he does at home. God knows how he earns his living, sponging off his uncle I suppose,' he added bluntly. 'How do you get on with him?' Janet hesitated, chewing her lower lip while she tried to think of a tactful reply. 'Aah, your silence speaks for itself. I expect he resents Brian having a girlfriend, especially someone as pretty and vivacious as you are. Do you have much to do with him? Is he always tagging along too?'

'I-I'm afraid we avoid each other if possible. I know he doesn't care for me but the feeling is mutual. Brian knows I think he is selfish so it's easier if we're not in the same company,' she said reluctantly.

'Now why doesn't that surprise me?' Jim muttered. 'I've known them both since we were all in our teens. Whether it was horses, girls or a friendly game of football, Leonard always had to be top dog. I suppose you know it was Leonard who caused Brian's accident? I'm convinced he did it deliberately. Brian was lucky not to lose his leg.'

'I-I didn't know it was so bad.'

'It was really awful. Brian regained consciousness for a few minutes, although he was still trapped beneath his horse, and the thing that upset him most was the mare's pain and that she had to be put down. Her hind leg was broken you see. Brian had reared her from a foal and trained her himself. He thought the world of her. She really was a fine animal.'

'Oh dear. Poor Brian. He has never mentioned anything about it.'

'Leonard wanted the mare for breeding at his father's stables but Brian refused to part with her. In my heart I've wondered since if that was the reason Leonard deliberately jounced his own horse into Brian's while he was still midway over the jump. You see there was a narrow stretch of the hedge where it was cut lower because there was a ditch on the other side. It was for experienced riders following the hunt to take a short cut, one horse at a time. Brian's mare was in front and sailing beautifully over when Leonard came galloping from an angle on his ugly brute of a stallion. He seemed to want to shove Brian's mare out of the way. The sickening thing was he knew he had caused Brian and his mare to take a nasty fall. He glanced back over his shoulder and saw them on the ground but he carried on following the hunt. I had been riding behind Brian along with another man. Sir Anthony was beside me. We were giving the ones in front time to clear the jump, as you do. We saw it all. I still see that accident in my head as though it happened last week.'

'No wonder,' Janet said, dashing away an unwanted tear. 'No wonder Brian still walks with a limp.'

'He was lucky not to lose his leg. When we got him out from under his mare his leg was broken twice below the knee as well as his thigh bone. Sir Anthony took charge. He knew what to do and he stopped us from moving Brian in case we made things worse.'

'The pain must have been dreadful,' Janet said hoarsely.

'Has Brian never told you about it? I believe Leonard dashed off home later that day. He didn't come back to stay until Brian came out of hospital.'

'Brian never mentions his injury. I had no idea it had been so serious or I would never have persuaded him to get up for a waltz that first evening.'

'Did you do that?' Jim grinned. 'Good for you. Maybe that's what he needed, somebody that knew nothing of his accident and treated him as a normal man.'

'I hope you're right.' Janet shuddered slightly. 'He says he is pleased now that he did it. I think he means it because we always dance the waltzes and any other slow dances now.'

'Show me the man who wouldn't be happy to hold a pretty lass like you in his arms. Brian deserves some good luck and you're the best thing that could have happened to him.' Jim chuckled, then gave her a wink which made her blush. She was aware of Leonard Shaw glancing frequently in their direction, then at Brian struggling to make conversation with old Lady Rogan and having to repeat every second sentence. Leonard seemed to have a permanent smirk on his face tonight.

## CHAPTER EIGHT

As soon as the dinner was over Jim Bennet made his apologies to Brian and Janet.

'They take the rents in alphabetical order but I asked to be one of the first. I'd like to get home soon to make sure Gillian is all right.'

'We understand that,' Brian said with a huge sigh. 'I'm exhausted. Thanks for looking after Janet for me. I couldn't very well ignore the old lady and she's not a bad old stick, if only she could hear.'

'Mmm, you drew the short straw tonight, Brian, but I have enjoyed meeting Janet here. She is as interested in cows and breeding as you are yourself. It's always a help if a woman understands what a busy life farming can be.'

'I would like to speak to Meg and Ranald before they leave, Brian, if that's all right with you?' Janet said.

'Of course it is. I shall be pleased to have a chat with them too. I'm gradually meeting all your family. I've often wished I'd had brothers and sisters but apparently my mother almost died getting me.'

'We understand about that. Jamie's wife was dreadfully ill before the twins were born and they cannot have any more children. Fortunately they already had Marguerite. Marie went up to Scotland to look after her so that Rina could rest. That's how Marie and Mark met. We all adore Marguerite but you will probably meet her next week. She has always come down to stay with us when Marie and Mark come.'

Brian took her arm and led her across the hall to a large room with lots of windows and plenty of well upholstered chairs and settees.

'We're over here,' Meg called softly waving a hand. 'We saved you a seat.' As they approached Brian realised his parents and Leonard were nearby with two vacant seats between. He seized the opportunity to introduce Janet to his mother and also her sister and brother-in-law. His father and Leonard drew their chairs closer so he introduced them all.

'Kerr?' his father said with interest. 'Kerrs from Wilmore? Blaketop Farm, Wilmore Village isn't it?'

'That's right.' Ranald nodded. 'Meg and I have moved in there now because that's where we have the dairy herd. My parents moved to a small farm owned by Sir Anthony. That's why we're here tonight to pay the rent.'

'I have met your father a few times at the market. He and his friend are both Scotsmen I think. They have an eye for the best Ayrshire heifers.' He chuckled. 'I'm glad we have Dairy Shorthorns so I'm not bidding against them.' Ranald looked puzzled.

'You mean William Sinclair? He and my father are half cousins. He is Megan and Janet's father.'

'My parents have not met Janet yet,' Brian intervened and threw his mother a reproachful look because his parents had had plenty of opportunity to meet Janet before tonight's dinner. His mother flushed.

'I see . . .' Dan Shaw looked at Janet and Megan. 'We noticed how alike you two look. So you're sisters, and Sinclairs. Of course! It must be your brother who won the local sheep dog trials recently? I'm told he is a first-class dog handler and trainer. You never told us that Brian.' He held out his hand to Janet and then to Megan. 'I'm very pleased to meet you both. This is a real surprise.'

'It is indeed,' Mrs Shaw echoed and smiled as she shook hands all round.

'Hadn't you better take your guest home now Brian since we shall have to wait for you to come back for us?' Leonard interrupted with a scowl.

'Oh dear.' Janet looked guiltily at Brian, then at his mother. 'I'm so sorry if I'm being a nuisance. I did suggest I should drive myself here in Dad's van but . . .'

'You're not a nuisance. I want to take you home, Janet,' Brian said swiftly, throwing an irritated glance at Leonard. 'We'll wait until the end and drop them off at Thorley Grange on our way.'

'That sounds a good plan,' Ranald chuckled. 'I never wanted to be in a hurry either when I was taking Megan home.'

'You can drive yourself?' Mrs Shaw asked in surprise looking at Janet with new respect.

'Both my sisters can drive,' Megan said proudly. 'Lord Hanley taught them. Dad felt he was being left behind so he asked my brother-in-law to help him choose a van and give him some driving lessons too. I hear it has been a big benefit, Janet, now he can take the milk to the station instead of getting soaked in the pony and trap on wet mornings.'

'It is. Dad wishes he had tried it ages ago.'

'Janet's brother-in-law knows quite a bit about cars and engines, Father' Brian said. 'He is coming down to Moorend to visit next week, isn't he Janet? I thought we might ask him if he would look over our car and give it a check.'

'That's a good idea, lad, if you think he'll have time.'

'You don't know Mark,' Megan laughed. 'He'll make time if there is a strange car to look over. He owns a small estate in Scotland but he leaves most of the administration to our sister, Marie. She helped Lord Hanley and his agent in the estate office before they married. Mark has built himself a garage and now people bring all their motors to him if they're not going well or making strange noises.'

They were interrupted when the names Kennedy and Kerr were called to pay the rents.

'We'll say goodnight now then because we would like to get home soon, in case our youngest rascal has not behaved,' Megan said. 'It has been lovely to meet you all.'

'Don't forget to bring Brian over for a meal soon, Janet,' Ranald called as they left. 'We'll have a proper chat then and maybe a walk around the cows.'

'Thank you,' Brian said. 'I shall look forward to that.'

'The whole family intend to trap your son and heir,' Leonard muttered in his aunt's ear, but they all heard.

'What do you mean by that?' Brian demanded.

'You know damned well what I mean,' Leonard sneered. 'The first night she saw you at that dance she stuck to your side all evening. I expect the blacksmith had told her your father owns Thorley Grange. She set out to snare you.' Janet stared at him in dismay. Her face paled.

'I don't understand. If your family own your farm why are you here as tenants?'

'Don't pretend you didn't know,' Leonard sneered. 'Why else would you choose Brian to sit beside and cling to him instead of dancing with me when I asked you?' Janet's green eyes flashed with temper.

'Even if it was true that Brian's father owned land it would make no difference to me. My eldest brother and our uncle own a big farm in Scotland but they're just as busy as we are and they work hard, a lot harder than you ever seem to do. They may not pay rent but they still have to pay for repairs and any improvements they want to make. The only time it would be a benefit is if they sold the land. They'll never do that because they have two sons.'

'There you are, Leonard. How often have I tried to explain that to you?' Daniel Shaw declared. 'It is true we do own some of our land, Janet, but we rent a small farm from Sir Anthony too.'

'That doesn't explain why she clung to Brian all night. She refused to dance with me twice,' Leonard said sullenly. He sounded so like a spoiled child that Janet might have laughed if she had not heard so recently that he had caused Brian's accident.

'I befriended Brian that evening because he was the only person there who was not dancing. He had only come to please you. He didn't know anyone to talk to but you never even looked his way to see whether he was feeling lonely or miserable.' She fixed a steely green gaze on Leonard. 'That was bad enough, but you of all people should have kept him company, at least some of the time, when it was you who caused the accident which has made him reluctant to dance because he has a limp.' Janet dashed away angry tears. 'I'd like to go home now.'

'You told her!' Leonard hissed glaring at Brian. 'You told her it was me. Where's your family loyalty now?' Brian's face went white and a pulse throbbed in his lean jaw. For several seconds his grey eyes held Leonard's before he turned away with a look of disgust. Leonard caught his arm and pulled him round roughly. 'Why? Why did you tell her? She's not part of our family. She's only . . .'

'I didn't tell anyone because I didn't know for sure it really was you — until now. You have condemned yourself.' Brian's voice was like ice.

Mr Shaw moved closer and took his wife's arm, seeing how shocked and pale she looked.

'Leonard and I will walk back to Thorley Grange . . .' Leonard opened his mouth to protest but he closed it when he saw his uncle's expression. 'It's only a couple of miles. It will give us time to talk,' he added coldly. 'Brian will you drop your mother off at home on your way to Silverbeck?' He turned to Janet and took her hand in both of his. 'I'm sorry the evening has ended so badly, my dear, but I hope we shall see you again soon. We shall try to make amends.'

Janet was relieved when Brian led her and his mother out to the car.

'Did you really not know it was Leonard who caused your accident, Brian?' his mother asked quietly.

'I thought it was but I never said anything because I couldn't be certain,' Brian said quietly. 'I suppose I hoped it wasn't Len because whoever it was did it deliberately.'

'Dear God!' Mrs Shaw breathed. 'This is terrible. I have been so misled. I thought Leonard was being kind and considerate coming to spend time with us after you came out of hospital. I am beginning to wonder if your father may be right after all. He thinks Leonard has always been a bit jealous because his father was not as wealthy as yours but that was because Daniel's maternal grandfather settled money on him when his mother died while he was still a baby. He thought his father, your grandfather, might marry again, which he did of course. Daniel and Bert always got on as well as if they were full brothers. There was never any jealousy between them. It is all so upsetting.'

'Don't fret about it, Mother, I am glad things are out in the open now.'

'I will try to put it all behind us,' Mrs Shaw promised. 'Will you be free to come for a meal with us on Sunday, Janet? It is time we got to know you properly.'

'Thank you. I would like that but I help with the milking morning and evening so it would depend what time you have in mind.'

'Brian usually helps with the milking too so we could make it in the evening or for Sunday lunch. Brian can tell me when you have decided between you.'

As soon as they were on their own Janet apologised for getting angry and saying more than she had intended about Leonard and the accident.

'Don't be sorry. I'm not,' Brian said, reaching for her hand and giving it a gentle squeeze. 'I was sure it was done deliberately but Leonard was not there when I opened my eyes, even though he must have known what had happened. I don't think he came back to see whether the mare or I were hurt, but everything was a blur of pain. Now we all know the truth, and I am glad my parents know, especially my mother.

It is not the only malicious thing Leonard has done. Recently he said if I was not around he would inherit more money when my father died.' Janet gasped.

'That's a dreadful thing to say, even in fun.'

'He didn't say it in fun. He has gradually grown more resentful since we were teenagers, although he often stayed with us and my parents treated us both the same, even when they bought me new clothes. Mother has been inclined to believe whatever lies or excuses Leonard uttered. I think Father will send him home now. It is time he helped his own father with training the horses. So you will come on Sunday, Janet? I would prefer evening then we can take our time.'

'All right, but I will drive myself to your house if Dad says I can borrow the van.'

* * *

It was strange that Lord Hanley always seemed to know when Marie and Mark were visiting Moorend and he always called to see them. Rick was a regular visitor whenever he was not at school but he always accompanied his grandfather as an additional visit and he invariably asked if Marguerite had come with Marie. He and Fiona still discussed topics, and sometimes disagreed, as they had when they were at school together, but Fiona never forgot how kind and gentle Rick had been with Marguerite when she was a three-year-old flower girl at Marie and Mark's wedding. They were still the best of friends whenever they met again, although Marguerite was now a feisty twelve-year-old and growing up fast. Marie said she needed to have plenty of spirit to stick up for herself with her two brothers. Although the twins had been delicate and frail as babies they were sturdy nine-year-olds now and already keen to help their father at Bonnybrae. They each had a collie dog and were eager to learn to handle them as their father did but they scorned attempts by mere girls.

Marguerite had done well at the East Lowrie village school. The teacher in charge had sent a letter to Jamie and

Rina to say she could no longer teach her the subjects which would be of benefit to a girl with her intelligence while she had so many other less able children at different stages. She suggested they might pay for her to attend the small private school in Strathlinn run by two sisters, the Misses Lyall. They engaged tutors on certain days of the week for those children who wanted to learn special subjects. She suggested Marguerite might benefit from learning Latin because she had expressed a desire to study medicine, either as a nurse or as a doctor. She was more than proficient at both sewing and cookery which she said her Great-Aunt Maggie Greig had taught her since she was a small girl, and also at keeping account of household expenses which she had apparently learned from her mother and her Aunt Marie.

If Marguerite had been able to choose for herself, she would have left school completely so that she could visit her Yorkshire grandparents every month of the year until she was old enough to train to be a nurse as her mother had done. This suggestion upset Jamie and Rina because they knew Marguerite already felt a great love for her Yorkshire relatives and they didn't want her leaving home and going so far away. Jamie himself had done exactly that and now he understood how hurt his parents must have been at the time. Rina had not wanted to go away anywhere but her mother had insisted she go to a school for young ladies many miles away in the south of England, the plan being that she should attract a wealthy gentleman for a husband.

'I have no regrets about marrying the man I love,' Rina said, smiling mischievously at Jamie. 'I'm afraid my mother was sadly disillusioned, so much so that she has vanished out of my life and I don't even know where she is. I wouldn't like that to happen to Marguerite.'

'Neither would I,' Jamie agreed. They compromised by agreeing Marguerite could spend half the school holidays with her grandparents in Yorkshire provided she worked hard at school and passed examinations in French, Latin and science as well as the mathematics and English, which the

Misses Lyall insisted on and taught to a high standard. They also included basics in geography, history and nature study but these subjects pleased Marguerite as she had a thirst for knowledge of all kinds.

Marie and Mark always tried to arrange their visits to Yorkshire to coincide with Marguerite's holidays, both to please her and because they both adored her bright smile and happy nature. They also took turns with Rina at driving her to school in Strathlinn during the winter months. In the summer months she could ride her pony there and Jamie paid for her to graze it in one of the small paddocks belonging to the station master during the day.

* * *

Janet spent a happy Sunday evening at Thorley Grange with Brian and his parents. Mrs Shaw had made a lovely meal, but more importantly the atmosphere was warm and friendly and both Mr and Mrs Shaw did their best to make her feel at ease. She didn't know Leonard had been intent on blackening her character, hoping to thwart his aunt from inviting her to visit, or welcome her as Brian's girlfriend. Both Mr and Mrs Shaw experienced twinges of guilt for listening to his opinions.

Brian told her Leonard had left to catch the early morning train back to his home in Lancashire the morning after the tenants dinner.

'I was glad in a way,' he admitted. 'There was no time for recriminations or any more of his peevish comments. I think it will be a long time before my mother can forgive him or welcome him as another son, the way she has always done.'

'Well, she has certainly made me feel welcome,' Janet said as Brian kissed her a lingering good night before she climbed into the van to drive herself home. He had tried to insist on collecting her in the car so that he could keep her much later if he was seeing her safely home himself, but he had to accept that Janet valued her independence.

'It's not a bad thing these days, Son, if a woman has her pride and wants to be a bit independent,' Brian's father said. 'Your mother enjoyed Janet's visit and I liked the way she was willing to help with the meal and the clearing up afterwards. I heard them chatting like old friends over the washing up. I've heard the Sinclair family are all hard workers.'

'They're certainly all brought up to help with whatever needs doing,' Brian said. 'All the girls can cook and bake, even their granddaughter from Scotland who comes to visit regularly. She will be down next week with Janet's sister and her husband — the one who knows about engines.'

'Then we must invite them all to lunch during the week,' his mother said, entering the room and hearing the end of the conversation.'

'That would be a good idea,' his father agreed. 'Mark Blackford might have a look at our old Hillman and see whether he knows what it needs to stop it chugging and coughing so much.'

So it was that Mr and Mrs Shaw met more of Janet's family and were further convinced that their son had made a good choice. Janet was certainly not a gold digger as Leonard had insinuated. Brian was pleased by his parents' delight in Janet because he knew in his heart she was the girl he wanted for his wife. His main concern was how he would persuade her to leave the life and the home she loved, especially since her family seemed to depend on her to help with the milking every day and her father had recently increased his milking cows to forty. Alan was married and had his own farm and milking to organize. Fiona, the youngest Sinclair had often helped with the milking while she was at school and during the holidays but in September she was going away to the teacher training college and they could no longer count on her for an extra pair of hands.

In comparison to Moorend, Thorley Grange was fortunate to have two cottages on the far side of the farmyard and the two men they employed both assisted with the milking. In addition, one of the wives helped when Brian or his father needed to be away. Her name was Amy and she had been invaluable during the time Brian had been in hospital after the accident and the months following while he recuperated. There was a small lodge belonging to the farm too but it was badly in need of repair so it had not been occupied for some years. It was quite pretty from the front. Dan and Emily Shaw had bought the farm when some of the farms were sold off the Thorley Estate to pay death duties and from the first time she saw it Emily had dreamed of repairing it someday and extending it at the back so they could live there when Dan retired. It was surrounded by a small woodland and a garden which was seriously overgrown but that did not deter her. Since meeting Janet and her family her plans for renovating the lodge and moving in there had resurfaced along with dreams of several grandchildren who would run across the fields to see her and be welcomed with loving arms.

# CHAPTER NINE

Peter knew he had reason to be grateful to Brian for suggesting he and Helen make up a foursome with himself and Janet that first time he asked Mr Barclay's permission to take his daughter out for the evening. The fact that Peter had sought his approval first, plus the four of them going out together, had allayed Mr Barclay's paternal qualms and ensured their relationship had got off to a good start. As he got to know Helen's father better Peter found he was always welcome at Upperwood Farm, but he made sure he did not keep Helen out too late when they went out for an evening on their own and he never took advantage of Mr Barclay's hospitality.

Sometimes it was hard to remember that Helen was not yet eighteen because she was mature for her years and capable, making a good job of keeping house as well as helping with various tasks outside and keeping accounts for the farm. Mr Barclay realised early on that their friendship was serious and it was mutual, in spite of the nine years between them. Part of him was relieved Helen had fallen in love with a decent man from a good family but the other half of him dreaded her marrying and being left on his own. He often wondered what his wife would have advised, but in his heart he knew she would have been relieved to see Helen so happy.

He and Ellie had known each other from their school days and neither of them had ever had, or wanted, anyone else. They had married when his wife was eighteen and he was twenty-two and he was glad they had had those extra years together when they were young.

When his brother called to see him just before Christmas to invite him and Helen to join his own family for Christmas dinner he asked if Helen was still courting the Sinclair lad.

'Aye she is. I've never seen her so happy since Ellie died. In fact I'll tell you, Adam, he's almost like the son I never had the way we can talk together and discuss things about farming and the changes the government are making introducing the new Milk Marketing Board and such like. He's a farmer through and through. His youngest brother won the local sheep dog trials recently but Peter seems able enough at working his own collies.'

'I expect it's bred in the lads. Sinclair has a reputation for being a hard worker and a good farmer but he has bred and trained good working collies ever since he moved down from Scotland. I heard he brought his original bitch with him on the train. Even the gypsies will tell you he's damned good, but he's nobody's fool. They say the eldest brother, the one who went back to farm in Scotland, was the best dog handler of all.'

'Scotland? Aye, now that's a thing that's bothering me. Helen will be eighteen next month and I can tell she's set her heart on marrying Peter.' He sighed. 'I reckon he feels the same, but I wouldn't like him to take her off to Scotland to get a farm to rent up there.'

'Why would he do that?'

'He might if he can't get a tenancy on the Silverbeck Estate. William Sinclair seems to be well in with Lord Hanley and Bob Rowbottom, the land agent, but they already rent two farms. Alan Sinclair and his wife are in Mountcliffe, the big farm in the village. There's a limit to how much land the estate will rent to one family however good the Sinclairs might be. If Peter can't get a tenancy in this area he might be tempted to go to Scotland. His brother-in-law owns an estate up there. Peter is no longer a boy. He's nine years older than Helen so I don't see him wanting to wait too long. Ellie was only eighteen when we married so I can't claim Helen is too young to marry.

'I can't see there's such a problem,' Doug Barclay mused. 'You have always got on well with Bob Rowbottom yourself and you only have one chick. You approve of the man she wants to marry. Why can't you ask Lord Hanley if he would take Peter on as a joint tenant with you and make him a partner in the farm? It will all be Helen's one day. We're not getting any younger, lad,' he chuckled, slapping his brother heartily on the back. 'You'd like to see Helen settled and happy, wouldn't you?'

'I don't know whether Peter would want that. He has his own ideas about the things he wants to do. On the other hand, his father has been farming the Mountcliffe Hill land since Alan got the tenancy. They're running sheep there. Peter says he's enjoying working with them for a change, better than he expected, but his younger brother is the shepherd in the family. We have sixty acres of hill land here which is best suited to sheep. We have a bit of everything with sheep and pigs and Helen has the poultry, but the dairy cows bring in our main income. I think Peter might fit in with the work alright but it wouldn't do for him and Helen to live too far away.'

'The way I see it this house is big enough for two families. You even have the extra staircase the single men used to use to their sleeping quarters. If Lord Hanley will agree you could convert the far end into a small house for yourself without too much expense. It would probably make Helen happier to know you were near at hand so she can cook you a meal now and then and clean for you.'

'Aye,' Albert Barclay said slowly. 'Aye maybe . . . I'll think on what you've said.'

As things turned out Albert didn't have long to think about anything because Peter asked Helen if she would promise to marry him when she was eighteen. She had no hesitation in accepting his proposal so Peter suggested buying her an engagement ring for Christmas to let both their families see their intentions were serious. Helen agreed with joy in her heart.

'The thing which worries me most,' she admitted, 'is I know my father likes you Peter, and he respects your ideas about things, but I hate the thought of leaving him alone. In fact, I don't know how he would manage all by himself.'

'I have thought about that sweetheart, but I do love you and I do want us to marry. I don't suppose my family will be very happy either. It will make another pair of hands less for the milking, but that is why I want us to get engaged and it will give everyone time to plan things.'

'I have wondered if that's what is worrying Janet,' Helen said. 'It's plain as anything that Brian loves her and I'm sure she feels the same, but if you both leave home how would your parents manage?'

'I don't know. My father has often wished we had a couple of farm cottages to employ married workers. But Helen my love, we have to live our own lives and do the best we can to fit in with our families. I'm sure our parents wouldn't want to hold us back.'

* * *

As things turned out Brian and Janet had already discussed these problems and reached no satisfactory conclusion. Brian felt he must make a firm stand. They needed to let everybody know they were serious and wanted to marry.

Once Mrs Shaw had got over the shock of discovering how false and insincere Leonard had been both she and her husband welcomed Janet warmly into their little circle and they made no secret of the fact they were planning to renovate the lodge and retire there when Brian got married. Since they had got to know her they were convinced Janet would make Brian a loving, caring wife, but they understood how deeply she loved her home and family and they admired her loyalty. They knew she played a large part in looking after the Moorend dairy herd too and she was always there for the milking. Everyone depended on her more since Alan married and moved to Mountcliffe. Fiona was intent on a career in teaching. David spent all his spare time working with the sheep and training his dogs but William insisted his youngest son must learn to plough and do all the jobs about the farm, including milking. The cows provided the main income at Moorend but David made no secret of the fact that he hated milking and had little interest in dairy cows.

Brian was twenty-six on the thirtieth of November, he knew Janet loved him. Their relationship was growing increasingly passionate. 'I really do want to be with you all the time, Brian. I want us to have children too, but I've helped with the milking every morning and evening since I was eleven years old and neither Polly nor Mother are as fit as they used to be, although I know Mother still enjoys milking.' Brian knew all this but the time had come to stand firm. He had never cared so deeply for anyone as he did for Janet. He was delighted when she finally agreed they should announce their engagement on his birthday, and he whisked her off to Wakefield before she could change her mind. They chose a beautiful diamond engagement ring and Brian insisted on buying the wedding ring at the same time while they were in the jeweller's.

Brian knew his own parents had been hoping for their relationship to progress and their delight at the news was boundless. Mrs Shaw immediately made plans for a celebration party. She invited as many of Janet's family as were able to come. Her plans for altering the lodge were already drawn up and she looked forward to welcoming Janet as a daughter while she and Daniel spent their retirement there, close enough to the farm for Dan to work, but not too close to the main farmhouse to be a nuisance.

It was a splendid party and a very happy evening with Megan and Ranald there, as well as Lynn and Alan, Peter,

Helen, David and Fiona, William and Emma. Marie had written to say she was truly sorry she and Mark couldn't be there, but they would definitely be there for the wedding once they knew when it would be. Jamie and Rina rarely travelled down to Yorkshire but they sent their congratulations and good wishes.

* * *

Not for the first time William wished there had been a worker's cottage near to Moorend Farm so he could employ a man, preferably with a wife, who might help with the milking. He wished it even more when he and Emma received a letter from Albert Barclay inviting himself and Emma for a meal and a discussion about Peter and Helen's future because they had asked for his approval to become engaged. The date was fixed for the week before Christmas although Albert Barclay had already given his consent to the engagement provided they waited until the autumn to marry. He wrote that he had a few ideas which he hoped might help the young couple but he had not discussed anything with either Helen or Peter until he heard their own views. He did not want to stand in the way of their happiness but neither did he want his only child to live far away in Scotland if Peter planned to ask his brother-in-law for a farm to rent. Emma shuddered when she read that but she was pleased when he said how much he enjoyed Peter's company and he felt he would be a caring and trustworthy husband.

'It feels like all our bairns are fleeing the nest,' William said as he drew Emma into his arms in bed that night. 'I'm almost wishing I hadna encouraged David to spend so much time on his dogs and looking after the sheep. I don't know how we're going to manage the milking without Janet, if Peter is not here either.'

'I share Mr Barclay's fear that Peter might take himself off to Scotland to get a farm of his own to rent,' Emma said. 'I hadn't thought of that until Albert Barclay mentioned it, but I know we can't expect Lord Hanley to let our family have another farm to rent yet, even if there were any coming up for lease, and we know there aren't any. Alan will miss Peter's help too.'

'Aye but there's two cottages belonging to Mountcliffe. Alan can apply for a married man to help them.' Emma was silent for a while then she said diffidently, 'How would it do if we hired a man to work here for us and live in Alan's second cottage? I know it's a long way to come here in time for milking every morning but perhaps we could buy him a bicycle?'

'A bicycle?' William echoed in surprise. He considered Emma's suggestion. 'We would need to be sure he could ride one or was willing to learn. It's worth considering though. Aye it's certainly better than selling off half the cows when Peter and Janet leave home. I'll discuss it with Alan. Maybe we should consult Mr Rowbottom. We shall probably need to pay a rent for use of the cottage.'

* * *

Helen was nervous about cooking a dinner for Peter's mother and father. She spent a long time cleaning and polishing the furniture in the dining room. They rarely used it since her mother died but with the fire lit and the curtains drawn it always looked warm and cosy. She laid the table with a beautifully ironed white damask cloth and washed and polished her mother's best china and glasses.

'Come and have a look, Dad,' she said anxiously. 'Do you think everything looks all right? Have I forgotten anything? The vegetable dishes and the dinner plates are warming in the oven and I've lit the paraffin stove to roast the beef and bake the potatoes crisp. I've made the batter for the Yorkshire puddings but I need to cook them last and get the oven as hot as I can. Everybody says Mrs Sinclair is a wonderful cook . . .' she trailed off disconsolately.

'You're a wonderful cook too lass, so don't get flustered. Anyway Mrs Sinclair has lasses of her own so they'll have had to learn. You've made this room look a real treat. Your Ma would have been proud of you.' For a moment his voice was husky but he coughed and cleared his throat. He was nervous about tonight's encounter himself but he had decided to put his brother's suggestions to the Sinclairs. Anything was better than his lass going off to live in Scotland however much he approved of Peter. He had mentioned the idea of making Peter a joint tenant and a partner in the farm to Mr Rowbottom confidentially and he had promised not to say anything except to consult Lord Hanley. He had returned the following day to say Lord Hanley would be in favour of the arrangement provided he paid for whatever alterations he wanted to do to the house to make it into two separate dwellings.

William, Emma and Peter arrived in their van. Albert Barclay welcomed them inside.

'My word something smells good,' William declared appreciatively. 'Do you have a housekeeper Mr Barclay?'

'Oh call me Albert. Everybody else does. Helen has been housekeeper and everything else since her mother died.' Helen came through to greet them with a nervous smile but Peter gave her a reassuring grin.

'Would you like to come through to the dining room? The meal is ready and I don't want the Yorkshire puddings to spoil. Will you carve the meat, Dad?'

'Can I carry anything through for you Helen?' Emma asked. Although she had met Helen a few times at Moorend they did not know each other intimately. It worried her a little that Peter had chosen a bride so much younger than himself.

'I'll come and carry a tray for you, Helen,' Peter said immediately, jumping up to follow her through to the kitchen. As soon as they were alone he seized the opportunity to steal a kiss. 'You've gone to a lot of trouble my love,' he said gently. 'Everything looks lovely, and you best of all. Have you any idea what your father wants to discuss with my parents?'

'No, he has been very quiet lately. I think he has something on his mind, but he has given his permission for us to marry when I'm eighteen and he never goes back on his word. Oh Peter, I'm so nervous in case there's anything wrong with the food.'

'You've no need to be nervous, Helen. Everything you have cooked for me has been delicious. I've brought your ring with me. I thought you might like to wear it tonight and let my parents and your father see it before everyone else sees it on Christmas Eve. When you're feeling nervous look at it and think "Peter loves me. Nothing else matters". Will you do that?'

He slipped the ring onto her finger and she smiled up at him with love and gratitude.

'You always make me feel better, Peter. Will you carry this tray through with the vegetable dishes and I'll bring the roast and the hot plates. I'll come back for the gravy and sauce and the Yorkshire puds. Dad loves them as much as the meat.'

'Mmm, so do I, and so does my father for all he still claims to be Scottish.'

'My father has bought a bottle of whisky especially for tonight. He asked me to find the whisky glasses for him. He usually likes ale himself.'

Everything about the meal was cooked to perfection and Emma praised Helen sincerely and asked if she would mind giving her the recipe for the apricot and almond flan. Helen blushed at her praise but she firmly refused when both Emma and Peter offered to help with the washing up.

'I have never known Peter offer to wash the dishes before,' Emma chuckled.

'That must be what love does to a man,' William teased, earning a frown from his son and a shy smile from Helen.

'Is that so?' Emma asked drily. 'I don't remember you ever offering to wash dishes.'

'That's why I got so many daughters to do it for me,' William winked at his wife, and followed Albert through to the sitting room. He accepted a generous tot of whisky and laughed when Albert topped his own up with lemonade and declared that was the only way he could find a liking for the stuff. William and Peter both sensed his nervousness and his diffidence as he began to tell them what was in his mind. After he had explained his idea of taking Peter into partnership with himself and also Helen, and getting Peter accepted as a joint tenant, he looked at Emma with a steady gaze.

'I know it's not a good thing for a young couple to set up house with an in-law, male or female. However much they're in love all young couples have to adjust and learn to give and take and they don't want anyone interfering. So . . . I er took the opportunity of asking Mr Rowbottom about the possibility of a joint tenancy, and if we could get permission to divide the house into two separate homes. I asked him in confidence,' he added hastily. 'I know Peter, or yourselves, might disagree with the whole idea, or think I'm a possessive old man where Helen is concerned.'

'I would never think that,' Peter assured him quickly. 'You have made me welcome here from the beginning, and — and I think we get on well enough.' He looked at his father. 'I know it's a different matter when we have to work together. Father and I sometimes disagree about the way things should be done.' William had been silent so far but Peter knew he was taking time to mull things over. He liked to discuss serious matters with his wife too and tonight there was no opportunity as the suggestion had come out of the blue, even for Helen and himself. But it was a generous offer on Albert Barclay's part.

'Did Mr Rowbottom give permission to divide the house into two,' Emma asked, 'and would it be possible?'

'Lord Hanley gave permission so long as I pay for any alterations myself. I don't need a big house just for me. We have a back stairs with a good big room at the top — big enough for two bedrooms really. When we had workers living in, they slept up there. Downstairs I could make the washhouse into a little kitchen and the maid's room could be my sitting room.'

'But Dad, that would be very small,' Helen protested.

'It's better than us all living together, lass,' Albert said firmly, 'for my sake as well as yours and Peter's. It has a fireplace and room for a couple of easy chairs. I can afford to pay for it and I know you will help me make it comfortable.'

'Could we make room for an indoor water closet?' Peter asked. 'You don't want to go down the garden on a cold morning.'

'No-o lad. I wouldn't want to go back to that. I hadn't thought about that.'

'Perhaps the bedroom could be divided to make a small bathroom?' Emma suggested. 'That's what they did at Bonnybrae where our eldest son lives, if — if it wouldn't cost too much money . . .'

William cleared his throat and looked at Emma.

'My wife and I usually like to discuss anything which affects our family,' he said.

'Aye, as me and Ellie did,' Albert nodded sadly but with understanding.

'Well I'd like a bit of time to think things over but you've made a very generous offer as far as Peter is concerned. I know there are no farms coming vacant on the Silverbeck Estate because I'm always asking Bob Rowbottom. He knows I'd like to get all my laddies into farms of their own.

'We wouldn't want Peter going back to Scotland to get a farm either,' Emma added, 'any more than you would want Helen to go away.'

'Oh no,' Helen gasped. 'I wouldn't want to go so far away and leave Dad.'

'We've never considered going to Scotland,' Peter said firmly. 'I think your father has made us a more than generous offer,' he assured her. 'I have to admit I would feel more secure if Lord Hanley will agree to put my name on the rent book as a joint tenant and I would be responsible for paying half the rent.'

'Aye. I agree, lad,' Albert said quickly. 'I wanted to be sure you and Helen would be able to carry on here if anything happened to me. That's why I asked Mr Rowbottom first to make sure.'

'As I said I'd like time to discuss things with Emma,' William said, 'but I agree you have made a generous offer. If we had been taking over a new tenancy from scratch for Peter it would have cost me a fair sum to pay the tenant's out goings and buy stock and machinery, to get started. What I would like time to consider is whether I can give Peter enough capital to buy his third of the partnership. Would you be willing to get a valuation done and then meet with your solicitor and ours to have things done legally?'

'Oh but there's no need for that,' Albert said quickly. 'I reckon I've enough put by to pay for the alterations to the house and everything will go to Helen someday so . . .'

'I know Albert,' William interrupted gently, 'but we Scotsmen are a proud race and we like to be a bit independent. I try to treat all my laddies equally so if we did this for Peter it would be his share paid out. Do you agree Peter?'

'I certainly do, but only if you and Mother can afford to do that,' Peter said slowly. 'I didn't expect any of this from either side.' He reached for Helen's hand. 'If I was paying for a third share of the stock and farm equipment and responsible for half the rent then nobody could say I'm marrying Helen for her money or to get a farm.'

'Hey lad, I know you love my lass or I wouldn't have offered you anything, and . . .' Albert looked at William and Emma, 'I know Helen is marrying a man from a decent family. I'm grateful for that. But I understand how you feel — the pride, and all that. I would probably feel the same. So I'll get a valuation done and see where we can go from there. What do you think about the new Milk Marketing Board?'

They went on to have an amicable discussion about the pros and cons of the government taking charge of collecting and marketing all the milk.

'I shall not be sorry if they can arrange collections of all our milk churns at the farm road end instead of having to take them to the station,' William said with feeling. 'It's always a worry in the winter in case we miss the train if we've had delays due to frozen pipes and other problems. It's not so bad now we take them in the van instead of the pony and trap but I don't like icy roads or snow.'

'I agree with you there,' Albert Barclay said with feeling. He looked across at Peter and smiled. 'I shall be pleased to acquire a son to help me.'

When Marie heard that both Janet and Peter would be getting married within the next twelve months and leaving Moorend she wrote to Emma, pleading with her and her father to come to Scotland for a visit before Janet and Peter left home.

> *You will manage without them when they move out so please can you take time to come and see Mark and I, and Jamie and Rina and their children. We would all love to see you. Then you both have your brothers and sisters to visit too. Neither of you have seen them for years. I know Uncle Jim would love to see Dad and have a good old chat. He often reminisces about the old days. You will see a big change in Aunt Maggie and Uncle Joe I think. They are getting frailer and I know they would really love to see you both one more time. Mark and I have plenty of room for you to stay and you have never seen our home or where I live. You will adore Jamie and Rina's boys too and Marguerite will be thrilled to show you her pony. Please try to come soon or you will never manage it when Janet and Peter leave, especially when Fiona will not be living at home next year either.*

Emma showed William the letter but he did not say he would visit Scotland. Later when they were in bed Emma broached the subject again. All afternoon she had thought about Marie's plea for them to visit. It was not the first time both Mark and Marie had tried to persuade them to visit in their new home. This time the letter had been only from Marie and addressed only to herself. All Emma's motherly instincts made her feel there was a hint of desperation behind

Marie's carefully written lines. Marie had never been one for moods or feeling disheartened but Emma felt she was in low spirits for some reason, even though they all knew how happily married Mark and Marie were and how well matched.

'Something tells me William that I should visit Marie,' Emma said, her voice firm. 'If you cannot find time for a short visit I think I must go alone.'

'You would travel to Scotland on your own Emmie?' There was a note of consternation in his tone.

'It's not something I look forward to but it would not be the first time. I went alone when Mother was dying.' Her voice shook at the memory.

'Yes, you're right. I will try to go with you this time. It would be good to see Jim again and I suppose Marie is right, Maggie and Joe are not getting any younger.'

'Then there's the rest of your brothers and sisters, and my two brothers and their families. It was not their fault we moved to Yorkshire.'

'No, you're right. That was all down to my mother and her bitterness. All right, tell Marie we hope to visit her in the New Year. It will probably not be until April when we have the spring ploughing and sowing done and if we're lucky the cows will be out to grass again. That makes the work easier.'

'That's wonderful, William. I will reply to Marie tomorrow,' Emma said warmly and turned into his waiting arms.

'I'm a lucky man,' William murmured against her hair, hugging her closer. 'I hope my mother is looking down on us to see how wrong she was to condemn our youthful love.'

# CHAPTER TEN

As another year dawned Emma and William talked long into the night as they often did when there were changes afoot or problems to solve. They were happy for Janet and Brian and accepted they were to be married in June. Until their meeting with Albert Barclay they had not realised Peter would also be getting married and leaving Moorend before the end of the year when Helen was eighteen, but William knew Albert Barclay was giving Peter a great opportunity as well as welcoming him into his family as the son he had never had.

'We have to be happy for Peter,' William mused, 'and Helen is a lovely lassie.'

'She is, and she's very capable and mature, and more importantly they clearly love each other,' Emma said. 'We must adapt to the changes and accept that our family are all making lives of their own.'

'Yes,' William sighed. 'It is the way of life. I think that is what my mother could not accept, me being the youngest and intending to marry. I have been thinking of the changes we must make at Moorend. I would have considered sending some of our own herd to Alan and Lynn at Mountcliffe to reduce the number of milking cows to what you and I, David, Polly and Tom can manage on our own,' William said uneasily, 'but Alan will miss Peter's help at Mountcliffe as much as we shall, especially with another wee Sinclair on the way. He turned restlessly in the big bed and drew Emma into his arms. 'As it is I shall sell . . .' he yawned, 'sell some of the newly calved heifers in the spring. They will raise some of the money towards paying Peter his share as well as reducing the work a bit for us.'

'It makes me sad when any of our children move out,' Emma said softly, 'but we have always known it must happen and we do want them to be happily married and with our blessing. Don't you agree?'

'Aye, aye my lassie, I do. We never had my parents' blessing and I always vowed I wad do ma best for all our bairns. I just didn't expect two of them leaving within the same year, but they have all been lucky so far — except for John.'

'At least he died for his country,' Emma said sadly. 'He wouldn't have wanted us to grieve for him.'

'I expect we shall find a solution eventually. You and Polly have more than enough to do with two men living in the house as well as helping with the milking twice a day and looking after the poultry.'

'I expect it would have been the same if the men had slept in a bothy as they do in Scotland. They would still need their meals and their washing done.'

'Aye, if only Moorend had a farm cottage for a worker . . . Maybe yours is the best idea, Emma to try and get a man to live in the Mountcliffe cottage and cycle to work. I have seen adverts for workers on the front of one of the local papers. I'll ask Ranald if he knows how they go about it. The hiring fairs don't seem so popular down here.'

'I think a lot of the old customs have changed since the war,' Emma reflected. 'There seems to be a lot of men unemployed so you would think there must be somebody who would be glad to do farm work.'

'You're right, Emmie.' William gave her a hug, then tried to smother another yawn. 'I'll enquire from Bob Rowbottom about renting the cottage in the village. We'll get things started as soon as things get back to normal now Christmas and New Year are over, but first we shall have the thrashing mill. I think Billy Hurst is starting at Silverbeck on Monday, coming to Moorend first, before making his way through the village to those who have corn still to thrash. Alan has a stack of oats so Hurst will be going to Mountcliffe.'

Thrashing days were busy for everyone, both inside and out. The man who owned the thrashing mill, and his mate who stoked the big steam engine, always came in for all their meals, starting with breakfast as soon as they had manoeuvred the mill into place beside the stack to be thrashed and set the belts at the correct distance between the mill and the steam engine which drove it. There were always extra men following the mill from village to village and they came in for the midday meal. Those who were from neighbouring farms often came in for their evening meal and a chat at the end of a busy day unless they were needed at home for the milking. Alan would be coming during the day and both Peter and David would go to help at Mountcliffe the day the mill was working there.

Emma and Polly had been busy plucking and cleaning one of the old hens which was no longer laying. It would make a large pot of jellied stock for a tasty soup, thick with vegetables and soaked peas or barley. This was followed by generous wedges of beef pie served with carrots, parsnips, onions and potatoes served with a large jug of beef gravy. All the men seemed to have a sweet tooth and always had room for a pudding which was often creamy rice with homemade raspberry jam, or a fruity sponge pudding and custard. Cliff Barnes was known throughout the district to have the largest appetite of any man they knew but he was also known to be one of the strongest and most willing of workers. He always chose the hardest task which was forking the sheaves of corn up to the top of the mill where the band cutter fed in the loosened corn at a steady pace. At the beginning of the day Cliff's task was relatively easy because the stack of corn was as high, or often higher, than the wooden mill but as the day wore on and the stack got lower the task grew more strenuous, lifting sheaf after sheaf up to the top of the mill at the same steady rate. Every man depended on keeping the mill going so that the thrashed grain poured down the spouts at the end of the mill where men were ready to fill it into bags and carry the grain to the lofts to be stored for stock feed through the rest of the winter. Other men were ready to carry away the newly thrashed sheaves of straw, while yet another raked up and carried off the chaff to the bullock shed for bedding.

Cliff ate a hearty lunch as usual, but when he came in for the evening meal he slumped into his chair and Emma noticed he did not eat with his usual relish.

'Is anything wrong Cliff?' she asked with concern.

'I'm tired. I want to go to bed,' he said, sounding like a small boy. Some of the men smiled but they all knew the Sinclairs did not allow anyone to mock Cliff Barnes, however foolish or slow witted he might seem to them.

'Off ye go and get some sleep then, Cliff,' William said kindly. 'Don't worry about the horses,' he added when Cliff opened his mouth to protest. 'I will see to them myself. You've had a harder day than any of us.'

When Cliff had left the kitchen one of the men said he had offered to change places with Cliff for a short break but the big man had declared it was his job. He didn't need help.

'It is true he has always wanted to do the same job whenever the mill comes,' William said. 'He likes to keep to the same routine whatever task we're at, but he's not getting any younger. We have no idea how old he is. He couldn't tell us his age when he first came to Moorend but he must have been about twenty. How long has he been with us now Emma?'

'It's thirty-seven years since we came to Moorend and Cliff and Polly have been with us from the week we arrived here,' Emma said.

'None of us are getting any younger,' Billy Hurst said with a grin. 'I remember my father bringing me to Moorend for a day's thrashing when I was thirteen. I'd wanted to come because he said he got the best food he ever tasted at Moorend Farm. He said I'd need to work and he set me on hooking the bags onto the spouts and changing them when they were full of corn. He was right about the food, Mrs Sinclair. You still give us the best meals and all our men want to come here.' He pushed back his chair. 'It's time we were moving to the next farm now though, ready for an early start in the morning. It's cold enough for snow but I hope it holds off for a while. We'll say good night now.'

It was true it had been a bitterly cold day and everyone was glad to get to bed early.

'I can't believe it is thirty-seven years since I came to Moorend,' Polly said as she and Emma washed the dishes and cooking pots and tidied the kitchen. 'I was fourteen and I had never been anywhere except to school. I've silently thanked Aunt Ivy often for getting me a job here.'

'You're a good worker Polly or you would never have stayed this long.' Emma smiled. 'And the same goes for Tom. We have been glad to have you both.'

The following morning Polly was raking out the fire and Emma was putting on her clogs and work apron to go out to the milking when Tom came clattering down the back stairs in a dreadful state, scarcely able to speak as he gasped for breath. His face was white.

'Hey Tom, slow up,' Emma said. 'Did you think you had overslept?'

'It's Cliff, Mistress Sinclair. I-I-I think he's d-dead. I can't waken him. He's lying still with his arms across his chest. He looks as though he's sleeping b-but . . .'

'Poke up that fire Polly. Put a drop of water in the kettle to get it boiling and make Tom some tea. He seems to have had a shock. I'll go up and see what's got into Cliff. He did seem to be very tired last night, quite exhausted in fact. It's not like him to sleep late.'

Emma climbed the back stairs to the room where the two men slept. It did not take her long to see that Tom was right. She felt her knees go weak and the colour drained from her own face. Cliff must have died in his sleep. He looked so peaceful, but it was a terrible shock to see him lying there so still. She ran down the stairs and out to the cowshed where William and Janet were already bringing in the cows ready to begin milking. She told them what had happened. Janet stood and stared at her in disbelief.

'Good God above!' William exclaimed. 'Are you sure, Emma?'

'Yes, I'm certain. Wh-what should we do? Shall we send for the doctor?'

'Yes. If you will help Janet finish getting the cows into their stalls I'll take the van and go down to Doctor Finch's house.'

Tom came out and automatically helped fasten the chains around the necks of the rest of the cows. He brought in the milking pails and stools as though in a dream. His face was pale and he looked as stunned as Emma felt. She was glad to see Polly coming into the cowshed carrying enamel mugs of hot strong tea, one for each of them. Emma cradled hers between her hands finding comfort in the warmth and the scent of the tea.

'Mr Sinclair wouldn't wait for his. He said he was going for the doctor,' Polly said, her voice shaking.

'Aye, he's gone in the van. Poor Cliff. It's a dreadful shock, and yet . . . and yet he looks at peace. Perhaps God has been kind to him at the end. It is better this way than going through pain and suffering. Try not to be too sad, Polly.'

'It ain't a good start to 1934 though, is it?'

'No, it is not.' Emma shook her head in regret. 'We shall all miss Cliff. But right now we had better get on with milking these cows or we shall be too late to get the milk to the train.' She sighed heavily. 'Life must go on. Cows must be milked and fed.'

The doctor declared Cliff had died in his sleep. His heart had given up on him but he said he would not have suffered as far as he could tell. Since Cliff had never mentioned any family and no one had ever contacted him in all the years he had been at Moorend, Emma and William arranged the funeral and the burial in the village churchyard. Emma didn't expect many people would attend but she and Polly baked fresh bread and scones and a fruit cake to provide a cup of tea for anyone who cared to come. There was always her own family and Polly and Tom. Perhaps the Wrights would attend too. Apart from being Polly and Tom's Uncle, Joe Wright had known Cliff well because he had often taken the horses to be shod at the forge. Alan, Lynn, Janet, Peter, David and Fiona, who was still on holiday, were all present, as well as Meg and Donald who had travelled from Wilmore Village. They had known Cliff all their lives. Emma and William were surprised and touched when Mr Barclay and Helen arrived, then Mr and Mrs Shaw with Brian. Mr Nichol, the baker, and Mr Robertson, the butcher, also attended the service before hurrying back to their respective shops. Mr Thorpe, the old school master was there. Emma felt humbled and grateful that so many had turned out to see poor Cliff on his last journey, especially when Lord Hanley arrived with his grandson Richard, as well as Bob Rowbottom and their trainee land agent, Michael Watt. Rick and Bob Rowbottom had known Cliff almost as well as her own family, considering all the years he had spent at Moorend and the times they had both visited, handed their horse over for Cliff's attention, and eaten tea at the same table.

Emma was glad she had instructed Polly to light the dining room fire and lay the table with her best damask cloth and the tea service she kept for special occasions. She had two apple pies in the pantry which she had intended serving for their own evening meal, but she was determined everyone would be welcome when they had come to give Cliff a final farewell. Meg caught her up and whispered in her ear.

'I thought Lord Hanley and Mr Rowbottom might attend. I've brought a sponge cake for tea and some shortbread.'

'Oh thank you, Meg. That is thoughtful of you. How surprised Cliff would have been. He never expected anyone to pay him attention.'

* * *

Three weeks later Emma had good reason to echo Polly's feelings that they were having a bad start to the year. The weather was bitterly cold and the paths were icy everywhere. Polly and Emma were clearing up after the midday meal and washing the dishes when Joe Wright burst into the kitchen. He didn't wait to greet Emma so she knew something had upset him badly. However rough he could be while working at the Smiddy he was always polite to her, and other women in the village.

'Oh Polly lass, I need yer. It's yer Aunt Ivy. She fell on't ice. Must've bin down't garden at t'privy. I didn't know. I-I didn't know she was lying there . . .' Emma thought the big man was going to burst into tears. She shoved the kettle back over the fire to make some tea — her mother's cure for all ills.

'Sit down Joe and steady yourself. Tell us exactly what has happened,' she said quietly. He stared at her as though she was speaking a foreign language.

'Tell us what's happened, Uncle Joe,' Polly said. 'Couldn't Aunt Ivy get up?'

'Course she couldn't bloody well get up!' he wiped his brow with the back of his grimy hand and sniffed hard. 'Broken her hip, hasn't she?'

'Broken her hip? Are you's sure, Uncle Joe?'

'That's what Doctor Finch says. Don't know how long she'd bin lying there, do I? Frozen she is. He's sent her to hospital.'

'Oh goodness!' Polly flopped into the chair beside him. 'She must be bad . . .'

'She is bad. Doctor Finch says we'll be lucky if she doesn't get pneumonia . . .'

'Here Mr Wright, drink this tea,' Emma said, handing him a large mug of strong sweet tea but his hands were shaking badly and she steadied the mug while he took a grateful gulp. 'Have you had anything to eat?'

'To eat?' He stared up at Emma like a bewildered child. 'I went in for't dinner. That's when I found me lass, lying on't garden path.'

'You help him drink some tea, Polly. I will make him a meat sandwich and there's soup left. Things might seem a little better if he has some food inside him. He is in shock.'

'You'll come 'ome wi' me, Polly?' He pleaded when he had eaten half a sandwich. 'I can't do things on me own. Last thing Ivy mumbled was about a clean nightie.'

'Aye,' Polly frowned and looked helplessly at Emma. 'She'll want her own nightgown . . .'

'Polly, I think you will have to go home with your Uncle Joe. You will have a better idea what Ivy will need and where to find her clothes. Maybe you could both go on the train to visit her at the hospital and see for yourselves how she is.' Both of them gave an instant sigh of relief. Emma was alarmed and touched to see a big strong man like Joe Wright blinking back tears of gratitude.

'I'll get back soon as I can,' Polly mumbled anxiously as she followed her uncle outside. Emma patted her shoulder.

'Don't worry, Polly. I think you may need to stay with Joe for tonight. Thank goodness we still have Janet and Peter here. There will not be many of us left to do the work this time next year when they're both married.'

Polly was at the station when William took the milk next morning. She looked pale and tired and he could see she had been crying.

'Have ye been at the hospital all night lassie?'

'Aye. Uncle Joe is still there. I hoped I'd get a lift to Silverbeck with you b-but I can't come to work. I've to collect some clean things for Uncle Joe b-but Aunt Ivy doesn't know us, Mr Sinclair.' She stifled a sob and William wished Emma was here. 'I have to go back . . .'

'All right Polly, I'll tell you what we'll do. I'll drive you back to Moorend and . . .' he held up a hand to silence Polly's protest. 'Emma will give you a decent breakfast for a start. A body aye feels better with food in their bellies. Ye can have a warm bath upstairs if ye feel like it. That's the best thing to refresh ye when ye havena slept. We're fortunate indeed that Lord Hanley put in a bathroom for us. Your clothes are at Moorend anyway. When ye're ready I'll drive ye to the Smiddy House to collect what ye need and take ye back to the hospital. Ye can stay with Joe for as long as he needs ye.' William had no idea then what he was promising.

Meanwhile Bob Rowbottom had agreed William should rent the empty Mountcliffe cottage if he could get a suitable man who was willing to cycle to work at Moorend. Lord Hanley had promised to send a couple of estate workers to clean out the cottage and whitewash all the rooms and generally tidy up because the cottage had been empty for some time, well before Alan and Lynn had taken over the tenancy. There was a couple in their sixties in the adjoining cottage. They had both worked for Gerry Wilkins at Mountcliffe until Thora had forbidden her husband to employ the man after he had fallen from a corn stack and broken his leg, leaving him with a pronounced limp and no longer able to follow the plough. She was afraid he might try to claim compensation. Unknown to his wife Gerry had continued to give whatever work he could to Sam, provided he kept out of Thora's sight, which meant no more milking, a job Sam had enjoyed and could easily do irrespective of his limp. He had repaired fences and cleaned ditches, trimmed hedges and general tidying until Gerry Wilkins retired himself and moved away.

He and his wife had reared their grandson, Tim, since he was four years old. His mother had died in childbirth and later his father had moved to Liverpool, hoping to make his fortune working at the docks. True to his word he had sent money to Sam and his wife each month to help pay for his young son's keep but Tim was now fourteen and ready to leave school. All he wanted to do was work on a farm and since Alan and Lynn moved to Mountcliffe he had followed them around like a lost puppy whenever he was not at school. Sam had heard that Alan's father was looking for a man to replace Cliff Barnes and when he and Ada saw the adjoining cottage being prepared for occupation again they were alarmed, fearing they would need to move out of their own cottage, if Alan also needed a worker when his brother left to get married. Not much went on in Silverbeck without everyone hearing about it. Sam lost no time in approaching Alan and telling him Tim was almost ready to work if Alan would give him a chance and teach him everything he would need to do.

'And I'm still able to milk cows and help look after the calves. I would be glad to do most jobs except plough. We know Mrs Sinclair will be getting near her time. Will you let me help?' He explained his situation with Gerry Wilkins. 'Ada used to help Mrs Wilkins in the house but she was not an easy woman to please and her lass, Irene, was a spoiled madam. When we had to make a home for young Tim Mrs Wilkins said she didn't want any children about her home so Ada had to stop working there. She was pleased to leave the bad-tempered old besom. Tim is an independent lad now so if your wife needs any help while she's lying in my Ada would be happy to do whatever she's asked. She keeps a clean house and she's a good cook.' Sam looked pleadingly at Alan.

Alan smiled at Sam and patted his shoulder in a reassuring gesture.

'It's my father who will be renting the next-door cottage from Lord Hanley because Moorend does not have any farm cottages. He's hoping to hire a man who can ride a bicycle and who is willing to cycle to Moorend every morning in time for the milking. But now you mention young Tim we know how keen he is to help, in fact he helps Lynn a lot already, carrying her buckets of milk to the dairy and helping her feed the young calves, and he loves the piglets. We shall need some help when my brother Peter gets married in the autumn. He'll be going to live at Barclay's place at Upperwood.'

'Will you give Tim a try then Mr Sinclair?' Sam asked eagerly. 'I'm more than willing to lend a hand with the milking every day until Tim learns to milk, or for as long as you want me . . .'

'Right then,' Alan grinned. 'Tell Tim to come and see me and let me know when he'll be leaving school. He told

Lynn he can leave at Easter. The sooner he starts the better it will be for my wife. I don't want her to take any risks.'

Sam and his wife went to bed with a feeling of relief and Tim was overjoyed to know he would soon have his first job and earn some money towards his keep. He loved his grandparents dearly but he knew they had made sacrifices to care for him. He also knew there were thousands of men who could not get employment and Mr Thorpe, his school master, had explained there was terrible strife in parts of Europe, especially in Germany where young men and boys like him were being trained to be soldiers.

Within days of Ivy Wright's accident she had developed pneumonia and subsequently died. It was a big funeral because the Wrights were well known beyond Silverbeck and although they had both been eager to know everyone's business they had both helped whenever anyone was in trouble. Emma was missing Polly's help both in the house and at the milking because she had been like a member of the family for so long. Nevertheless she baked cakes and scones and took them to the blacksmith's house to help with the funeral tea. Polly was too distressed to thank her properly and Emma got the impression there was more than her aunt's death upsetting her.

The day after the funeral Emma understood why Polly was so disturbed. Joe Wright called to see William and he would have preferred to talk in the farmyard.

'I've horses waiting to be shod, two ploughs to mend and a score of other jobs waiting for me,' he muttered. 'I-I can't manage without Polly. Truly I need her Mr Sinclair. Ivy did everything in the house — washing, mending, keeping things clean and she allus had a hot meal waiting for me.' He gulped and his large Adam's apple moved up and down.

'Are you saying Polly doesna want to come back to work at Moorend?' William asked incredulously. 'She's leaving Emma — and without any notice?'

'You have lasses of your own to help . . .'

'Fiona is due to go to college and when she's finished there she'll not be coming back to Moorend. She'll need to get a job and earn some money befitting her education, like other young women. As for Janet she will only be here until her wedding in June. We're really going to miss her badly, with or without Polly. I think you'd better come to the house and tell Emma yourself.' Joe followed him reluctantly. He wondered if Ivy would have approved of him taking Polly away from Moorend.

Emma stared at Joe Wright in dismay. It had never occurred to her he would want to keep Polly permanently. She looked helplessly at William, then shrugged resignedly, trying to hide her disappointment in Polly.

'If Polly wants to live at the Smiddy there's nothing we can do about it.'

'That's the trouble, Missis. She doesn't want to stay with me. She's drowned the place out since I told her how badly I need her and that it's her place to stay and look after me. She's all I've got. Her mother and Ivy were sisters. We wanted to adopt her and Tom when their mother died. Their father wouldn't agree. He married again within a twelve month and filled the house with more kids.'

'Yes, I remember,' Emma said quietly. 'Ivy was keen to rescue Polly from her stepmother and have her living in Silverbeck.'

'I've promised to offer Mr Rowbottom more rent if he'll get us an inside water closet and a bath like yours but she says that's not what she'll miss. She says you're like her mother and sister and friend all in one and she doesn't want to leave you. Polly's half-brother has a lass just leaving school if you'd take her on as a maid and show her what to do?' He looked hopefully at Emma. 'I don't like to leave you in the lurch any more than Polly does but a lass like Eve would be no use to me, especially with a lazy slovenly mother like she has as an example. She needs a good woman to set her right.'

'I suppose I could consider her,' Emma said slowly, 'especially if we can't get a man willing to live at Mountcliffe and cycle here to work. We would probably have another man living in the house needing washing done and his meals . . .'

'That's another thing. Polly says she'll miss Tom. I've told her he can come and live with us. She can look after both of us and I'll buy him a bicycle to get to Moorend for his work. We're nearer than Mountcliffe.'

* * *

Emma and William were relieved to hear Alan was willing to replace Peter with Tim Jacobs, a young boy he could train himself, plus some part-time help with the milking from Tim's grandfather Sam Jacobs.

'I know it will be a few years before the lad can do everything Peter does,' he grinned at his brother. 'I shall miss you for the ploughing old boy.' He gave Peter a friendly thump.

'Aye, you will that,' Peter nodded. 'You'll need to do that yourself for a year or two until young Tim grows a bit and gets some muscle.'

This relieved the pressure at Moorend following Cliff's death but they all knew it was temporary with Peter's wedding looming in the autumn. William knew he must search for another worker soon. Both Tom and Cliff had come to him looking for work and both had stayed for many years.

'Can you help me write a notice to put in the local paper?' he asked Emma. Together they drafted an advertisement for a farm worker and William took it into the office in Wakefield.

On Sunday afternoon Polly arrived at Moorend. She was clearly upset.

'I didn't tell Uncle Joe I was coming,' she muttered. 'He always eats a big Sunday dinner after we come back from church and then he falls asleep.'

'It's better than falling asleep in church,' William chuckled. 'That's what I'm often tempted to do, especially when the weather gets warmer and we've been working hard all week.' Both he and Emma could see Polly was struggling to hold back her tears and she had never been one to cry easily. William made his excuses and left Emma and Polly alone.

'I didn't want to leave Moorend,' Polly said. 'You've both been so good to me, and to our Tom. Do you think I've done the right thing? Uncle Joe says family should come first b-but everybody here feels more like my family . . .' Polly wiped away a few tears with the back of her gloved hand.

'Dear Polly, you know we shall miss you. You have been like one of the family since we first came to Moorend, but I believe your Uncle Joe really does need you and he says you're the only family he has, you and Tom, even though it was your mother and Ivy who were blood relations.'

'Aye. He made me feel real bad when I told him I didn't want to stay at the Smiddy. B-but what I came to tell you was about Eva, my step brother's lass. Uncle Joe says you're going to give her a trial. My father, he's her grandfather you'll understand, he says she's light fingered and that I ought to warn you.'

'Light fingered?' Emma frowned.

'Yeh, she — she steals things. He says he's ashamed of her. She got into trouble at school and he says she's always falling out with her mother and her three sisters because they say she steals their clothes and things.'

'Oh dear,' Emma said, her face troubled. 'I have already written to the address Joe gave me and offered to give her a six month's trial as soon as she leaves school. I can't go back on my word.'

'Uncle Joe barely knows her. Well neither do I really, only from what my father told me. I do know she's never been near a cow in her life.' Emma bit back a smile remembering how nervous she had been herself the first day she went to Bonnybrae and heard she would have to learn to milk a cow. Her face softened. Even then William had been patient with her. Polly herself had never been near a cow either when she came to Moorend but in spite of her fears she had proved to be good at milking and learned to enjoy it.

'Don't worry, Polly. If Eve does not do her work and behave herself she will have to leave.'

'I'm missing the company I had here,' Polly said with a huge sigh. 'I thought it might make a bit less washing and cooking for you if Tom came to live with me at the Smiddy. Uncle Joe said he would buy him a bicycle.' She looked beseechingly at Emma.

'I shall leave that to you and Tom to decide, Polly. He is a good man and we wouldn't want to lose him. He is very tidy in the house so I could never complain, but if he is agreeable we shall not mind if he goes to live at the Smiddy with you so long as he gets here for the milking each morning. He will have his midday meal here with us each day of course, as will the new man when we get one.'

* * *

William and Emma were surprised at the number of men who applied for the farm worker's job, some writing letters which had obviously taken great effort, but most of them arriving at Moorend in person, some walking many miles to reach the farm, even though they had never worked on a farm or had anything to do with animals. They were desperate for work. Emma thought some of them looked too frail to do a hard day's work and none of them went away without food and a hot drink. Eventually William narrowed the applicants down to three and of them, a man named Steve Walker, was the one he preferred. None of them had ridden a bicycle but most were certain that would not be a problem, except for the one William favoured.

'Even if I can't learn to ride a machine I promise I will walk and be here before 'tis time to start the milking.' He had worked on a farm a few miles from Blakemore, where the Kerrs lived and William thought Ranald might know of him. Also, he had a telephone number written down on a scrap of paper which he gave to William so that he could telephone his present employer who had promised to give him a reference.

'He's retiring from the farm. Sale is at the end of March. I never worked anywhere else,' the man said dejectedly. 'His wife is ill so they're moving to a little house near Mrs Evans, that's their daughter. They have no lads to carry on.' He sighed heavily.

'You must have started work there when you left school?'

'Aye, I started a month afore my fourteenth birthday, but I always ran about the farm before that after my grandad. He had worked there all his life for my boss's father.'

William felt that was a recommendation in itself so he promised to telephone the number he had been given and let Steve Walker know within a few days.

'I think I'll drive over to Ranald's and see if he knows anything about the man, or the family he has worked for,' William decided, 'but I will go down to the village and telephone this number first. As soon as they bring the telephone lines to this end of Silverbeck I think we should get one. It would often be useful.'

'It would be lovely,' Emma agreed with a wistful smile. 'I could talk to Jamie and to Marie, as well as Maggie and Joe. I'm surprised they got a telephone at Bonnybrae before we have it here. It is far more isolated.'

'I suspect, from what Mark said, that Joe and Maggie joined in with James and Jamie and paid for the extra line and poles up from the road to Bonnybrae. It will be useful now Joe and Maggie are not so fit and Joe has stopped driving.'

'Yes, I suppose so. Jamie bought their car and both he and Rina have learned to drive so they or Marie take Maggie and Joe wherever they need to go whether it's shopping or to the doctor's.'

# CHAPTER ELEVEN

Emma and William gradually became accustomed to the changes which were taking place in their family and household. Tom moved out to live with Maggie and their uncle in the house attached to the Smiddy. He cycled to work each morning but he still had his midday meal at Moorend. Steve Walker, their newest employee was proving a conscientious stockman and always arrived for work on time. An unexpected bonus was his skill as a ploughman, a quality William appreciated since David had yet to learn to plough and William felt he was getting too old to do all of it himself.

The girl, Eve, on the other hand was totally unreliable. Emma felt it was almost like teaching a child how to wash and dry dishes. She had to insist they must be stored tidily and with care in the same cupboards every time, worse she had to instruct the girl to have a bath and change all her clothes at least once a week, and clean and tidy her own bedroom, as Polly had always done. Emma couldn't believe it when she lost her hairbrush and comb and found them on top of Eve's chest of drawers. The same thing happened with Fiona's writing case when she came home at Easter. Emma realised it was not so much that Eve was dishonest, but more that she had never had anything to call her own and she craved for possessions. Her younger sisters and their mother all seemed to use each other's belongings, even clothes, as well as stockings and shoes if they fitted. Eve had never had a bedroom to herself or possessed her own hairbrush or comb.

'She is like a magpie,' Emma said to William. 'I shall buy her a brush and comb of her own when I go to town. I must try to make her understand she cannot take things which belong to other people.' True to her word the next time Emma went to Wakefield she bought a brush, comb and matching hand mirror, plus two pink face cloths. Eve was ecstatic and promised to take care of them and not borrow anything from other people without asking permission.

Polly had felt ashamed that her niece had no suitable dresses for working in, or for anything else, so she had left two of her three maid's dresses and pinafores for Eve. They were well washed and getting shabby but Eve had arrived wearing the only dress she possessed and that was getting too small. Emma had already bought material to make two maid's green dresses plus white cotton for three pinafores. It did not take her long to cut out and sew the first dress to the simple pattern she used which was comfortable and could be pulled in with the matching belt. When she asked Eve to try it on for length the girl couldn't believe she would have a new dress of her very own and that she must wear it for working.

'Did you learn to sew at school?' Emma asked.

'Oh yes. I liked sewing and knitting but we had to pay for the materials we used and Ma would never give me the money to make anything much. Miss Dewer usually gave me things to hem or buttons to sew on. Sometimes she gave me scraps of wool to knit into mittens or a scarf for the winter. I never got to keep them for myself though once I took them home,' she added dourly. 'Miss Dewer showed me how to sew flowers on a handkerchief once. She said I would be good if only I had more practice. Course I never did,' she sighed.

'Do you think you could hem this dress for yourself if I pin it up?' Emma asked.

'Is it only for me? Will anybody else wear it?'

'It is just for you. It will be yours to wear and for you to take care of, to wash, iron and mend,' Emma said firmly. Eve couldn't believe that could be true. She had never had anything she didn't have to share or borrow. That evening she settled to hem the dress as soon as the evening chores were finished and the kitchen tidied. She was gradually learning that she had to work to a routine and things must be done the same every day whether it was sweeping the floor or washing the dishes.

When Emma checked how the hemming was coming on before Eve got too far and made a mess of it she was astonished.

'Eve that is as good a piece of sewing as I have seen,' she declared. Eve looked up at her and her cheeks grew pink with pleasure.

'Is it really all right, Mrs Sinclair?' she asked earnestly. She had done so many things badly and disappointed her new mistress. Sometimes Emma had struggled not to lose her temper when Eve was slovenly or skimmed over things and Eve had sensed her displeasure even though she often didn't know what she had done wrong.

'It is excellent hemming. I shall leave you to finish all of the hem and the bottom of the sleeves and I will make a start on another working dress for you. Then you will have two good dresses for afternoons and you can wear the two Polly left for you in the mornings for the dirtier jobs, like cleaning out the range and black leading.'

'You seem better pleased with your young maid,' William said when Emma curled in beside him in bed that night.

'She is improving. I don't think she has had anyone to teach her how to keep herself clean, even less clean a house. Her teacher at school has taught her to hem though and she is making an excellent job. I don't think she is truly dishonest either . . .' Emma frowned. 'She sees things and wants to hoard them to herself. I don't think she means any real harm but I am struggling to teach her that some things are private.

I am glad you brought me a cash box with a key for the egg money and the spare cash we usually keep in the house. I have moved the box from the usual shelf in the pantry. It's in our wardrobe now in case you want it some time when I am not in.'

'Did you leave the spare key in my sock drawer as you said?' William asked.

'I did. It is kinder not to put temptation in her way. I don't think she has ever had anything which belonged only to her. We have had a large enough family but none of them have ever taken each other's possessions without permission.'

'I reckon she's never had anyone to set an example,' William said. 'In spite of what Polly said she has taken well to the animals. I think she will be quite good at milking when she has had a bit more practice.'

'Yes, I must say she loves to collect the eggs and feed the hens and chickens and Janet says she is very patient at teaching the young calves to drink.'

'Maybe she'll turn out alright eventually,' William said optimistically.

'I hope so. This is the third phase of our lives,' Emma said with a sigh. 'I suppose we should have expected changes.'

'Third phase?'

'Well the first phase of our lives was when we were young at school, working and single, then we married and had our children, now they are all growing up and leaving the nest and giving us grandchildren.'

'You sound sad, Emma,' William said softly and drew her into his arms, stroking her soft, silky skin. He had always enjoyed the feel of her and his touch seemed to soothe when Emma was upset.

'I am a bit sad,' she admitted, 'but I'm really looking forward to our visit to Scotland. At the beginning of the year I wondered whether we would manage to keep our promise to go what with losing Cliff and then Polly leaving. Steve seems to have settled in well and even Eve is improving but I don't know whether she will keep it up when I am away. I have told Janet she will need to stay in the house as much as she can to keep an eye on her. I think Eve likes working with Janet anyway. I expect they are nearer in age and possibly understand each other better.'

* * *

Marie understood about the upheavals at Moorend and she hardly believed her parents really would visit so she was overjoyed when she received her mother's letter giving the date and time of their arrival at the end of April.

Both Marie and Mark were at Strathlinn station to meet them and Marie was almost in tears as she hugged them both.

'I really couldn't believe you would manage to come after having so many upsets.'

'Hey, lassie, dry your eyes. Your mother and I always keep a promise when we make one,' William said gruffly. He was surprised that the visit meant so much to Marie because there was no doubt she and Mark were happy in their marriage.

'Everyone is looking forward to seeing you both. We're going to our house for lunch, then you can relax and have a rest for a while — at least you can when Marguerite and the boys return to school, but they will be having their meal with us too and they are so excited. Mr Mason is hoping you will have a stroll along to the Smiddy, Dad. He remembers you when you were a boy, he says. He's looking forward to seeing you again.'

'It will be lovely to see the bairnies,' Emma said, feeling a bit choked with emotion. 'In fact it is lovely to see old haunts again. I'm looking forward to going down to Locheagle to see my brothers David, Richard, and their families, and where we all went to school.'

'Tonight we're all invited to Bonnybrae for our meal. Uncle Jim can't wait to see you both and Jamie is looking forward to showing off his collies, Dad. They have a lot of lambs and some ewes which should lamb anytime. Aunt Maggie and Uncle Joe will be there as well. They are both a bit emotional about you coming back together after all these years.'

'Aye, the time has fairly flown since the day we married,' William mused.

When Marie and Mark went to bed Marie curled into her husband, holding him close.

'Dearest Mark, you're so patient with me and with my family. I'm sure you will be tired to death of us by tomorrow night.'

'Marie, my love you know I would do anything for you, but entertaining your family is a pleasure. You don't know how lucky you are to have such loving parents and brothers and sisters who never seem to bicker or get jealous. You're all so close and they have all made me welcome at one time or another, even your cousins.' Marie hugged him tightly in response.

'I have not told my parents yet that we are having a big family gathering here tomorrow night with all the uncles and aunts and as many cousins as are free to come. Aunt Maggie and Uncle Joe have promised to entertain them tomorrow afternoon while I prepare. Mrs Mason is coming to help at night with two of her friends. She seems quite excited about it. That was a great idea of yours to design our two drawing rooms so that we could push back the dividing doors and make one spacious room. It will probably be the only chance for Mam and Dad to see some of their relations when they are only staying four days.'

'I have a feeling already they may come back more often now that they have come together once. They both seem elated at the prospect of visiting old haunts. I heard your father telling your mother he would like to take a walk up the hill again, just the two of them, as they did when they were young. It clearly holds precious memories for them both.'

'Then I must make sure they get the opportunity to do it — maybe tomorrow if it is a lovely morning, before they go to Aunt Maggie's, or they might never get away. I can't tell you how happy I am that they have come at last.'

'I can see that sweetheart,' Mark chuckled.

'I'm so proud to show them our lovely home and how happy we are. I love you so much Mark. I've been luckier than I ever dreamed.'

'I've always known I'm the one who is blessed to have you for my wife my dearest,' Mark said, his voice deepening with passion as he caressed her with increasing desire.

It was a beautiful morning and William welcomed Marie's suggestion that she would drive them as far as the Bonnybrae track where it turned up the hill.

'I'll continue up to Braeside and tell Aunt Maggie where you are and to expect you back in time for a meal about twelve.'

'If we drink the flask of coffee, Marie, and eat the scones and cake you have packed for us we shall not need any dinner,' Emma said with a smile.

'The exercise and good Scottish air will give you an appetite.'

When Marie told Maggie and Joe what her parents were doing before they came to Braeside for lunch, Joe threw back his head and chortled.

'What's so funny about that?' Marie asked bewildered. 'I expect Dad wants to reminisce about his young days.'

'Now Joe,' Maggie cautioned, frowning at him, but Joe went on grinning. 'Marie is a big girl now and a respectably married woman as well.'

'Maybe she is but you don't know for sure what happened . . .'

'Come on Uncle Joe,' Marie aimed a fist gently at his chest. 'Stop chuckling to yourself and tell me what you were going to say.'

'Aye well why not,' Joe laughed, 'Mind it's only speculation, Marie, because neither of them ever told us.' He went on to tell her how her father had taken Emma up to the top of the Bonnybrae hill to show her the view and help him gather the sheep. 'Your mother was a pretty young lassie, not much more than sixteen and as innocent as the morning dew.

I believe William had meant it to be an innocent enough pleasure. Unfortunately the mist came down, as it often does on the hills in these parts. They couldn't find their way back. They had to spend the night on the hill. I expect they snuggled up to each other to keep warm. They were young and healthy . . .'

'That's enough Joe,' Maggie chided.

'Aye well Marie doesna need me to tell her what was only natural temptation,' Joe said, 'but Jim told me his father saw William guiding Emma to the boundary fence early the next morning when the mist lifted. He saw her running across the fields to the house and creeping in at the back door. William went back up the hill to gather the sheep himself. You told me yourself, Maggie lassie, that Emma didn't realise she was expecting William's bairn until you told her what was wrong with her and that was nearly four months later.'

'Emma was so innocent and Mother didn't even give her a chance to say anything.'

'Aye, she was a bitter woman, sending William away to Yorkshire to work as she did, but my own father had his fair share o' pride and shame. He packed poor wee Emma off to his brother's so nobody would know the sin she had committed. Even my brothers and I didn't know what had happened until a while later. Thank God he got her home and her and wee Jamie were both safe.'

'Phew . . .' Marie whistled through her teeth. 'So that's why Granny Sinclair called Jamie a bastard and said he was not a Sinclair,' Marie mumbled. 'No wonder he was so upset when those boys at school started taunting him. That's why he ran away. I never understood what had upset him so badly.'

'Ye have to remember, Marie none of us knew who the father of Emma's baby was. She wouldn't say. Our two families didn't know each other so well then either.' Joe put an arm around Maggie's shoulders and drew her close, his face gentle and loving. 'Maggie and I have been lucky even if we did have to wait a long time for our own happiness.'

'The sad part was William told me the baby was his as soon as he knew Emma was expecting a baby. He wanted to marry her immediately but our mother had banished Emma from Bonnybrae. He didn't get the chance. We didn't know where she was and he was despatched to Yorkshire to work for a living. I know he never forgave Mother but I've thanked God many times that things turned out well for both William and Emma. They're happily married and they love all their children. They have worked hard and done well too. Maybe God does work in mysterious ways. To tell the truth I believe things have worked out well for Jim having Jamie here too, and they both love Rina.'

'We all love Rina I think,' Marie said.

'Aye well let's hope William can show Emma the view from the top of the hill today.' Joe said with a grin. 'It's a glorious morning and they seem happy to be here at last. Marie, lassie, you've done a good job persuading them to come.'

Maggie brought two large fruit pies and a tin of shortbread and gave them to Marie on a tray.

'Joe has forced some early rhubarb and I remember how much your father loved a rhubarb pie, so I have kept a smaller one back for today's lunch. I thought you would be able to use some extra food. It will be a fair gathering with all seven of us plus our other halves and their families and four of Joe's. It will be a real celebration. We're both looking forward to it. Your Mark is a generous man, and a tolerant one to put up with all of us in his home.'

'Oh I know, Aunt Maggie. Mark has been wonderful about it all. He really enjoys Cousin Billy's company and I get on so well with Fran. We see them quite often and I know they are coming with Uncle Robin and Aunt Evelyn.'

'Will Fran be bringing the two wee ones?' Maggie asked.

'No, her mother is looking after them.'

'Aah of course,' Uncle Joe said with a wicked smile, 'I remember now. Mark travelled all the way up from Yorkshire to be at their wedding, but he really came to ask you to marry him.'

'Uncle Joe! You're doing too much remembering about other people and their courting days,' Marie remonstrated. 'Who will tell us about yours I wonder? I must ask Uncle David and Uncle Jim. They must know what you and Aunt Maggie got up to. I must go now though. You will remember it's a surprise? We're not telling Mam and Dad until everybody is due to arrive.'

'Ye'll be going up to see Jamie and Rina now though? I know Rina has been baking a bit extra too,' Maggie said.

'It's very good of both of you,' Marie said gratefully. 'I will call at Bonnybrae before I go home then.'

Up on the hill William and Emma stood together and enjoyed the view they had intended to see all those years ago when Emma was sixteen.

'We can even catch a glimpse of the Clyde,' William said, gazing into the distance with his arm around Emma, holding her close. 'I know I should have taken better care of you that night Emmie,' he said, his voice unusually husky. 'You were such an innocent wee lassie then but I've been a lucky man the way things turned out, even though we did have our unhappy patch and a lot of damned hard work when we first married.'

'It is all in the past now, William, and I've no regrets either, so let's not spoil such a lovely day with any bitter memories. I can't believe how ill-informed I was then. If I had not been so stupid things might have turned out differently but it never occurred to me I could be expecting a baby.'

'Dearest Emmie you were as innocent as a babe in arms but you were never stupid. Let's sit a while and enjoy our coffee and the view.' They sat side by side and enjoyed their picnic like children escaping from school. When they had finished eating William sprawled full length on the springy turf, pulling Emma on top of him. He held her close and kissed her with as much passion as when he was a young man.

'Oh William,' Emma laughed softly, 'aren't we a bit old for this now.'

'We shall never be too old for love, you and me, my Emma. There's no one here to see us now and at least age has the advantage of not making any more babies.' He chuckled softly and rolled Emma onto her back. 'This is for old times' sake, my lassie,' he murmured against her ear.

It was a while before they drew apart and sat up to straighten their clothes.

'No one would believe you could still blush, Emmie,' William chuckled, 'and you a mother and grandmother. How lucky we are.'

'I never thought we would ever climb this hill again,' Emma said dreamily.

'No, but I'm glad we have, my love. And I'm glad Marie persuaded us to come. It will be a short visit but maybe we shall come again before too long, once the weddings are past and we settle into a routine again back home.'

'Yes, I do hope so. We shall not have time to visit all our relations this visit, but Marie was right, Maggie and Joe have aged since we last saw them and Maggie was always so kind to me even after she realised I was expecting a baby. She didn't condemn me as so many did. Your father was generous to my parents too. I'm so glad we came.'

'So am I but we'll go down to Locheagle tomorrow so you can see your brothers, Richard and David at least. We could take a look at the church where we married too.'

'Yes, I'd like that, and a look at the school where I first learned to sew. I'm glad I made two new dresses for myself before we came.'

* * *

It was a huge family gathering but a very happy one. Everyone was full of praise for Marie's organization and the lovely buffet meal she provided and they were grateful to Mark for opening up his beautiful home and making them all so welcome. Several times Emma had to wipe away a tear as she greeted loved ones she had not seen for so many years.

'We didn't expect we would be able to see all of you on such a short visit,' she said as she received hugs and kisses from one after another. Emma rarely wore pink but Mrs Hill had recommended the fine wool material in a dusky pink and Emma was pleased with it. In spite of being fifty-one her hair had barely a hint of grey and it was still thick and wavy. The deep pink of her dress seemed to give added bloom to her fair skin and happiness added a brightness to her eyes. William had made her feel almost like a girl again while they were up on the hill and Joe had done his fair share of teasing them both.

'Why Emma lassie, ye hardly look any older than when you were married,' her eldest brother, Richard, greeted her with a happy smile. 'It's really good to see ye looking so well.'

'It is that,' her brother David agreed. 'Nobody would believe ye were the mother of nine bairns.' No one ever mentioned the still born baby which had so grieved Emma at the time of his birth.

'Your brothers are right, Emma,' two of William's brothers complimented her, bending to kiss her cheek. 'That young brother of ours must have treated you well,' Robin Sinclair grinned. 'And how many grandchildren do you have on top of your own brood?'

'We have six and another on the way,' William told his brothers proudly. 'And we're proud of every one of them.'

'Does that include me, Grandad?' Liam asked.

'And me, Grandad?' His twin echoed.

'Of course it includes you two rascals,' William chuckled. 'I see you'll soon be able to handle your collie dogs better than your father.' Although the men folk tended to gather together and discuss farming and the world in general while the women talked of their families and homes, it was noticeable that William rarely parted from Emma's side, either keeping an arm around her shoulders or holding her hand as he might have done when she was a young girl. It was Jim and Joe who eventually remarked on this with teasing smiles, but Robin and Jack overheard.

'Aye, you'd think the pair o' them are still as much in love as when they were youngsters,' Robin teased, loud enough for those around him to hear. Emma blushed rosily, thinking of their time together on the hill earlier in the day. She wondered why people thought couples shouldn't still love each other as the years passed.

It was a good thing Marie had arranged the gathering for a Friday evening because it was almost midnight before the party began to break up and still Liam and Reggie were running around, while big sister Marguerite helped Marie and Mrs Mason fill up last drinks or cups of tea. They all agreed it had been a wonderful evening and thanked Marie and Mark sincerely for arranging it.

The four days of their visit seemed to have flown by and when it was time to leave on Sunday morning Emma had a struggle holding back the tears as she hugged Marie and bid Mark good bye.

'It will not be too long before we see you again,' Mark assured her. 'We shall be down for Janet's wedding in six weeks' time.' He said it as much for Marie's sake as her mother's. He understood how flat and sad she would feel when her parents had departed and things went back to normal. That night he loved her with extra tenderness. Although she never mentioned it or moaned, he knew she longed for a baby of her own. When they were first married they had talked freely about having children but it had never occurred to them that they might not be blessed with any of their own. They were happily married and very much in love and gradually Mark had begun to accept there would always be only the two of them. He knew his natural mother had died in childbirth giving him life so part of him was relieved that he would not lose Marie in such tragic circumstances. He never wanted a child of his to suffer the misery he had suffered at the hands of a foster mother, especially one who had pretended she was his real mother for the sake of money. He was not a bitter man by nature but he could never think of her, or his two so-called brothers, with any vestige of joy.

# CHAPTER TWELVE

When they returned home to Yorkshire Emma felt unusually flat and tired after all the excitement of seeing so many relations, especially her beloved Jamie and Marie, in their own homes. She was proud of all her children so why did she feel so dejected?

Snuggling down next to William that evening she turned to him for comfort.

'I'm happy for all our children, truly I am, seeing them making a success of their lives, and perhaps it was meant to be that some of them should return to their Scottish roots but they all seem to have grown up so quickly and now they are all flying the nest.'

'It is natural,' William soothed.

'I expect it is.' Emma still had a feeling that Marie was not entirely at ease with life, even though it was evident to all that she and Mark were well matched and happily married. Marie also had stimulating work with the Stavondale Estate, even though it was much smaller than it used to be. Emma was not sure whether it was a mother's instinct, or her imagination, so she didn't mention her doubts to William again.

'I know we should rejoice for them, but Janet will be married soon.' She sighed. 'Then it will be Peter moving out. I want them all to be happy but the house will feel empty without them. I don't think Fiona will return home to live either. Even when she finishes at college she will need to live where she can get a teaching post. That could be miles away. There will only be David.'

'We shall always have each other,' William whispered, nuzzling her neck as he drew her even closer and began to love her as they had done so often through the years in sad times and glad times.

* * *

Janet was feeding colostrum to three young calves at the end of the milking when Rick Fortescue appeared and made her jump. He had remained a constant caller at Moorend but he usually called in at the house first to say hello now that he was away at school during the week. On this particular day he went straight to the farm buildings searching for Janet. He gave her his usual smile and she thought what a charming young man he had become, although he was still only sixteen years old. He would likely break several hearts before long. She was surprised when she realised he had sought her out specially to wheedle an invitation to her wedding. She couldn't resist the look in his wide blue eyes, half pleading, a little wistful and yet mischievous too.

'I never thought you would be interested in our wedding, Rick. You're almost the young laird now,' Janet said, half serious but with a teasing note in her voice.

'Ah but Marguerite will be a bridesmaid surely?' he asked with his old roguish grin.

'She is, but she will not be playing hide and seek and chasing each other round the bushes as you both did at Marie's wedding. You're such a handsome fellow now and Marguerite is a spirited twelve-year-old going on twenty.'

'You never know what we might do. I'm going to marry Marguerite you know when we're older.' Janet almost laughed aloud, but when she looked up she realised he was deadly serious.

'Oh Rick, I expect you will meet lots of young ladies once you get to university,' she said gently. 'Meanwhile I know you and Marguerite have always been good friends and I will send you an invitation to the wedding if you really do want to come. In fact, Brian and I will be honoured to have you attend but the reception is only in the village hall you know, although I think it will be an excellent meal. We are having the caterers who were meant to cater for the Mountcliffe sale until Mrs Wilkins cancelled them at the last minute. Mr Rowbottom has heard several reports of them being very good. He and his wife will be there.'

'Yes, so I heard.' He grinned. 'I may get a lift with them.'

'Aah, I see . . .'

'Thank you, Janet. You and your family are the nearest I have to a family you know.'

'We are?' Janet's dark eyebrows rose in surprise at his sincerity.

'Yes, I always feel welcome here. I am thankful Mother agreed to come and live with Grandfather Fortescue. I know it must have been a difficult decision for her now I understand about the past, especially when everyone here knew my father, my natural father I mean.'

'Will you be going to study at university soon?' Janet asked changing the subject.

'Yes, next year I think, if my exam results are as good as the headmaster is expecting. I want to study mathematics and physics,' he said decisively. 'Grandfather says I should study what interests me so long as I don't waste my time and I work hard. He says knowledge is never lost and he will teach me what I need to be a good landlord, with help from Mr Rowbottom. We hope Mike will still be our land agent.'

* * *

Fiona was the chief bridesmaid and the wedding was arranged for the first Saturday in June so that she could get home for the weekend. Emma wrote to ask which train she would be getting on the Friday evening so that William could meet her at the station. She replied immediately.

> *Harry will be collecting me in his car. He plans to drive up as soon as he has finished school on the Friday afternoon. We shall stop on the way home to get a meal, so we may be a bit late. Harry has everything planned so there's no need for you and Dad to worry. I do wish Janet had sent him an invitation to the wedding though.*

'Gosh! I'm amazed at Harry Thorpe bothering to drive up to the college to get Fiona home,' Janet said in surprise. 'We never thought of sending him a wedding invitation, did we? I-I didn't know he and Fiona were so friendly. I thought he must still be giving her help with her studies.'

'So he was,' Emma said slowly. 'They got on well when she was working at the school as a pupil teacher but . . .' She frowned. 'I expect he is just being kind. He is a very thoughtful young man. He has given Fiona a lot of free coaching. I expect he wants her to do well. I don't think there is anything more than that. After all he's a man now.'

'Yes he is, but Fiona is not a child any longer either,' Janet mused. 'She is intelligent and very pretty. We tend to forget she's nearly eighteen. She has matured rapidly since she had responsibility for the younger children at school.'

'Ye-es, I suppose you're right, but Harry Thorpe must be eight or nine years older than Fiona.'

'Maybe he is but I believe he's a very decent young man. Anyway, one more invitation will not matter, if it would make Fiona feel better?'

'It's a bit late,' Emma murmured. She deliberated a moment or two. 'Perhaps you could give him an invitation if you see him when he drops Fiona off. Thank him for delivering your chief bridesmaid, or something? Say we would look forward to seeing him there if he can come.'

'Yes, all right. I'll look out for them.'

* * *

There was no doubt about it, Janet's wedding was a very happy day for everyone concerned and for the first time since Jamie had run away to Scotland Emma was delighted to see all her children together. Since the family gathering which Marie and Mark had organized for herself and William during their visit to Scotland it seemed to have drawn William's brothers closer again and Robin had volunteered to send one of his own sons to stay at Bonnybrae to help Jim and so allow Jamie, Rina and the boys to attend the wedding with Marguerite. They agreed to have a family photograph taken, plus another which included all the partners who were now part of their wider family.

Mr and Mrs Shaw were delighted with their son's choice of bride and the warm and loving family which welcomed him into their circle, especially since he had no brothers and sisters of his own. Although Janet had never mentioned Leonard, she had been relieved when Brian told her his best man would be one of his old school friends. Leonard's parents were at the wedding and proved to be a lovely, homely couple. Janet heard them saying their son had gone to America to seek his fortune training horses.

The improvements to the lodge where Mr and Mrs Shaw were going to make their new home were not quite completed and Mrs Shaw was anxious to move out and leave the main house spotlessly clean and tidy for Brian and Janet to begin their married life. Consequently Mr Shaw suggested his son should borrow the family car and take Janet for a two week honeymoon.

'You both deserve it. I heard Janet say she had never had a holiday. We thought we were going to lose you after that dreadful accident . . .' He shuddered. 'We never thought we should see you so happy but you've risen above the pain and trouble, son, so have yourselves a good holiday and go wherever you want. It might be a long time before you get another.'

So Brian and Janet had booked into a posh hotel for one night within a few miles of home but they had kept it a secret.

'After that,' Janet told Marie and Mark, 'we are going to Scotland. I want to see Loch Lomond and Mark wants to go to John O'Groats. We shall not book anywhere. We'll stay wherever the fancy takes us,' she declared happily. 'It will be an adventure.'

'But you must come and stay with us before you head south again,' Mark declared.

'Oh you must, you really must,' Marie insisted. 'Two nights at least, but you can stay as long as you like. Aunt Maggie and Uncle Joe will be so pleased to see you both, and so will Uncle Jim. He'll want to hear all about your farming, Brian.' So it was agreed. Brian and Janet managed to escape at the end of a gloriously happy day with no more pranks than a few noisy tin cans tied to the back of the car and a notice on the back window announcing they were just married.

Janet was very shy on their first night together, but Brian had known she would be because she had always blushed so easily and he knew she had never had other boyfriends. He resolved to be patient and gentle and his tender loving was rewarded by her passionate response. 'I'm the luckiest man alive,' he whispered against her ear a while later as they snuggled into each other's arms and settled down to sleep.

* * *

The summer passed with all the usual work of turnip hoeing and hay making. All too soon it was time to get out the binder, sharpen the knives and harvest the wheat and oats.

Emma was disappointed when Marie wrote to say she and Mark were postponing their usual autumn visit because it would not be long until they were travelling down to Yorkshire for Peter and Helen's wedding at the end of October, but they hoped to stay for a whole week then, instead of the usual long weekend. Marie had a secret which she was resolutely trying to keep to herself and she had sworn Aunt Maggie and Rina to secrecy too. She hoped her mother would understand and be happy for them when they eventually arrived at Moorend two days before the wedding.

They all knew Helen had inherited a well-equipped house so it was difficult to think of suitable wedding presents which would be useful or give the young couple pleasure. In one of her letters to Marie, Emma had mentioned that Peter and Helen would not be going away on honeymoon, partly because they wanted to spend money on redecorating their part of the house to make it their own, and also Peter was keen to pay his share of the rent from the beginning. Helen would not be happy leaving her father on his own for long either, although he seemed to have settled well into the renovated part of the house which was now his home. Both Peter and Helen had worked hard to make it comfortable and cosy with two new carpets and a small comfortable settee with two matching chairs. They had painted the sitting room and the bedroom with its newly attached bathroom, and lime washed the tiny kitchen. It had once been the wash house so it had a good chimney for a new range and Albert Barclay did like to see an open fire.

Marie decided to write to Peter and tell him how Uncle Joe had arranged for herself and Mark to escape secretly from their wedding reception to a very clean and comfortable house on the outskirts of Wakefield for two nights after their own wedding at Silverbeck Hall

*He drove us there in his car and collected us again after two blissful days on our own. He and Aunt Maggie kept it a secret from everybody, even Mam and Dad. The lady who owns the house used to work for Lady Hanley at Silverbeck Hall. She is very homely and provides really good food. Mark and I plan to stay for a whole week at Moorend this time so if you and Helen would like that as our wedding present I will arrange it and Mark and I will take you there and bring you home again. It will be our secret so Helen will not be embarrassed by David, or anyone else, playing tricks — which they would probably try if you were staying at Upperwood Farm. Also we'll make sure Mr Barclay gets home safely after the wedding celebrations are over.*

*Marguerite is excited and looking forward to being a bridesmaid again. She is not superstitious about this being three times a bridesmaid never a bride. Please write soon and let me know what you think.*

*Love to both of you.*

*Marie and Mark*

'How understanding and considerate Marie is,' Helen said gratefully. 'I feel nervous enough as it is, Peter. I don't want to be a disappointment to you.'

'Dear Helen, you could never be a disappointment to me and I love you too much to want to hurt you.' They both felt secretly relieved to be having at least one night away from everyone they knew and they agreed that was the best wedding present they could wish for. Helen wrote to thank Marie and accept gratefully. They did confide in Mr Barclay, knowing they could rely on him to keep it a secret. He had been a bit concerned for his only daughter, with no mother to explain anything about being married and what to expect so he considered it a splendid idea. He knew Peter would treat her gently if they could be left in peace.

* * *

It was a lovely autumn day when Mark and Marie made a leisurely journey down to Yorkshire, breaking the journey for lunch beside a river and stretching their legs with a short walk. William and Emma had just finished their afternoon tea, prior to starting the milking when they heard the car. They went out together to greet the pair with their usual warm welcome.

'Marie!' Emma squeaked, as soon as she saw her daughter climbing out of the car, smiling widely. 'Y-you — you're expecting a baby?'

'Well I hope it's not a baby elephant,' Mark said chuckling as he hurried around the car to put his arm around his wife's shoulders.

'That's wonderful news!' Emma was struggling to keep back a tear or two. 'And you both look so well and so happy. Oh I am glad.'

'And so am I lassie,' William whispered in her ear as he drew Marie into his own arms for a hug. He alone knew how much Emma had felt Marie and Mark's happiness would be complete if only they could be blessed with a child of their own.

'Come in, come in,' Emma urged, her words falling over each other. 'Why didn't you tell us? When is it due? Have you been keeping well?'

'Hey Emma,' William chuckled. 'Give the lassie time to get inside. She can only answer one question at a time.'

'I know, I know, but I'm so pleased for you both,' Emma said, putting out clean cups and saucers and pouring tea while Eve brought fresh scones and some shortbread, without being prompted for once.

Emma poured herself another cup of tea and sat down again.

'I shall be there to help with the milking soon, William.'

'I know — when you have heard all their news,' William grinned and winked at Mark.

'So when is the baby due?' Emma asked, turning to Marie.

'In January.'

'January . . .' Emma pondered. 'You must have known around the time of Janet's wedding?'

'We have had so many disappointments we didn't want to tell anyone until we were absolutely sure,' Marie said.

'It's a wonder Maggie never hinted in her letters,' Emma mused. 'You look well but maybe you were not so good at the beginning?'

'I have been perfectly well,' Marie smiled reassuringly at her mother.

'We swore them all to secrecy,' Mark grinned. 'But we are pleased you are happy for us, aren't we dearest Marie.'

'Oh I am truly pleased. I can't think of any couple more suited to being good parents than you two.'

'That's the reason we decided not to come earlier and make two journeys. We do want to be at Peter's wedding so we're here now and staying for a whole week if you can put up with us.'

'You know we can. We shall be pleased however long you can stay,' Emma said warmly. 'Now I'd better let you settle into your old room while I go and help with the milking, although Eve is turning out to be much better outside than we expected.'

'I'll carry the cases upstairs then leave you to unpack, Marie. I'm ready for a walk so I shall see if I can find Peter and tease him a bit.' Mark grinned wickedly but Marie knew her husband was going to discuss with Peter how they would get him and Helen away from the reception without anyone suspecting. 'Don't forget to tell him I will help Helen dress and do her hair while the bridesmaids are getting themselves dressed,' Marie said. It was all part of the plan for Helen to hide their suitcase and put it in the boot of Marie's car without anyone knowing.

Marie had always been a caring and considerate person, even as a girl, as Lady Hanley had quickly discovered, and she knew Helen had no mother or other close female relatives and every bride was a bit nervous on their wedding day. Sure enough Helen was grateful for Marie being so calm and helpful, and for her reassurance. She knew she would always remember Marie with special affection.

'You must write to me sometimes and tell me all the news,' Marie said. 'Peter has never been much of a letter writer but I love to hear what all my family are doing. And Helen . . . if ever there is anything troubling you, or just things you want to ask, I know you have no mother to turn to, but I would do my best to help, or advise if it is a woman you need, and I promise I would never tell anyone else, not even Mark, or any of my own sisters, if you say it is confidential.'

'Oh Marie, thank you, thank you so much. I confess I have missed Mam not being with us these past few weeks. Dad has been ever so good and done his best but . . .' she shrugged her slim shoulders helplessly.

'I do understand, Helen. However good they are sometimes men cannot possibly know how we women think or feel about personal matters.' Marie hugged her, then slipped the lovely white wedding dress over her head. Mr Barclay had insisted she must get a new dress specially made and on Emma's recommendation she had gone to Mrs Hill and her sister and they had been delighted to dress such a young and pretty bride. They had even made her a head dress of white roses and silver leaves to hold in place the veil which Helen's mother had worn, and her father had given her a beautiful string of matching pearls which had also belonged to his wife.

'You have something old and something new, Helen. Now you want something borrowed and something blue. Here you are. Borrow my silver bracelet. It has blue stones in the centre of the flowers. It was a gift when I was a bridesmaid for my cousin and his wife.'

'You're so kind,' Helen said with a tremulous smile.

'I must drive to the church now and meet up with Mark. Your father is waiting for you downstairs with the bridesmaids.' Marie kissed her on both cheeks. 'You look so beautiful, but Peter knows he's a lucky man. I'm sure he will be good to you, Helen.'

It was a lovely wedding even though it was not so big as Janet's and Brian's had been and afterwards Mark and Marie left a little early on the pretext that Marie needed to rest. None of them guessed they had smuggled away the bride and groom until David searched for them, determined to play some tricks. He and his friends were even more disappointed when a smiling Mr Barclay told them they would not be returning to Upperwood Farm either because they were spending a few days at a secret rendezvous.

# CHAPTER THIRTEEN

In January Marie and Mark became the parents of a fine baby boy. They named him William Rupert after Marie's father and Mark's oldest and very close friend, who had agreed to be one of the godparents.

Emma and William kept their promise and travelled up to Scotland to see their new grandchild at the end of March. It was a surprise to everyone, including Marie and Mark, when almost a year later there was a baby sister for baby William. They named her Margaret Emma which pleased both Aunt Maggie and her mother. In June of that year Janet and Brian had a baby boy and on Christmas Eve Helen had a baby girl named Christine Emma after both her grandmothers, much to her Grandfather Barclay's delight, although he called her Chrissie from the beginning.

On Boxing Day Bob Rowbottom rode over to Moorend especially to congratulate Emma and William on their ever increasing family.

'How many grandchildren is that now then?' he asked, smiling broadly. 'It must be good reason for a toast?'

'I thought you didn't like whisky,' William grinned, bringing out a bottle of the best malt whisky and a couple of glasses.

'I've had so many toasts at Moorend welcoming your extended brood into the world that I've acquired a taste for it,' Bob said with a chuckle. 'Lord Hanley sends his congratulations too. Young Rick was in at the time. You'll never guess what he had to say, the rascal. His mother was quite shocked.'

'I expect he's picked up all sorts of ungentlemanly expressions since he's been at university but I hear he's doing very well by all accounts,' William remarked.

'Oh it wasn't anything rude. He simply sounded so very confident. He said when he marries Marguerite they will give you great grandchildren to be proud of too. Lord Hanley asked him what made him so sure the young lady would accept him as her husband. "Oh" says he, "I decided ages ago Marguerite is the girl I want for a wife." We were all astonished. "Mm . . . I see," Lord Hanley, said, winking at Thea and doing his best not to smile. Rick took himself off and Lord Hanley shook his head and chuckled. "Oh the confidence of the young. What a lot the boy has to learn." There's no doubt he'll have plenty of lessons ahead but he sounded quite sure about having your granddaughter for his wife.' Bob Rowbottom grinned. 'I'm glad I shall not be the land agent for Silverbeck Estate then, William. You will be taking over all the farms for your family.'

'Och, Rick is a grand laddie but things rarely turn out like our youthful dreams,' William said drily. 'When his time comes to look for a wife Lord Hanley will have several well-bred, wealthy young ladies lined up for him as prospective brides.'

'Mm, I'm not so sure. The boy's happiness is always his main priority. It will probably depend more on whether your granddaughter agrees.'

'I'm sure Lord Hanley will want someone with more standing than the granddaughter of one of his tenants.'

'Marguerite's mother was from a land-owning family, wasn't she? I seem to remember you and your wife being worried when Jamie wanted to marry her. You didn't think he would be good enough for her, yet from what Marie says they couldn't be happier together.'

'That's true I suppose, but I doubt if Lord Hanley or Rick's mother will see things that way.'

'Thea is not a snob, not at all. Anyway, the class system has changed since the war, and if Lord Hanley is right, there will be greater changes still if we have to live through another war. He seems convinced it's a possibility with the unrest in Germany and the number of people without food or work in this country.'

'Aye, things are very unsettled, but I pray it will not come to war.'

* * *

As Emma expected, Fiona spent most of the term at her teacher training college, returning home for the holidays and sometimes for a weekend when Harry Thorpe collected her to go to one of the village dances with him.

Marguerite continued to visit regularly, travelling on the train with calm confidence when Marie and Mark and their little family could not come. They all enjoyed her cheerful nature and merry dark eyes. She made a point of visiting her aunts and uncles and all her young cousins. Even the youngest babe in arms, seemed to adore her.

'I know I shall have to train as a general nurse and get a proper qualification, but you know Granny, I think I would really like to work with children after that,' she said to Emma on one of her visits.

'Your mama will be able to tell you about that, my dear,' Emma said with a smile.' I believe her patients were often children when she worked at the Fever Hospital.'

Fiona had to spend a year in a school to do her teaching practice and earn her parchment before she became a fully qualified teacher. The nearest post she could get to home was in a school on the other side of Doncaster but she found pleasant lodgings with a kindly widow and settled down to prove herself. Now that she was nearer, Harry Thorpe collected her most Friday evenings and brought her home to Moorend, but Emma felt it was only a matter of time before her youngest child left the nest completely. Harry had become as welcome as all the other members and friends of the Sinclair family. Everyone expected he and Fiona would marry when she had gained her full qualification as a teacher but there was a cloud on the horizon. As a married woman Fiona would not be allowed to continue teaching and she loved her job. She excelled during her year's training and she was offered a contract to teach for another year at the same school. She agreed to accept the opportunity, much to Harry's disappointment.

Mrs Thorpe had died eighteen months earlier and his father's own health was gradually deteriorating without his wife to need his care and take up his attention. Although one of the women from the village went to the School House each morning to cook a meal, clean and do their washing, Mr Thorpe had taken to wandering off for walks. This was becoming a worry for Harry, although his father was well known to everyone in the village and they all kept a friendly look out for him. Often someone accompanied him back home if it was cold or wet, or getting dark. Emma did not voice her own concerns but she felt there was a danger Fiona would become a full-time nurse to old Mr Thorpe, instead of doing the job she loved, if she and Harry married. Consequently there was a growing tension between the young couple, especially now Harry was thirty-one and longing to make Fiona his wife. The pressures in the government cast further uncertainty throughout the country as the threat of another war increased.

* * *

Marguerite had also worked hard and done extremely well at the school run by the Misses Lyall. Using her own initiative she had discovered a hospital in Yorkshire which would allow her to start her nurse's training slightly earlier than usual due to her excellent academic record and the reference from her teachers pledging her practical attitude plus her sense of responsibility towards younger pupils in the school. Rina and Jamie were hurt and shocked when she announced she had secured a place to start her training and she intended to go to Leeds. She would be required to live in the nurses' home but she hoped to stay with Granny and Grandad Sinclair at Moorend whenever she got time off.

Jamie rarely got angry with any of his children but he was hurt when Marguerite, feeling proud of her successful application, innocently presented them with a fait-accompli.

'I suppose this is the result of the letters you exchange with that fellow at university? He lives in Yorkshire doesn't he?' he demanded.

'You mean Rick? Rick Fortescue?' Marguerite asked.

'Of course I mean him! Lord Hanley's grandson, isn't he? Don't think he will want anything to do with you when you're living there all the time and he returns home to be a gentleman. He's been amusing himself, wanting a girl to write him letters so he can boast to his friends.'

'Oh Dad, Rick's not like that. Anyway, he has nothing to do with where I do my training. He doesn't even know yet that I shall be going to Leeds, and neither do Granny and Grandad Sinclair. As a matter of fact Rick doesn't want me to be a nurse.' She didn't tell her beloved father that in Rick's last letter he had shocked her by asking her to marry him. He was sure there was going to be a war soon and he would be joining the forces. At seventeen her thoughts had so far centred only on becoming a nurse as her mother had been. She liked Rick, she had always regarded him as her friend, and she liked him even more now she was in her teens and Rick was a perfect young gentleman of twenty-one, but she had no thoughts of getting married to anyone until she had completed her training. One thing did make her uneasy concerning Rick though. She read the newspapers so she knew that war was almost inevitable. The thought of Rick going to fight sent a chill down her spine and filled her with dread. He could be killed, as his father had been. Until now her own little world had been happy and secure within a circle of loving family and friends. She had never considered death, or its consequences.

Rina shrank from the idea of her beloved daughter going to live and work so far away but she remembered how opposed her own mother had been when she had wanted to train to be a nurse. She had been derisive and bitter. Rina silently vowed she would never oppose Marguerite's plans to the extent where she no longer felt welcome in her own home, as she had felt herself. In bed that night she explained her thoughts and feelings to Jamie and pleaded with him not to alienate Marguerite. Jamie remembered Rina's struggles and the misery her mother had caused. He understood and drew her tenderly into his arms. He was lucky to have her as his beloved wife. She could so easily have died giving birth to the twins. He also considered the sorrow he must have caused his own parents when he ran away from home himself, and that had been due in part to his grandmother's bitter resentment. He promised Rina he would try to accept Marguerite's plans, but he admitted he was not happy that his only daughter had chosen to live and work so far away. He blamed his parents and his family for welcoming Marguerite so warmly and so often but he silently admitted both he and Rina had encouraged her to visit whenever the opportunity arose. They had wanted her to be part of a loving family, more so because Rina had no family to call her own, except for Aunt Maggie who had never made any claim to relationship because she had been born as the result of Rina's grandfather's youthful indiscretion. Consequently she had never been accepted as a relative by Rina's parents. Even before she discovered their tenuous connection Rina had learned to love Maggie for the kind and loving person she was. They both cherished the mutual affection and friendship which had grown with the years.

* * *

Emma's heart beats raced when she recognised Jamie's writing on the letter which the postman had just delivered. Ever since he married Rina he had left the weekly letter to Rina to write, adding only a few lines to the bottom of her letters himself. Rina was a good correspondent and often gave them Maggie and Joe's news when Maggie was too tired to write herself. Even William had noticed how his sister and brother-in-law had grown frailer since they had begun to make an annual visit to stay with Marie and Mark. Emma tore open the envelope and gasped as she read.

'What's wrong Emma? Is it bad news? Is it Maggie, or Joe?'

'No one is ill,' Emma said, her mouth tightening. 'As you've guessed the letter is from Jamie. Marguerite has secured a place in Leeds to train as a nurse and Jamie is blaming us for encouraging her to come down here. He believes she is coming to be closer to Rick Fortescue and that we have nurtured their friendship. Here you can read it for yourself. It is short, even for Jamie, but he sounds quite bitter that his only daughter wants to move so far away from home. He ought to be proud Marguerite has done so well.'

William took the letter and frowned as he read.

'I didn't even know Marguerite was applying for places. She is not eighteen yet. You weren't aware . . . ?' He looked at his wife over his new reading spectacles. Emma shook her head. 'How the devil can he blame us?'

'I don't know,' Emma said, 'but I do know we shall welcome the lassie here as we have always done, when she gets time off.' Her manner was determined.

'Maybe Jamie will understand now how we felt when he ran away to Scotland without even telling us where he had gone. Both he and Rina have overcome difficulties and striven for what they wanted to do with their lives so it's to be expected that Marguerite will have the same grit and determination.'

'Oh yes?' Emma smiled wryly and nodded at William. 'I see a man across the table who has had more than his fair share of both to get where he wants to be and prove himself a success.'

William grinned at her. 'We didn't have much option, did we, my lassie?'

'Oh William, I'm hardly a lassie anymore.'

'You'll always be a lassie to me,' he assured her. 'By the way, Jamie also seems to think we're responsible for Marguerite getting too friendly with Rick Fortescue, but I don't think we ever influenced either of them. The laddie has come around Moorend since he and Fiona went to the village school together. He often calls even when neither Fiona nor Marguerite are here.'

'Yes, he makes himself quite at home in my kitchen,' Emma smiled. 'He told Janet we are the nearest he has to a family after his grandfather and his mother. He has grown into a nice young man with polite manners and kindly ways.' She chewed her lower lip thoughtfully. 'I must admit he always seems to have had tender feelings for Marguerite, ever since she was a flower girl at Marie's wedding, and she always asks if he's around when she comes down here on holiday. I've never seen anything more than friendship between them though. I shall write to Jamie this afternoon and put him straight on a few matters,' Emma declared firmly.

When Rick reached his twenty first birthday Thea had not wanted an elaborate celebration, knowing the date would revive all the old speculations. Rick was in agreement because he was at Oxford and working hard at his studies. Consequently his grandfather decided to buy him a motor car instead. He had taught Rick to drive around the estate in his own car when the boy was still sixteen so he knew Rick was capable and steady. Having his own vehicle would make his journeys back to Yorkshire easier.

Neither Emma nor William knew that Rick had twice driven up to Scotland and stayed with Marie and Mark. The visits had been short but Mark had given Rick some instruction on the basic maintenance of his car which he said could prove useful when he was driving long distances on his own. Marie had never thought to mention the visits in her letters to her parents now that she had three adorable children of her own to write about. In any case Marguerite had taken Rick to visit Aunt Maggie and Uncle Joe's and twice to Bonnybrae so she had not seen so much of Rick herself. While they were at Bonnybrae, Rick had sensed a certain coolness in Marguerite's father and a wariness in her mother. He was puzzled and a little hurt after the warmth and friendship he received at Moorend. He had never been over familiar, nor anything but gentlemanly with Marguerite, although he longed for more than giving her a friendly kiss on the cheek when he said goodbye, but in comparison with the young ladies he had met at Oxford, Marguerite was sweet and innocent.

Rick was not responsible for Marguerite's decision to do her nurse's training in Yorkshire either. It was one of the few hospitals which would accept her before her eighteenth birthday, and even then her application had had to be approved by several dignitaries. Her academic results and excellent references had swung the balance in her favour, plus the fact that everyone was on edge, believing war was approaching and with war came an urgent need for doctors and nurses. Rick was delighted when he heard. He would be finished at university by the time Marguerite started her training in September and he would have more opportunity to see her when she was living nearer his own home.

* * *

Although Harry was disappointed at being unable to marry Fiona as soon as he had hoped he was a kind and understanding man. He was well launched on his own teaching career so he understood that Fiona wanted to teach for at least one year before they married. They spent a lot of time together during the long hot summer of 1939. Every morning, while Mrs Williams was working at the School House, Mr Thorpe seemed happy to work in his garden. She was a kindly woman and always took him out a mug of coffee and a bun or biscuit. She often sat beside him on the bench and drank her own and chatted a while. Harry seized these times to drive to Moorend. If Fiona was not required to help her mother with cooking or baking she went to help the men working with the hay and then the harvest. Harry joined in, enjoying the fresh air and sunshine, feeling his muscles strengthen and most of all spending time with the woman he loved. Emma assured him he was always welcome to have his meals with them at Moorend but Harry insisted he must return home to supervise his father and let Mrs Williams attend to her own household tasks.

'Your father was always a countryman at heart, Harry. I often saw him walking his dog, even as far as the Common sometimes,' William said one day while they were working side by side piling the rows of hay into heaps or haycocks. 'Maybe he would like to come with you sometimes and wander around the field while we're working.'

'I'm sure he would,' Harry mused. 'Wouldn't you mind him wandering about?'

'Of course not.' David was working nearby and overheard.

'Perhaps it would be a good idea to get your father a dog again?' he said. 'I have an elderly collie who would probably be good company for him. She likes to be with people but she's too old to work the sheep now.'

'That's kind of you David,' Harry said gratefully. 'I know how much you love your dogs. If this good weather keeps up maybe we could try it out tomorrow afternoon?'

'Certainly, it's worth a try,' William agreed. 'I reckon we all need a bit of companionship whether we're old or young.'

So every afternoon Mr Thorpe arrived with Harry. Sometimes he fell asleep in the sun with Patsy the dog lying beside him, and sometimes he and the dog wandered slowly round the field.

'We're going to have a good crop of blackberries this year,' he announced. 'Maybe I could pick some soon for Mrs Sinclair to make a blackberry and apple pie?'

'We would all like that,' William said with a laugh. 'Emma makes good bramble and apple jelly too if you get plenty. She's sure to give you a jar to sample.' None of them realised the momentous events which were hovering over them all.

It was the last Sunday afternoon in August and Fiona and Harry were sitting together in the garden at the School House. A few yards away Patsy, the elderly collie, lay sprawled at Mr Thorpe's feet while he slept in his canvas chair, or at least they assumed he was sleeping. Sometimes he found it easier to close his eyes on the world and let his thoughts drift. He was easily tired these days but he had felt content since he had spent time in the fields again, as he had done in his youth. They had all been to church that morning but Harry had been unusually silent since they returned.

'Are you troubled about anything, Harry?' Fiona asked.

'No more than anybody else, I suppose,' he mumbled. 'I'm convinced we shall be at war very soon.' He turned to Fiona and drew her into his arms, burying his head against the silky warmth of her neck. He shuddered. 'You know I shall have to join up . . .'

'Join . . . ? Oh Harry!' Fiona gasped and the colour left her face, leaving her freckles standing out against her sudden pallor. She turned into Harry's arms and clung to him.

'God knows, Fiona, I dread the thought of leaving you. I'm worried about my father too. He is my responsibility. I don't know how I can arrange things, but it's my duty to fight for our country.'

'God forgive me! How thoughtless, how selfish I've been,' Fiona groaned. 'I never thought of you having to go away to fight when I agreed to continue working at the school another year.' Her arms tightened around Harry's chest and she buried her face against his open shirt neck. 'I couldn't bear it if anything happened to you Harry. I do want to marry you, you know that, don't you?'

'Yes, I know my love.'

'I wish . . . Oh how I wish I had not signed that contract. We can't wait if — if. Oh Harry can you forgive me? W-would they allow me to break the contract? I could look after your father if I was not staying away all week. Wh-what would they do if I write and tell them I must withdraw?'

'I don't know.' Harry's arms tightened around her and he kissed her fervently. Eventually he lifted his head and stared into the distance. 'I do know there will be more young men than me called to do our duty. Some of them will be teachers too, and every other profession. I wouldn't be surprised if they will be pleading with married women to take our places and fill the breach.'

'Then let us get married now,' Fiona said urgently, 'or as quickly as it can be arranged. If we have a quiet wedding I don't need to tell the staff at the school. And if they find out and object I shall resign.'

'You would do that for me?' Harry asked gruffly, nuzzling the warm skin at her neck before moving back to find her mouth in a tender kiss.

'I should have done it when you first asked me,' Fiona said with remorse. 'I just so wanted to feel like a real teacher, and I wanted to earn some money of my own.'

'I know. I understand my darling girl,' Harry said emotionally. 'After all my father and I encouraged you and we're proud of your success. Even if they do break your contract for getting married I'm sure it will not be the end of your career as a teacher. We shall all be needed eventually.'

Later that evening Fiona told her parents she and Harry had discussed having a quiet wedding immediately.

'Harry says he will have to join up when war is declared and — and he thinks that could be any day now.'

'Did he say when — not if — war was declared?' William asked.

'Yes, but Dad, you said the same yesterday. Harry is convinced there will be no other way. He reads several newspapers. Yesterday they reported that Hitler is demanding Danzig and the Polish Troops are gathering at the border. Britain and France have pledged their support to Poland.'

'I think the politicians are all prepared for war,' Emma agreed. 'In yesterday's paper it said we are all to be issued with an identity card, and they are already planning to evacuate hundreds of children from the cities into the country. Poor wee souls. They will feel so lost without their parents. They are moving all the precious items from the museums and galleries in London too.'

'Maybe they are,' William said, 'but this war will not be confined to London now the Germans have aeroplanes the same as we have. Last time they attacked our ships bringing food. This time they'll attack the factories where weapons and aeroplanes are made as well as the ships. They'll attack wherever there are big populations too.'

As ever William waited until he and Emma were in the privacy of their own bed before he mentioned what was really on his mind.

'Both Tom and Steve are over forty so I don't think the government will recruit them for the army but I'm worried about David. At twenty-four he's exactly the type of fit young man they will recruit.'

'Oh William!' Emma whimpered softly. 'I hadn't thought of David going. He's the only strong young man we have left.'

'I doubt if they'll consider that,' William said grimly.

'I am worried about Mark. Whether they send for him or not I think he may want to join the RAF. You know how much he likes anything mechanical.'

'Aye,' William sighed wearily. 'It's a bad business all round.'

* * *

The following Sunday was the third of September 1939. It was another beautiful autumn day with the leaves beginning to turn from green to gold. A few fluffy clouds floated gently in the clear blue heavens. The world seemed so peaceful. Birds were twittering together as they gathered in flocks, ready to begin their long flight to warmer climes.

The Silverbeck church had a large congregation on Sunday morning and the service was almost over when a church warden approached the pulpit with a piece of paper. The vicar read it carefully then he looked on the anxious upturned faces of his flock and cleared his throat.

'The prime minister announced today "This country is now at war with Germany. We are ready". Let us say one more prayer before we depart God's House and return to our homes and families.'

The congregation moved slowly out of the church, gravely shaking hands with their new vicar as they filed past him at the door. Standing to one side of the path further along Lord Hanley and Thea stood waiting. As William, Emma and David approached, closely followed by Fiona, Mr Thorpe and Harry, Lord Hanley moved to William's side, indicating he wanted a word.

'We shall wait beside my car. It is parked outside Mr Robertson's shop and I saw your van nearby.' Thea gave them a wan smile and Emma thought how pale she looked. She had not seen much of Lord Hanley recently but they had heard he had been attending the House of Lords more often than usual. He seemed to have aged and she had never noticed how grey his hair had become.

As they left the people behind and approached the car Lord Hanley moved towards them.

'Thea and I would be obliged if you would all join us for Sunday lunch at the Hall. This situation affects us all. There is much to discuss.' Fiona and Harry looked at each other, their expressions registering their disappointment as William accepted graciously.

'Harry and I will see you both later then,' Fiona said urgently. 'We — we mean to go ahead with . . .'

'You and Harry and Mr Thorpe must come too. You too David,' Lord Hanley insisted. 'Richard should be back from Oxford by the time we get home. This war is going to affect all of us and I want to help if I can, wherever I can, though I fear the one young man I would give my life to help will be beyond all my influence and powers of persuasion.' Emma thought she heard Thea stifle a sob and her heart went out to her. Surely Rick would not be sacrificed to war as his father and uncle had been.

Emma and William followed Lord Hanley's car in their van while Harry drove his father, Fiona and David.

'I know Dad would not want to offend Lord Hanley by refusing,' Fiona muttered to David, 'but I can't understand why he wants to see us. We have affairs of our own to discuss. We intend to get married by special licence on Tuesday, before the school holidays end in ten days' time, and before Harry receives his call up papers.'

'Married? So soon?' David repeated. Harry caught his eye in the mirror.

'We have mentioned it to your parents, David. I don't think they will object in the circumstances. We wondered if you would be one of our witnesses. Janet has agreed to be there for Fiona.'

'Gosh!' David exclaimed. 'I know the war will mean a lot of changes but you two are certainly moving fast. I expect they will send for me too,' he added unhappily. 'I don't know how Mother will take that, or how Dad will manage all the work. We shall have to sell the sheep I think, just when I am building up a good little flock of breeding ewes.' He sounded young and disconsolate so Fiona didn't mention the wedding again. They all knew the war would change lives everywhere. Mr Thorpe was very quiet and Fiona wondered if he had dozed off to sleep. He had seemed weary in church but Harry had told her he had seemed more withdrawn than usual all week. She knew he still read his newspaper every day and listened to the radio so he understood the threat of impending troubles and upheaval. There was little wonder if he felt dejected. Fiona felt a bit the same herself. They would both miss Harry dreadfully. Her own career as a teacher no longer seemed important in comparison.

Lord Hanley ushered them into the large entrance hall at Silverbeck Hall and Thea pointed out a downstairs cloakroom then showed them into the drawing room.

'Lunch will be ready,' she said. 'Cook is expecting us but we assumed Rick would have returned.'

'I thought he had finished at Oxford,' Fiona said. 'He told me how well he has done, getting a first class honours degree in mathematics and physics. I didn't think there was much further he could go unless he wants to get a doctorate?'

'He enjoyed studying once he settled down,' his mother said. 'He had already begun further studies in his spare time, something to do with cryptograms, I think. He was planning to go further. I believe it was you, Harry, who first awakened his interest in simple codes when he was still a boy.'

'Oh yes!' Fiona exclaimed. 'I remember — sort of puzzles with numbers and letters? Rick was always a lot quicker to get the answers than I was — though I never admitted that to him, so please don't tell him,' she added with a grin. 'We always enjoyed an argument.'

'He was very happy when he started school with you and your brother so your secret is safe with me.' Thea gave a faint smile. 'He — he has had a l-letter requesting him to r-report to the offices of some army general or other in London.'

'Oh no! Already?' Fiona asked, her own face paling. Now she understood why his mother looked so drawn and unhappy.

'A request is more of an order in the present circumstances,' Lord Hanley said grimly, overhearing their conversation. 'Richard knew he would have to join up if we went to war. I so hoped we could avoid another one. My sons were in the army, but Richard fancied the air force. I believe Marie's husband intends to join the air force according to the last letter we had from them. It will mean giving up his garage business.'

'Yes,' Emma said reproachfully. 'We hoped he would wait and see whether or not he was called up. He will be forty in December. I-I hoped he might avoid it now he has three young children.'

'Ah lunch is ready. Thank you, Mrs Scott. We shall start without Richard. After his interview he was going to Oxford to clear his rooms and bring everything home. It must have taken longer than he anticipated.'

It was a delicious lunch but Fiona was sitting next to Mr Thorpe and she noticed he only picked at his food, although everyone else ate with relish.

'Please congratulate Mrs Scott. She has made a lovely meal for all of us,' Emma said. 'It makes a change not to have to start cooking the moment we get home from the kirk. I expect food supplies will soon be short.'

'I'm afraid you're right. There will be shortages of human and animal feed, as well as imported fertilisers but the government are a bit better prepared this time than they were during the last war,' Lord Hanley said. 'Ration cards have already been printed. Prime Minister Chamberlin was hoping Hitler would settle for peace right up until this morning's ultimatum, but he hoped in vain. Sir Reginald Dorman-Smith, the Minister of Agriculture, has already been granted wide ranging powers allowing him and his assistants to take possession of any land which is not farmed with maximum efficiency. He had already delegated many of these powers to the County War Agricultural Executive Committees. They are being referred to as the War Ag. The government has no desire to see the country come as near to starvation as we did in the last war but it will not be easy when the Germans have so many submarines ready to sink our merchant shipping. We depend on imports for sixty percent of our food so it is vital that we grow more of our own. Many of the politicians have been aware of the situation for some time, hence the introduction two years ago of a subsidy on lime and basic slag to try and improve yields. Many of them understand improvements are not instant.'

'It has helped,' William agreed. 'We have taken advantage of the subsidy and spread lime on the Mountcliffe Hill. David says he sees a difference except on the steeper parts where it was too risky to spread anything. Fortunately the sheep graze everywhere so at least they leave some manure behind.'

'David, ah yes, my boy. I expect they will be sending you for a medical any time now. The French called up all their reservist troops more than a fortnight ago and they have evacuated sixteen thousand children from Paris. All our eligible young men can expect call up papers any day now. I believe, David, you are more needed to help grow the nation's food. Should I assume you would prefer to get on with that rather than join the armed services?'

'I would prefer to do the job I know but I don't suppose the officials would listen to my preference, even if I dared tell them,' David said drily.

'Maybe not, but we can try. I shall do my best to convince them you are needed here. I hope you will agree to the suggestion I am going to make, William? Bob Rowbottom and I have already discussed it, in fact it was his idea. We believe we should put the tenancy of Mountcliffe Hill into David's own name, along with the land belonging to Beckside, the small farm adjoining the lower fields and Alan's. I understand you once told Bob Rowbottom that it would make a decent sheep farm with the addition of the sheltered lower fields for lambing ewes and fattening lambs?'

'I did yes,' William flushed and chewed his lip. The suggestion had been partly in jest at the time. His landlord knew far more about his tenants than he had thought. 'But Beckside is still occupied, isn't it?'

'Yes, but I'm afraid if Mr Taylor, the present tenant, doesn't give up the tenancy of his own accord, the War Ag will take it over. Whoever has it will insist the accessible land is ploughed and put into cereals for the duration of the war, whether the owners or tenants agree or not. Hopefully they can be persuaded that it is better to crop the land in rotation, but not all those in charge will understand farming and the countryside as we do. I think Jed Taylor may agree to give up the land if we allow him to rent the house, at least until such times as David marries and needs the house himself. I understand you erected an appropriate boundary fence between the fields which Alan farms and the Mountcliffe Hill, William?'

'Yes, we did. We have kept it completely separate. Alan pays rent only for the land he farms. We pay the rest.'

'Then I believe if we make a separate tenancy for Mountcliffe Hill Farm and put it in David's name, back dated to March, the officials will accept that he is responsible for the farm and the land cannot farm itself. Hopefully they will leave him to do the job he does best. How you arrange the money, the bookkeeping and division of labour will be up to you and your two sons, William. I am not asking you to be dishonest because at the end of the day you and your family have always paid your rents on time. In spite of all the years you have lived in Yorkshire I know you're still a canny Scotsman so you will find a way.' Lord Hanley summoned a smile.

'Oh, I do so hope you're right, Lord Hanley,' Emma said, gratitude shining in her green eyes. 'And I wish you could save your own grandson, the way you're trying to save David. Rick is a fine young man.'

'Yes, we are grateful for your efforts to help our family,' William said.

'I certainly appreciate your help, Lord Hanley,' David said with a sigh of relief.

'It may not be all to your liking I'm afraid. There will be a severe shortage of labour,' Lord Hanley continued. 'There is to be a subsidy of two pounds per acre for ploughing up grassland to grow arable crops — cereals, potatoes, sugar beet and so on. According to the present figures we need one and a half million acres of extra land under the plough by the spring, including many acres of beautiful parkland belonging to wealthy estates.'

'Good Lord!' William protested. 'We don't have enough horses or ploughmen in the country to manage that.'

'Nevertheless, if we are not to starve, we must do our best. There are suggestions we make use of tractors and milking machines to compensate for the shortages of manpower. They are already recruiting women for the Women's Land Army.'

'As far as milking machines are concerned I have been looking into them already because my own family are all leaving home and we still need to milk the cows. My relative, Andrew Kerr, is considering trying one too, or rather his son is. I don't know how we would manage a tractor though, even if I could afford one. The ones I have seen look more like small thrashing machine engines, although Mark tells me they have better ones in America that are more compact. He is convinced if we can manufacture tanks, we should be able to make tractors.'

'Yes, I have heard that too,' Lord Hanley said. He turned to Harry, 'Are you expecting to join the services too Harry?'

'I am Sir. I shall volunteer for the army if they give me a choice. I don't want to be in the navy.'

'Oh no,' Fiona shuddered, 'not the navy. Harry and I plan to get married on Tuesday, by special licence. We — we did mention it to you both,' she added, looking at her parents. William and Emma nodded acknowledgment.

'We understand, dear,' Emma said softly. 'You have known each other a long time and I'm sure you will be happy together, but everything is so unsettled. It will not be much of a wedding at such short notice,' she added sadly.

'Thank you both for your approval,' Harry said quietly. 'Maybe Lord Hanley can advise us what we should do for the best?'

'I will try,' Lord Hanley said.

'I signed a contract as an unmarried woman to teach for another year at the school where I was working before the holidays,' Fiona told him. 'I wonder whether I should confess to getting married, or keep it secret. Shall I be in serious trouble for breaking my contract?'

'Surely with you away fighting for your country, Harry, it would make sense for your wife to take over Silverbeck Elementary School, especially now the older children are being moved on to secondary school? The vicar was telling me his wife trained as a teacher. She teaches the Sunday school children, of course. She might be willing to help with the younger ones some of the time. I'm sure the country will need married women teachers to replace the men. Would you like to do that Fiona? I know most of the men on the County Council. I could have a word with them on your behalf?'

'We never thought of that,' Fiona said with a note of excitement. 'It would be so much better if I could stay in Silverbeck at the School House.' She turned to Mr Thorpe with a wide smile. 'Mrs Williams and I will take care of you between us. I don't want to get into trouble, but more than anything, I want to marry Harry before he is called up into the services.'

'Oh yes, I do agree with you my dear,' Thea said with feeling. Lord Hanley gave her an understanding smile.

'You're a good lass, Fiona . . . always were.' Mr Thorpe patted her hand. His voice sounded weak and distant, little more than a whisper and Fiona clasped his hand and squeezed it gently. He hadn't touched his dessert. 'God bless you both, you'll make Harry happy,' he murmured softly. Fiona looked into his weary face with concern. 'Harry!' she gasped and put her arms around the old man's shoulders, holding him up in his chair. 'Harry! I th-think your father feels faint.' Harry rushed to her side while Thea hurried to the window and swiftly swept cushions from a chaise longue in the recess.

'He needs to lie down. Help him onto here,' she instructed. Harry and David lifted him gently onto the long seat and put a cushion beneath his head. 'We should send for Dr Finch,' Thea urged anxiously. 'I fear it is more than a faint.'

'Yes,' William agreed promptly. 'I'll drive to the village and ask him to come.' He squeezed Harry's shoulder. 'I'll go, you stay at his side laddie.'

'We should have been able to telephone for the doctor by now,' Lord Hanley muttered, 'if the engineers had done as they promised a month ago and got the lines erected through the village and over the Common.'

Doctor Finch was finishing his lunch when William rang the bell but in no time he was in his car and driving up to Silverbeck Hall, leaving William to follow in his van.

Harry was kneeling beside his father, holding his hand while his free hand clasped Fiona's like a lifeline. She pressed it in support even as she struggled to hold back tears. They both knew the old school master had taken his last breath.

# CHAPTER FOURTEEN

Doctor Finch shook his head sadly as he confirmed what they already knew. He had known Henry Thorpe and his late wife for many years and enjoyed many a discussion with the old schoolmaster.

'I did try to warn him to take things easier. His heart has not been so good recently but he said he had enjoyed going up to the hayfield and watching the men work, it reminded him of his boyhood. It was the digging in his garden I tried to warn him about.'

'I know,' Harry said sadly. 'I wanted to do the heavier work myself but he would have none of it.' He summoned a faint smile. 'He told me to stick to my own part of the garden, cultivating Mother's roses and her rockery. After she died the garden was the only joy he had left.'

'One of his joys,' Dr Finch said quickly. 'He was very proud of you Harry. A couple of weeks ago he told me he wondered if he had done the wrong thing in encouraging you to change your employment and become a schoolteacher. I didn't know you were a Civil Servant for two years after university. He said you were brilliant at figures.'

'I don't know about that,' Harry said, 'but there was always someone else ready to take advantage or snatch the credit for completion of a good job.' Fiona was surprised to hear a slight bitterness in his tone. 'I tried to tell my father I had no regrets. I have found a lot more satisfaction in teaching the children and guiding young minds to be honest and kind, as well as learning their lessons. I don't think he really listened. He seemed worried about another war.'

'Yes, he was, but there are a great many people sharing his fears.' Dr Finch noticed Harry clutching Fiona's hand. 'I can tell you he was delighted that you were going to marry a fine young woman with a good family behind her.' He frowned, remembering. 'Your marriage is this week, isn't it? I'm certain your father wouldn't want you to postpone it. At times like this we must snatch every chance of happiness. He would have expected you to do that even though you may not feel like celebrating.'

'We'll see . . .' Harry said. 'Thank you for coming so promptly Dr Finch.' The doctor patted his shoulder and nodded.

'Shall I call in on Mr Johnson, the undertaker, on my way home? Mrs Tilson usually does the laying out but I think she is away visiting her sister this weekend.' He frowned, considering who else he could send but Lord Hanley intervened.

'I think Mrs Scott will be pleased to oblige,' he said quietly. He moved to Harry's side and laid an arm around his shoulders. 'Is that all right with you my boy? Will you ask her please, Thea? She usually copes with everyone connected to the estate, including my wife. There are new white sheets and a white laying out shirt.' He grimaced. 'My wife was always prepared since the death of our sons. We can soon replace them.' Harry felt as though he was in a trance but he shook his head and reached again for Fiona's hand.

'My mother was always prepared too, Sir. I shall be grateful if Mrs Scott is willing but I must go home and bring the sheets and shirt which have waited there since before my mother died. You will come with me Fiona?' he asked quietly. Emma stepped forward then and touched his arm.

'We're so very sorry, Harry. The three of us should go home now and leave Lord Hanley's household in peace but anything we can do to help, please tell us. You are welcome to stay at Moorend until after the funeral if you wish.'

'Thank you Mrs Sinclair. I-I don't think things have sunk in yet.'

'I'm sure they haven't, laddie,' William said, 'but remember we're near enough your family now and we will do whatever we can to help.'

Fiona flashed her parents a grateful smile as she went with Harry to his car.

'Before you go, Harry,' Lord Hanley said diffidently, 'Thea and I wondered whether you would agree to let your father rest in peace in the small private chapel here. There is a door to the outside and I can give you a key so that you may see your father at any time. Think it over. Tell me when you return.'

To Fiona's surprise Thea accompanied them out to the car.

'I do not mean to interfere,' she said softly, her expression deeply troubled, 'but I know you had intended to be married on Tuesday. I heard your father's last words giving you his blessing. It was almost as though he knew. I feel he would want you to go ahead, especially when it is to be such a private ceremony amidst a world in turmoil. You may feel it would be disrespectful, but I beg of you to consider what I say. Better to act now than leave a fatherless child behind,' she added the last words in a hoarse whisper. 'Please don't be offended . . .'

'We are not offended,' Harry assured her and Fiona took her hand and gave it a gentle squeeze and a smile of understanding.

When Harry and Fiona returned to Silverbeck Hall with the clothes for the laying out they were surprised to see the Rev Simms' car. He was speaking to Lord Hanley and Thea in the smaller drawing room.

'I met Dr Finch on his way home,' he said, turning to greet Harry and Fiona. 'I thought it would save you coming to see me. The undertaker told me he could deal with the funeral on Wednesday morning at eleven thirty. That would suit my schedule if it is convenient for you, Harry?'

'I-I,' Harry pushed a distracted hand through his hair. He knew everyone was doing their best to help him, but he could scarcely take things in, let alone make arrangements. Yet at the front of his mind was the possibility that his call up papers could arrive any day, and most likely by the end of the week. 'I must send some funeral notices, letters you know. Mother had some distant relatives. My father has a cousin . . .'

'I will help you, Harry,' Fiona offered quietly. 'If you write the letters I will address the envelopes.'

'Thank you.' He gave her a grateful glance. He looked at the Rev Jacob Simms. They were of similar ages and as schoolmaster Harry had welcomed him both to the parish and into the school. In the short time he had been in Silverbeck they had become friends. 'I do appreciate you all trying to help me. I know time could be short. It — it's . . . I can't take everything in.'

'I understand that,' the vicar and Lord Hanley said almost in unison.

'You will feel much better after a good night's sleep,' Thea advised. 'Allow everyone to do their respective tasks and make the arrangements. We have a box of funeral stationery which I can give you.' She looked questioningly at Lord Hanley and he nodded.

'They are right, Harry,' Fiona said softly. 'Everyone genuinely wants to help. Your father was known to everybody and he was so well respected. It will be a big funeral. Let us go back to the School House and write those letters. Mrs Whitelea is right. Things will not seem quite so bleak after a good night's sleep.'

'Before you go, Harry,' Rev Jacob Simms laid a hand on his arm, 'I am speaking as your friend now, not in my professional capacity as a clergyman. None of us know what each new day will bring, especially now. I believe you should continue with the arrangements for Tuesday. After all it will be a short and quiet ceremony, not a jubilant celebration. Only Fiona's sister and brother will be present as witnesses, plus myself and my wife, Angela. You will be glad of Fiona's loving support and comfort if she can be at your side as your legal wife at the funeral the following day. It is clear to me that you comfort each other.'

'Thank you, Jacob. Can we let you know tomorrow?' Harry asked. He gave an exhausted sigh. 'I don't seem able to take in what has happened yet, but I appreciate you taking time to come and see me here, and for arranging the funeral.' He turned to Lord Hanley and Thea. 'I can't begin to thank you both for your help and understanding, and for — for allowing my father to remain in your chapel until the funeral.'

Although neither Lord Hanley nor Thea had put their thoughts into words they both felt the young couple would feel awkward and uncomfortable if the first night of their married life was spent in the School House with Mr Thorpe in his coffin in the next room.

Harry was glad of Fiona's company as he entered the empty School House.

'It feels strange not to find my father sitting before the fire with his pipe or washing his hands at the kitchen sink after being in the garden.'

'I know, Harry. Let us get these letters written and we can post them at the postbox as we go through the village. I hope you will spend tonight at Moorend with us. Mother will have a meal for us, even though you probably think you can't eat a thing. I don't want to leave you alone in an empty house to grieve and — and I can't stay with you tonight, however much I would like to give you all the comfort I can offer.'

'I don't know what I would do without you Fiona,' Harry sighed. 'Suddenly you seem so mature while I feel like a bewildered small boy needing guidance.'

'It's the shock, Harry, but I am thankful your father did not suffer.' She took out the black edged envelopes and matching sheets of writing paper and laid them on the table. Harry came and sat beside her as she took her fountain pen from her handbag. He passed her the address book which had belonged to his mother and which she had kept up to date each Christmas. He pointed out the relatives he needed to inform of his father's death.

'None of them are close except his cousin so I don't expect they will attend the funeral. I feel I should let them know though. I've just remembered. I only have a couple of postage stamps and this is Sunday . . .'

'Don't worry about that. Mother always keeps plenty of stamps to keep in touch with Marie and Jamie, Aunt Maggie and Uncle Joe. In fact she writes to them all every week and to lots of other friends and relatives when she is in the mood.'

* * *

Harry did feel more like his usual clear-headed self on Monday morning. He had felt drained the previous evening, yet sure he would not sleep. Fiona's father had made him a large toddy at bedtime and insisted he drink every drop. The bed was warm and comfortable and there were none of the village noises at Moorend. He couldn't believe he had slept the night through when he saw bright daylight through the curtains. Emma insisted he must eat a substantial breakfast to give him strength and energy. 'And here are the postage stamps you will need to post your letters, Harry,' she added, placing her stamp box at his elbow, 'but before you go off to the post office William would like a word with you and Fiona in the sitting room, on your own.' She gave a sneaking glance towards Eve who was washing the dishes and preparing to peel vegetables at the sink. Emma knew her young maid never missed anything if she could listen in to conversations and she was inclined to gossip.

A little while later Harry faced Fiona's parents in their comfortable room.

'Have you decided whether you still want to go ahead with your wedding on Tuesday, as you had planned?' William asked, as Fiona came in to join them. She took a seat sat beside Harry on the sofa and he instinctively reached for her hand. Emma noticed and smiled at them. She felt they would have a good marriage together if only the fates were kind to them.

'We have not discussed it this morning,' Harry said. 'I feel torn in two. Half of me thinks we should go ahead when it is all arranged and it will be no more than a short, simple ceremony — almost a formality.' He gave Fiona an apologetic glance. 'It is not the kind of wedding we would have planned if war had not suddenly loomed in front of us. The other half of me thinks many people will consider us disrespectful if we proceed as arranged. We have my father's blessing but I scarcely know what he would have expected us to do in the circumstances.' He sighed heavily. 'Even before yesterday's announcement, he knew war was coming and that I would be called up for service. He was really pleased when Fiona and I told him we were getting married this week by special licence.'

'We're truly sorry your father will not see you married,' Emma said gently, 'but everyone knows you both had great respect for him, as did everyone in this area.'

'Emma and I think you should go ahead as planned,' William said quietly. 'Very few people will realise when or where the wedding has taken place, when it is so low key, but you two will know you are legally man and wife. You will be able to give each other comfort and I'm sure your father would have wanted that. We understand how important it is to be with someone you love at times like this, don't we Emma?'

'We do indeed,' Emma agreed.

'We understand being married may mean complications for Fiona and her work,' William said, 'but we'll give you both whatever support you need. Together you will overcome many problems which might seem insurmountable alone.'

Fiona and Harry looked at each other. 'Then with your approval we would like to go ahead,' Harry said.

'We appreciate you being so understanding, Mam and Dad,' Fiona said. 'We know we are flouting all the conventions and we shall probably be criticised.'

'Don't worry about people who have nothing better to do than gossip at times like these,' Emma said firmly. 'Now we need to change the subject. The funeral will be a big one, Harry. Your father was a popular figure in the community. I wondered whether you would agree to us providing some refreshments in the village hall after the service. Many people will wish to offer their sympathy. It is your decision of course.'

'You are right, Mrs Sinclair. I'm ashamed to say I had not even considered that aspect.'

'You are part of our family now and if you agree I will do my best to organize some food. I know my girls, Meg, Janet, Fiona, and Lynn, will all do some baking. I will order extra bread from the baker to make sandwiches. We could have ham, salad, cheese, egg . . . I think that would be enough variety. Maybe Mrs Williams would like to help us serve tea and coffee? She should at least be asked and included because she looked after you both so well.'

'She did. I would not like to hurt her feelings,' Harry said. 'I'm sure she will want to help. She was away visiting her sister this weekend so she does not even know yet. I must make haste and tell her.'

'Then we'll not keep you,' Emma nodded. 'I think Polly will do some baking and come to help serve teas. She still likes to be included.'

* * *

The Rev Simms and his wife had already booked a lunch for four in Wakefield before Mr Thorpe's death had occurred. They urged Fiona and Harry to stick to the arrangement and get away from the village for a little while and they knew Mrs Williams was anxious to prepare the house for their return.

Mr Thorpe had confided in Mrs Williams regarding Harry and Fiona's decision to be married quietly by special licence before Harry was called away to serve his country but she had been shocked when she learned of Mr Thorpe's death.

'Oh lad,' she sobbed, giving Harry a sympathetic hug, 'you'll go ahead with your marriage? Your father would have wanted that. He was so relieved you would have Fiona beside you whatever happened with this horrid war.'

'Yes we have discussed it with Fiona's parents and they think we should go ahead.'

Mrs Williams called in her niece to help her. They worked hard to make the old School House as spotlessly clean and welcoming for the young couple as the time allowed. She had already bought new sheets and matching pillowcases as a wedding present and she made up the bed with them and used the gift from the vicar and his wife which was a matching eiderdown and counterpane in pale blue satin. Her niece filled two large vases with sweet smelling roses from the garden and placed one in the hall and the other in the bedroom to welcome the new bride and her husband when they returned to the house. They made sure there was food in the larder as well as fresh bread, milk, eggs and bacon. It was the best they could do in view of the sad circumstances.

After the funeral Mrs Williams was glad to be busy pouring tea at the village hall. She had been fond of old Mr Thorpe and the funeral had upset her, but she also knew well enough there were those who would be avid for answers to their questions regarding the marriage of their young schoolmaster and they would try to detain her.

'I am so glad Harry has a fine wife and a good family behind him now, to give him help and support at a time like this,' she said to Emma as they cleared away the remains of the tea. 'Mr Thorpe always thought Fiona was a grand lass and a hard worker, even when she was a pupil teacher. I pray the two of them will be blessed with a lifetime of happiness, in spite of the dreadful state of the world and its wars.'

'Indeed we hope so too, Mrs Williams. I know Fiona will be glad of your continuing help. Neither of them are sure what will happen or where they will end up. They will both go back to school the same as they did before the holidays, until they hear from the authorities. For the time being Fiona will have to travel each morning on the bus from Wakefield and back again in the afternoons. Harry is going to teach her to drive his car but in the meantime he will be tied to taking her to the bus in the mornings and meeting her at the end of the day. He says that is better than being without her all week.'

'Aye well they love each other,' Mrs Williams said simply, 'and they may be parted all too soon if Harry gets his call up papers.'

Richard Fortescue was present at the funeral service with his mother and his grandfather. He waited until most of the people had spoken to Harry before he came to express his sympathy with great sincerity. Harry thanked him gravely.

'I hear you have heard about your call up from the government?'

'Yes, but for the army. I had volunteered though and I expressed a preference for the RAF, like Mark. They were damned cagey about it,' he said. 'I have to report to the same office in London in ten days' time, rather than start training at one of the local stations, or barracks, or whatever they are. One of the officials hinted they intended to make use of my administrative skills and intelligence and they were not interested in my preferences or my physical aspects, whatever that means. He made it clear I shall be forbidden to discuss any details of my work, even with close family. Any mail I receive must be sent to an address they will supply and it will be forwarded to me from there. It will all be censored. I wondered if they intend to train me as a spy but I have never been brilliant at languages, or travelled in Europe as some of the fellows at university have done.'

'I remember you had a natural leaning towards science and mathematics though, even as a youngster,' Harry said.

'Mm . . . well I shall have to wait and see, I suppose. I am sorry I was not back in time to see you both on Sunday afternoon.' He looked at Fiona standing close at Harry's side. 'Grandfather and Mother had got themselves into a panic by the time I returned so they were not very happy with me.' He grimaced. 'I drove on to Leeds to see Marguerite you see, instead of coming straight home. I wanted to tell her I had got my call up. I asked her to marry me,' he added in a rush, as though the words were drawn out of him. 'She — she refused.'

'Oh Rick,' Fiona laid a sympathetic hand on his arm. 'You're both so young and she has only just started her nursing training.'

'I know. That's what she said. She has promised to write every week. But I love her, Fiona. I think I've always loved her. What if I don't come back from this bloody war?' He sounded so young, so boyish. Fiona and he were the same age, they had attended Silverbeck School together, they had discussed and debated and competed against each other, but right now she felt like an elder sister and she almost cried at the sight of his dejected expression.

'We must try not to think like that, Rick,' Harry chivvied him. 'Hope springs eternal remember,' but Fiona saw his own face had grown a shade paler and knew her own was the same. They had discussed the future at length and they were desperately hoping Harry would not be called up for service until they had had some time together, even though they would both be working and in different schools, but at least they could spend their nights together now they were married.

The elderly teacher who was headmaster at Fiona's school had agreed to continue in his post until a suitable replacement could be found. The young man who had been appointed to take his place had been drafted into the RAF. Fiona was nervous when she was asked to report to the headmaster's room. She was sure he must have heard she was married but he smiled kindly and introduced her to a man who seemed to be some sort of official and she remembered Lord Hanley saying he knew most of the men on the Education

Committee and he would have a talk with them. Apparently he had kept his word because Fiona was to leave her present post and start teaching at Silverbeck Elementary School alongside Mr Harry Thorpe.

'This will give you time to become familiar with the working routine of the school before Mr Thorpe is called up for military service. I understand you and Mr Thorpe were married recently?'

'Yes,' Fiona admitted. 'We had intended to wait until I had worked another year here, but — but when war was officially declared we . . .'

'Yes, yes, I understand. I believe you also worked at the school as a pupil teacher before you did your training?'

'Yes I did, under Mr Thorpe Senior at first, then . . .'

'Of course. I am sure you will cope admirably. Mrs Angela Simms is presently helping with some of the younger children on a voluntary basis. Apparently she qualified as a teacher before she married. We expect there will soon be evacuees living with relatives in Silverbeck so we are arranging to employ Mrs Simms in an official capacity for three mornings plus two full days per week.'

Fiona was jubilant when Harry met her off the bus that evening.

'I am to start working with you at Silverbeck on Monday morning, Harry. Lord Hanley must have remembered us and used his influence and explained the situation at Silverbeck as he promised.'

It was six weeks before the official letter came for Harry. The night before he left there was little sleep for either of them as they clung to each other in a passionate embrace interspersed with Harry explaining that he had made his will and everything he owned would be hers.

'If I do not return, Fiona, there is enough money to buy a small house.'

'Oh Harry don't say that.' She turned into his arms to hide her tears. 'You must come back to me. I need you so badly. I love you more than life itself.'

'I know my darling wife, but if you had to give up work and vacate the School House I want to know you are comfortable and can buy a home of your own.'

'But you said yourself they need married teachers now. Why should I give up work?'

'Because my dear innocent, we may have made a baby Thorpe after so much loving. Seriously I hope I have not given you a baby, Fiona, at least not yet, but I want you to know that whatever I have is yours. I have a life insurance which my parents had taken out for me when I first started work. On my father's advice I doubled it before things became so serious and made such things either impossible or unaffordable.'

'Oh Harry, all the money in the world would never make up for a life without you. I shall pray every night for your safe return.'

As it happened it was the end of November before Harry was finally called up for military service and by the time he went Fiona was more than proficient at driving the car.

'The driving test which the government introduced in 1935 has been cancelled while the war is on,' Harry told her, 'but you would easily have passed the test anyway. Anyone would think you had been driving a car since the day you left school.'

'I'm glad you have faith in me,' Fiona said, giving him a hug. 'I had a good teacher, that's what it is. As things have turned out I shall not need to travel to work.'

'That's just as well since petrol is rationed and things are likely to get scarcer as time goes on. I miss my father terribly but now that it is time for me to go away to the war it is almost a relief to know he is not here to worry anymore.' His voice became husky as he drew Fiona into his arms. 'It's hard enough having to leave my dearly loved young wife behind.'

'I know. I shall try not to cry when you leave tomorrow morning Harry, but — but I'm not sure I shall manage it. I don't want to make it harder for you than it is already.'

* * *

Whenever Marguerite had a full day free from the hospital she travelled to Moorend as soon as she finished her shift the previous evening so she could spend most of the day with her grandparents. William drove her to Wakefield in the evening to catch the bus back to the hospital, but if she got at least two nights together she made the journey by train to Scotland to see her parents at Bonnybrae.

At Silverbeck, Fiona missed Harry terribly being in the School House on her own so she suggested to Emma that she would collect Marguerite from the bus and, if her niece was willing, she would be happy to have her stay overnight at the School House then she could walk through the village to Moorend the following morning. Marguerite was more than happy with this arrangement.

'I know I'm lucky to have family I can visit on my day off,' she said, 'and I'm grateful to have someone meet me off the bus.'

'We all love to see you, Marguerite. We look forward to your visits. I'm just being selfish wanting your company overnight. Do you mind walking up to Moorend in the morning when I go into school to work?'

'Of course I don't mind. I enjoy walking in the fresh air. As a matter of fact I'm pleased to have a chance for us to talk. Of all my aunts and uncles you're the one nearest to my age. I think you might understand how I feel about — well about some things.'

'You mean like missing Rick?' Fiona asked with a smile. 'Yes, I can understand that well. If it's any consolation he always comes to Moorend for a brief visit on the rare occasions he gets enough leave to travel up to Silverbeck. He always asks if we have seen you and how you are.'

'We do write regularly but sometimes our letters seem to cross in the post and letters are not the same as seeing someone and — and seeing each other face to face.' Fiona noticed the colour which had risen so readily in Marguerite's cheeks and guessed her young niece had only recently realised she loved Rick as a woman loves a man, rather than the very good friends they had always been. The passion which had flared between them when Rick was leaving for the army had awakened Marguerite to a depth of feelings she had never experienced and had not known she possessed. 'Rick asked me to marry him,' she said now in a low voice. 'I feel so torn in two, Fiona. I do want to do something worthwhile and train as a nurse, but — but now that Rick has gone away I wish we had been married . . .'

'I'm sure Rick understands, Marguerite. After all you are both very young.'

'I know, and I know Father would not have given his approval yet. Besides he thinks Lord Hanley will want Rick to marry someone rich and with a title and I don't think Rick's mother wants him to marry me.'

'Oh I'm sure that can't be true, Marguerite. Whatever gave you that idea?'

'It was something Rick told me she had said. Something about not leaving me with a baby and no father.'

'That doesn't mean she does not approve of you, Marguerite. I expect she was warning Rick not to leave you with the misery she must have suffered. Maybe you don't know that Rick's real father died before he could get leave to be married and he never knew he had given her a child. At least that is what I understand happened, though I hope you will not mention that to Rick unless he tells you himself. I only know because Granny Sinclair told me when Harry and I decided to get married a year earlier than we had intended and Mother said she was glad because she didn't want me to be left as Thea was with a child and no husband.'

'Oh? I-I didn't know that.' Her cheeks flushed crimson. 'I-I . . . we were so tempted to make love. Then we — we stopped at the last minute. Now I understand what Rick's mother must have meant. I have felt so guilty because I told Rick I wanted to finish training to be a nurse before I get married and he would be away and I would be left alone with nowhere of our own to live?'

'I think you were sensible to wait, my dear,' Fiona said. 'I am a few years older than you are and I have finished my training. Harry is much older than Rick too, and he could give me a home to live in. I confess I do miss him terribly and I worry if his letters don't arrive when I think they should, but I am so very glad we decided to get married, whatever happens.'

'But what if Rick never comes back, or if — if he is a prisoner of war . . .'

'Please try not to think like that, Marguerite. Maybe he will get a longer leave soon and then you will be able to spend more time together. I don't think Lord Hanley will disapprove as much as your father thinks when he understands you are the girl Rick wants to marry and the one who can make him happy.'

# CHAPTER FIFTEEN

Weeks passed into months. Christmas came and went and 1940 dawned with the nation in an anxious state knowing the Germans were already too close for comfort after sinking the Royal Oak in its home base of Scapa Flow and the crash landing of a Nazi aeroplane on a Scottish moor. Hitler had declared German U-boats were free to attack all shipping, including ships belonging to neutral countries. He was intent on diverting food supplies away from Britain so that he might add to the gloom and conquer the British spirit. The government were more prepared for such a strategy this time and rationing of butter, sugar and bacon was introduced immediately with all other food supplies and prices strictly controlled.

At Moorend Emma thought the food situation would not affect them too badly, at least as far as the bacon and butter were concerned but regulations were brought in limiting farmers to killing a maximum of two pigs a year for their own use and that of their workers, with severe penalties for anyone who flouted the law. All milk producers now had to be registered with the milk marketing boards. Supplies to the public were rationed with priority given to young children and pregnant women. Everywhere thousands more men were called up and the country seemed to be almost in perpetual darkness with the short days of winter and sheds, workplaces, and houses alike were forbidden to show any glimmer of light in case the German bombers were alerted. Blackout material sold out as women did their best to sew black blinds and linings to cover their windows and in factories and farms the windows were painted dark colours. These regulations were enforced by the police and the newly formed Home Guard. In spite of the gloominess people were determined to keep up spirits by singing popular songs such as Somewhere over the Rainbow and We're Gonna Hang Out The Washing on the Seigfried Line, rendering them with defiant gusto. In America a new, and very long film, called Gone with the Wind was proving extremely popular and London cinemas were taking advance bookings, determined to maintain a spirit of optimism and hope of a brighter future.

The Women's Land Army had been formed with a thousand volunteers and had swelled to twenty thousand within two years of war being declared, though not all were volunteers. Coal was desperately needed to supply the factories and some men elected to work down the mines rather than join the armed forces, but eventually one in every ten men called up was drafted to the coal mines to ensure a continuing supply of coal for the munitions factories. The government created three million new allotments and encouraged the households to grow their own vegetables to supplement rations and where possible some kept a pig, or a few hens. Household waste and vegetable peelings were boiled and blended with a little meal when it was available to make a mash, but animal feed was as severely rationed as that for humans due to the need for imports. Linseed cake for the dairy herds came in large sheets which had to be broken into small pieces in a machine wound by hand.

The School House garden was large and old Mr Thorpe had kept the ground in excellent condition. Fiona was determined to grow her own vegetables and Harry advised her which plots to use to vary the rotation.

'Father was strict about that,' he told her. 'He never grew onions on the same plot two years in a row and the same with the other vegetables. He said that helped avoid diseases.'

'*I would like to keep a few hens, or even a pig,*' she wrote in one of her weekly letters.

*Mother says the authorities are keeping a check on every farm and controlling the produce used. I'm sure some of the children are barely getting enough to eat. I know I can't feed them all but maybe I could add a little nourishment if I have vegetables for soup.*

'Farming is bred in you, my darling wife,' Harry chuckled, giving her a hug and a passionate kiss the moment he arrived on a forty-eight-hour pass. True to his promise he constructed a small wooden hut with a pen for half a dozen hens. Building materials were scarce but before he went off again he asked the local builder if he could spare some cement and bricks, even broken ones would do, so long as he could trim them to build a pig sty at the end of the garden.

'Aye, I'll do that,' the builder promised. He was an elderly man who should have been retired but his son and son-in-law had been taken into the army. 'That wife of yours is a grand teacher and she'll show my grandchildren how to be thrifty, aye an' some of their mothers could do wi' a lesson.'

'I hear some of the women are being drafted to work in the munition factories, kitchens and hospitals,' Harry said. 'Fiona tells me they have several children as young as three years old in school now and Mrs Simms is working full-time to help look after them.'

'Aye, she's another good woman doing her best for the youngsters. Every day before they leave the school she plays the piano and they all sing a hymn and say a prayer. I hear the vicar was told he is no use for the army. He failed his medical. Something to do with a heart defect, but he's volunteered for the Home Guard.'

Harry never knew when he would be home again, or for how long, but Fiona cherished every minute of his brief visits and dreaded the partings, however much Harry tried to reassure her he was in far less danger than many of the ordinary householders living in London or Birmingham. As time passed this appeared to be true because the German bombers seemed determined to wipe out Britain's capital city and its inhabitants. All the industrial centres were targets, including the ship building on the Clyde.

Emma and William prayed every night for the people who had lost their homes and loved ones, and their thoughts were always with their sons-in-law, Harry and Mark, as well as Rick Fortescue. He paid them a fleeting visit whenever he was home on leave and he always asked for the latest news of Marguerite. He made no secret of his desire to marry her as soon as she finished her nursing training. Marguerite confided in Fiona and admitted she loved Rick dearly, but she was like her father. Jamie always considered things from all angles and Marguerite knew, even if she and Rick were married they would be living apart. Unlike Fiona, she would not have a home of her own or a useful job to do. She did not want to live at Silverbeck Manor with Rick's mother and grandfather, however kind they might be, and her home at Bonnybrae with her own family would not be the same if she was married. She wanted to do something useful, like helping the wounded soldiers. She did admit she dreaded the journeys back to Scotland on the train.

'I usually have to stand all the way because the trains are packed with servicemen either on leave or being drafted to some obscure place. Some of them look so young and homesick but others are intent on flirting and trying to have a last fling. Some will barely take no for an answer and insist on a kiss and cuddle, even when I tell them I have a boyfriend in the army.'

Marie had a busy life of her own looking after her three children and running the Stavondale Estate, as well as manning the petrol pump which she and Mark had installed near his workshop before the war began and petrol rationing had never been considered. Mark seemed reasonably content with his life in the RAF. He had known he would not get to be a pilot at his age but he worked hard and had a natural grasp of all things mechanical. He had swiftly gained promotion because men like him were required for the continual maintenance of the aeroplanes. Mark had built a small team of reliable men around him. He was strict about the smallest details, drilling it into the trainee engineers that a screw left out or a bolt not tightened could mean the difference between life and death for an air crew. The pilots trusted him. Although he could not be a fighter pilot, he had learned to fly the planes which he maintained, insisting that by doing so he could become more familiar with the workings, engine noises and general performance of the aircraft he had to service. When he could be spared, he was allowed to deliver planes to other airfields where they were needed. Twice he had managed to get a forty-eight-hour pass when delivering a plane within easy travelling distance of Yorkshire and Marie and the children had packed up at short notice and driven down from Scotland to be with him at Moorend. Once he had managed to contrive a delivery to a Scottish airbase, and after standing two hours on a crowded train he had arrived home unexpectedly much to Marie's and the children's delight.

At Silverbeck the local War Ag Committee decided the lower stretches of the Common should be ploughed to grow more cereals. Everyone knew how hard that would be for it had never been anything but rough grass for as long as anyone could remember. Moorend bordered the Common and William was known to be one of the best farmers in the district so he was asked to undertake ploughing, cultivation, sowing and harvesting of cereals.

'God knows how I'm to manage it,' William confided to Emma when they were alone in bed. 'Steve is every bit as good at ploughing as I am but it is strength and endurance we're going to need. David doesn't enjoy ploughing but I know he'll do his share. His youth and strength might make up for his lack of skill but I can't see a way to getting our own fields ploughed and sown as well. The men on the War Ag may have sent us two land girls but they're no use for a job like this when the Common is so rough. In fact the one called Doris is no use for anything as far as I can see.' William rarely criticised people unless it was to their faces so Emma knew he was as frustrated by one of the land girls as she was herself.

'Bob Rowbottom might have had some suggestions to help us if he'd still been here,' Emma said doubtfully.

'I doubt if anyone can help much,' William said despondently. Bob had recently retired as the Silverbeck land agent and he and his wife had moved to Ireland to stay near their daughter who was now a war widow. Her husband had been one of the first casualties of war after being recalled to the navy. He was lost at sea when his ship was torpedoed.

Lord Hanley came to Moorend with Mike Watt, who had been appointed to the War Ag Committee on Lord Hanley's recommendation. Mike had also volunteered for the Home Guard so he had heard the objections of the locals claiming the Common should be left alone.

'You'll be wondering how you are going to manage to plough so much land in addition to your own,' Lord Hanley said to William as he buttered one of Emma's newly baked scones.

'It's just about an impossibility,' William admitted, 'and I'm not as young as I was when we came to Moorend and I tackled the old grassland here.'

'I agree, but Mike tells me the War Ag are being allocated tractors from America on a lease lend basis, that means we shall pay for them after the war is over but we shall have their use now when we need them. It is the only way the country will manage to plough the extra land we need. There are not as many horses in the whole country as there were during the last war.'

'I suppose a tractor might help.' William frowned thoughtfully, 'But we shall need more than a tractor. Alan and David were here for Sunday dinner and they must have heard something about bringing in tractors. Our plough would not do but Alan thought some of the other machines could be adapted to work with a single pole instead of shafts, if the blacksmith can devise a good strong link to attach the plough to the tractor. I shall need to ask Joe Wright what can be done. God knows how we shall get on ploughing a straight furrow if we have to look behind all the time, as well as steering the tractor. Mind you I got the impression David was looking forward to having a go.'

'I don't suppose he'll look forward to ploughing part of the Mountfield Hill, even with a tractor,' Mike Watt said dryly.

'Ploughing the hill land? You must be joking,' William scowled. 'It's far too steep.'

'Mmm, I have tried to tell the rest of the War Ag Committee that but they are scheduling even more land for the plough for next year and the south side of Mountfield Hill is on their list.'

'Yes,' Lord Hanley spoke up, 'and it's not only hill land they have their eyes on this time. We have to plough up the parkland adjoining Silverbeck Manor, right up to the garden fence. No one is exempt. I hear some of the King's land and gardens are to be cultivated.'

'Oh the lovely parkland,' Emma said. 'What about those magnificent trees?'

'I regret to say some of them will need to be taken down. The corn will not ripen where there is too much shade. We must all make sacrifices but the main thing is we must win this war.'

'We must but I'm sorry to hear about the parkland,' William said. 'The steep land on Mountcliffe is neither safe nor suitable for ploughing. Apart from that it constantly needs open drains to allow it to dry enough even for sheep. It is improving but it is not yet ready for cows to graze. Ploughing it would be useless.'

'Mmm, well they're bringing in grants for draining and they're not enforcing ploughing Mountcliffe Hill this year,'

Mike Watt said. 'I have told them exactly what you have just pointed out. Unfortunately some of the committee have never cultivated a garden, even less a field. They spend their time studying maps then decide what must be done.'

'It's always the way,' Lord Hanley said with a sigh. 'That's why I wanted Mike on the Committee and why I proposed you too, William. The country needs practical men who understand the land and the problems. I was sorry to hear you had refused.'

'Aah, so that's why they came to me?' William mused. 'It's not my scene telling other folks how to farm, but in any case I don't have time. I did say if anybody wants my advice I would try to help if they come to me but I'm not forcing my views on anybody.'

'It's a pity because you will know better than most farmers what can be done and what is unrealistic.'

Lord Hanley and William walked outside together still talking but Mike Watt hung back.

'Thank you for coffee, Mrs Sinclair, your scones are delicious, as always.' He lowered his voice. 'How are you getting on with the two land girls? Are they proving useful?'

'We were just discussing Doris last night,' Emma admitted. 'I don't think she has any intention of being useful, or ever learning anything about farming. At a time like this, with so many young men and women risking their lives, I can't believe a healthy young woman can be so lazy or unreliable.' Emma coughed and apologised. 'I'm sorry, I should not be criticising her to you, Mike.'

'As a matter of fact I know the supervisor. That's why I am asking for your honest opinion of her. Between ourselves this is the third place the girl has been and if she can't get on here she will never get on anywhere. Mrs Ramshaw thinks she would be better working in one of the factories but she got the impression she is only interested in men.'

'I did wonder about that when she arrived,' Emma said flatly. 'She is out of luck here. They are all too old for her, well except David, and he is not here all the time. Anyway, any spare time he gets seems to be taken up with his sheep dog training. The dogs have been invaluable for the steep parts of the hill with no men to spare to help.'

'What about the other girl? Mrs Ramshaw thought she might be too small and frail for the work of a land girl but she volunteered.'

'Oh Jean is fine,' Emma said warmly. 'What she lacks in strength she makes up for in intelligence and initiative. She is always willing to try things.' She paused, frowning. 'They have the two rooms up the back stairs. I thought they would be company for each other but to be honest I believe Jean would be happier on her own. She has a scar down one side of her face. I understand she was badly burned during the bombing and she lost both her parents and her young brother. Mrs Ramshaw told us she spent considerable time in hospital and then she was placed in a foster home, though I believe they were very good to her from what she says. Anyway, she is conscious of the scar and I suspect, when things are not pleasing her, Doris can be quite spiteful. She doesn't let me hear her though so I have no proof, only intuition, and once or twice I have noticed Jean has been in tears. Her sweet nature and her personality more than make up for any physical defects.' Mike nodded in understanding and went on his way to rejoin Lord Hanley. Emma thought how much he had matured and wondered whether it was since Bob Rowbottom had retired or whether it was due to the war and extra responsibilities. Either way Lord Hanley seemed to approve of Mike, both as his land agent and as a contact and representative with the War Ag Committee.

* * *

The arrival of the first tractor in Silverbeck was a novelty and Joe Wright was one of the first people to come to Moorend to see it.

'I reckon I'm getting too old to deal with these changes,' he said when he had walked all round it at least twice and inspected the broad metal mud guards and the heavy iron wheels with what he called their spud-lugs. These were iron triangles bolted on all round the large back wheels, and designed to help traction on the fields. 'They will make some mess on the road through the village if you're intending to share it with Alan, and I expect that's what you'll be doing?'

'It is,' William agreed. He was not particularly happy with the machine himself but David had shown a remarkable interest and so had Alan. 'We have some iron plates we can bolt on the big wheels to stop the lugs digging in for travelling on the road but they will take a bit of time fixing on every time we want to move the tractor between the farms. Anyway the main reason we have got it is because we have been instructed to plough up the Common. That's not going to be easy. I have ordered a new tractor plough but we're hoping you'll be able to convert the drill to a single pole to fix on here.' He bent to show Joe the place where the machines would be attached to be drawn behind the tractor. Joe Wright pushed back his cap and scratched his head.

'I'll need to think about it,' he said doubtfully.

'Well have a talk to David and Alan. They have some suggestions about how to convert our mower and the binder, maybe the hay rake as well. I can't afford to buy all new machines just because they've supplied us with a tractor and we shall still need to use the horses to get through all the extra work.'

'I understand that. Still maybe you're lucky to get a tractor,' Joe said. 'They say there's a shortage of iron. You'll have heard the grumbles and objections from the folk who live at the far end of the village? The government are taking all the iron gates and cutting off the iron railings from their garden walls. They have even taken the iron gates from Silverbeck Manor. The folks in the posh houses behind the church can't say they're the only ones being deprived. They'll have to get wooden gates made, that is if they can get any wood and a joiner to make them.'

'That's no great sacrifice in comparison to the thousands of people in the cities who have lost their homes and everything they possessed,' William said. 'Both Harry and Rick Fortescue told us things were pretty bleak wherever the bombs have been dropped.'

'Aye so I've heard, but they say our planes are bombing the German cities and factories in retaliation. I pity those young pilots taking their lives in their hands every night.'

'Ye're right, Joe. We have a lot to be thankful for in comparison.'

* * *

Marguerite was twenty years old in August 1942. She had two weeks to spend at Bonnybrae with her family after completing her nursing training, and before embarking on the next stage of her life. She had some news to give them but she knew it would not please them, any more than it had pleased Rick when she wrote to tell him in her weekly letter. She had already confided her plans to her Aunts Fiona and Marie and asked them to keep it a secret until she had broken the news to her parents and her beloved grandparents.

She had not expected Rick to wangle a four day pass and drive overnight all the way to Scotland but Rick was desperate to see her. He could not wait for letters to make his arrangements so he had managed to sneak out from the buildings where he worked in the strictest secrecy and found a telephone kiosk. He phoned Marie to ask if he could beg three night's accommodation with her.

'Of course you can stay with us, Rick. It will be lovely to see you, but I'm sure Rina would have been happy to give you a bed too so you could be closer to Marguerite.'

'I'm not sure Marguerite's father would welcome me though,' Rick said ruefully. 'I get the impression he does not approve of me as a prospective husband for his only daughter. He seems to think I'm an upper class good for nothing gentleman, but war is a great leveller of class — even if I did consider myself a gentleman and I don't. Grandfather Fortescue approves of Marguerite. He has given me the engagement ring he bought for my grandmother. It may be a bit old fashioned now but I think Marguerite will like it if she will agree to us being engaged.'

'Oh Rick, I know she loves you and I'm sure she will agree. I have heard her say how difficult it is to convince some of the young soldiers that she is already attached if they are persistent when she is travelling up to Scotland on the crowded trains. It will be easier if she is wearing an engagement ring.'

Marie was sure there would be good reason for a celebration after hearing of Rick's plans and in spite of the rationing she secretly planned a family gathering with a decent meal. She suspected Jamie would be a lot more willing to see his daughter engaged than he would be to hear of her plans to travel to France to help nurse wounded soldiers, especially now Marguerite had learned to drive an ambulance while working at the hospital. There was no telling what risks she might need to take. She had always been intelligent but the past few years and her work as a nurse had made her into a responsible and skilled young woman with a mind of her own and a fierce determination to do what she felt was right.

Marguerite was Emma and William's eldest grandchild and they had adored her bright eyes and big smile from the first time they had seen her as a toddler. She had stayed with them at Moorend so often they loved her as they loved each of their own children and their hearts were heavy and filled with anxiety when they heard she intended to go to France to nurse the soldiers.

Jamie did his best to hide his own dismay. In his heart Marguerite would always be his little girl and they all knew how dangerous working in France would be. He could only pray she would return to them safely. His own distress made him feel a deal of sympathy for Rick Fortescue now. He forgot his earlier bias against the fine young man in his army uniform. It seemed trivial to have opposed him because he was the grandson of Lord Hanley and would one day inherit an estate and belong to a class far above an ordinary farmer's daughter. Rick's love for Marguerite was obviously deep and sincere, and surely that was what mattered in this troubled world where no one could look to the future with certainty. Jamie remembered how hard he had found it to wait for Rina, and how he had feared for her safety when she was surrounded by disease at the Fever Hospital where she worked. Surely the danger from enemy bombs and guns was far worse? He and Rina did their best to find comfort together, holding each other close each night and praying for their daughter's safe keeping. They knew well that Marguerite had inherited their own determination to do what she considered right, but it did not calm their fears and they felt sympathy for Rick.

Marie made a splendid meal for all the family in celebration of the young couple's engagement and everyone admired the emerald and diamond ring which had belonged to Lady Hanley. All too soon Rick had to return to report to his superiors in London and Marguerite found it difficult to keep up her own spirits when he left. She knew now what love entailed and it was not only the passionate response she felt whenever they clung together, their bodies quivering and alive with desire. It was only his mother's pleas to Rick to cherish and protect Marguerite which kept him from making love on the last evening they had together.

'It is frustrating to think that I am still in Britain and yet I cannot give you an address where you can write to me direct my love,' he lamented. 'Not only that, but it cools a man's passion and his words of love, knowing every word he writes is censored.'

'I do understand, Rick,' Marguerite murmured against his warm neck as she clung to him in a final embrace. 'Fiona feels the same about the letters she and Harry exchange, but we do understand how dangerous it is for any information, however innocent and harmless it may seem, to leak to the enemy. Even at the hospital there were posters reminding us that careless words could cost lives.'

'It is true, my darling. Even the place where I work is never discussed.'

'Then we must store up our love until we can be together for ever,' Marguerite whispered, her voice trembling as she struggled to hold back her tears and wave bravely as the train carried Rick away.

Marguerite had promised to spend her last day in Britain at Moorend with her grandparents, arriving the previous night and leaving early on her last morning to catch the early train to London to join two nursing friends and a regiment of soldiers on their way to France. Rick had told his mother of her plans and that Marguerite would only be there for one full day, so Lord Hanley had ridden to Moorend two days earlier to persuade Emma and William to come to lunch at Silverbeck Manor and bring Marguerite with them.

'I have a feeling Lord Hanley wants to talk with her,' Emma said to William later that evening. 'I couldn't very well refuse without being uncooperative but I hope he doesn't upset her.'

'I don't think he will do that,' William answered with a frown. 'In any case we shall be there to protect her if he starts telling her it is her duty to consider Rick first, or something. I wish she was not going to France myself, and I know you feel the same, Emma, but we must accept her decision. The lassie matters more to us even than our landlord so we shall support her whatever he might say.'

As it happened it proved to be a very pleasant and informal lunch in a small room almost next to the kitchens at Silverbeck Manor.

'We're down to the minimum of staff like everyone else,' Lord Hanley explained, 'and cook is not so young to be carrying meals to the dining room.'

'This is much more to our liking,' William declared.

'And friendlier too,' Emma added with relief.

When the meal was almost over except for the coffee Thea turned to Marguerite.

'I know Britain seems to be in a very bad state with the German navy being more powerful than our government had expected and with their aircraft wreaking havoc with the lives of so many people, leaving them homeless and children without parents, even so Rick insists none of us should consider the possibility of defeat. He says we must come through, and we shall, though he believes it would help if we could have more support from America. Anyway he is looking to the future with great optimism and he is determined the two of you will be married the moment the war is over.'

'Yes, I know,' Marguerite said with a faint smile, and fingered the lovely engagement ring he had given her. 'We have to believe that we shall win. I have to believe it anyway. I can't bear to think how sure I was when I refused to marry Rick before he went away but . . .'

'I understand my dear,' Thea said gently and put her hand over Marguerite's where it lay on the table toying with her coffee spoon. 'Rick explained that you didn't want to live here at the Manor with us when he would be away all the time . . .'

'Oh but it was not that I didn't want to live with you!' Marguerite exclaimed in dismay, her cheeks colouring. 'I wouldn't mind if Rick and I had to live in a tiny flat or a rundown cottage so long as we can be together and fill it with love and make it a home. Living in the grandest palace without each other could never make it a happy home.'

'I know that my dear,' Thea said gently, 'and I think you were right to ask Rick to wait until the war is over and you can be together. I'm sure when that time comes you will agree it was worth waiting. Meanwhile I admire your spirit of independence and your determination to do a worthwhile job.'

'You wouldn't be a Sinclair without that independent spirit and damned Scottish pride,' Lord Hanley intervened with a chuckle and a wink at William. 'Thea and I are pleased Rick has chosen a girl with spirit and consideration for her fellow men and women. We wish you were not going away to France but Rick tells us you have made up your mind and we must not try to influence you so we shall wish you well and we shall not interfere, except to say I have bought you a ticket and booked a seat in first class for your journey to London.'

Emma breathed a sigh of relief and William squeezed her fingers beneath the tablecloth.

'We shall all look to a brighter future,' Thea said with determination, 'so I wanted to show you and your grandmother the west wing. We thought you and Richard would be happy living there as it is completely separate and private, with its own entrance. It does need freshening up in some of the rooms but, quite apart from materials being so scarce just now, I thought you and Richard would enjoy choosing your own colour schemes and furniture together and making it a real home.' She looked anxiously from Emma to Marguerite.

'That is very kind of you,' Emma said. 'I'm sure you're right. I doubt if Marguerite and Rick have thought that far yet, have you dear?' She turned to look at her granddaughter.

'It-it's all so lovely in here like a proper home,' Marguerite said huskily, and dashed away a stray tear. 'I-I thought Lord Hanley might expect us all to live together . . .'

'Men don't always understand how badly women need their own place and space,' Thea said with a smile. 'You may have to be firm with Richard over some things my dear. Never be afraid to come to me if you need a woman's point of view and support. I may be his mother but I know he is not perfect.'

'I-I am so glad you understand. You see already Rick assumes that we shall be married here at Silverbeck Manor but I know my father is expecting to make a wedding for me because I am his only daughter. I would hate to hurt my parents and my father already thinks I shall be marrying above my station. He plans to invite all our friends and relations and he says he will ask Lord Tannahill if we can hire Stavondale Manor. That is where my mother lived when she was a girl. Lord Tannahill bought it and his shooting parties stay there but he hires it out for functions sometimes. When he is in Scotland he lives in a separate wing, where my great grandfather used to live. Mother says it is much cosier and more like a home.'

'That all sounds splendid and something for all of us to look forward to,' Thea agreed. 'If only we can win this dreadful war.' Emma thought she sounded sad and guessed she was thinking of the price Rick's father and herself had paid in the last war, as well as his brother and thousands of other young men. What a waste war is but we all cherish our own country. Why did that man Hitler want to rule the world when all he causes is grief and devastation?

You're looking very solemn, Granny. Do you think it is wrong for Dad to insist on making a wedding for me?'

'No, no not at all, my child. He will want to walk you down the aisle himself, but he is also a proud man and he would not want anyone else to organize or pay for your wedding. You understand that don't you, Mrs Whitelea?'

'I do indeed and you will have my support, Marguerite. The main thing is for you to take care of yourself and come back safely. It would break Richard's heart if he lost you now.'

* * *

Although they had enjoyed a lovely lunch, and in spite of the rationing, Emma made a splendid meal that evening for all the family who could come to Moorend. To save petrol, which had gone up in price to one and eleven pence halfpenny, as well as being rationed, Meg and Ranald collected Janet and Brian and squeezed in Fiona on the way through the village. Alan and Lynn had opted to walk up to Moorend and David was still living there, although his time was spent between Moorend and Mountcliffe Hill and occasionally with Alan because he had somehow become the chief tractor driver for all their considerable acres. He knew his ploughed furrows were not as straight and neat as his father and Steve made with the horses and plough but with so many extra acres to turn speed was required.

Two days before Marguerite's visit Mrs Ramshaw had visited Moorend and taken Doris away. The atmosphere felt as though a cloud had been lifted when there were no more of her sullen scowls and sly manoeuvres to avoid work. Even

Eve remarked that harmony had been restored and she and Jean began to chat together more freely. Certainly, Jean was beginning to look much happier and Emma told the supervisor she felt they would manage with only one land girl so long as she could keep Eve, her maid, who already worked outside with the cows, young calves and poultry, as well as inside. The arrangement suited Mrs Ramshaw well. She confided that she had been more concerned about placing Jean, the girl being so small for the work of a land girl. William was in at the time and he chuckled.

'My wife was never very big but she never let anything beat her either. She has done more work than most women, as well as rearing a family. Jean has a willing spirit and a determination not to be beaten. She will do fine.'

'It pleases me to hear you say so, Mr Sinclair. Jean has had a lot to bear in her young life. Her home was one of the first to be bombed and she lost both her parents and her young brother. Her only relative is her father's elder brother who has been in the navy all his life and she has no idea where he is or even if he is still surviving.'

'That's so sad,' Emma said, 'but I am glad you told us. Now we shall understand why she doesn't ask for time off to visit her family. She will stay with us at Christmas, as Eve does. After all, the work still has to be done wherever there are animals needing care.'

# CHAPTER SIXTEEN

Marguerite was left in no doubt when she arrived in France that her work was required and worth the horrible journey. Nurses were in short supply with so many wounded men. It was hard to share Rick's optimism that Britain was bound to win this dreadful war with the noise of guns and shelling, tanks constantly on the move and ambulances bringing in more wounded day and night. Most of her new colleagues had taken to calling her Rita, saying it was easier to call for her than Marguerite and because she was already able to drive she was often called to drive an ambulance when wounded men were in desperate need, sometimes close to the front. None of this appeared in her letters home, or to Rick. She wrote cheerfully of the countryside and her new friends and a few of her patients. Sometimes badly wounded soldiers asked her to write a letter home for them, and twice she was asked to read his letters, and to reply, by a young man who had been blinded. He yearned for the company of family he knew and loved and whose faces he could picture.

There was little opportunity of getting sufficient leave to travel home to Scotland but twice in the two years she was in France Marguerite and Rick managed to snatch a brief time together in London. Each minute spent together was precious. Time was so short and meetings so rare. Their memories were a treasure to store and be relived when they were apart. Marguerite was aware of Thea's warnings and Rick's illegitimate birth due to his father's death in the last war but their love was precious and their longing to be together overcame all boundaries. They were young and passionately in love and the world was an uncertain place with air raids and bombing, submarines, guns, death and destruction. They had bonded together as children and they knew they belonged together for whatever remained of their lives. Rick made love to Marguerite with a tenderness impossible to resist. Indeed, Marguerite had no thoughts of resisting and she responded with a passion which carried them both to a world of their own, beyond wars and greed and suffering.

Towards the end of 1943 a new medicine called penicillin became more available for treating sepsis. Nursing conditions were often rudimentary and patients with severe wounds frequently became delirious, especially if they had had to wait for treatment. The result was often amputation of an affected limb, and even death. The first time Marguerite witnessed the improvement in a delirious, badly wounded soldier, she wrote home to her mother. 'The improvement was incredible. It made me believe miracles can happen sometimes after all.'

Early in 1944 Marguerite fell on a slippery path in the dark. She broke her wrist and badly sprained her ankle. It was snowing and by the time she had dragged herself to shelter she was wet and shivering with cold. She developed a high temperature as well as her injuries so it was decided to send her back to Britain along with three badly wounded soldiers who would benefit from her calming presence during the journey. A letter was waiting for her from Aunt Marie to say Mark was due to travel home on leave and he would meet her at the hospital in London and drive her home to Scotland to recuperate. The doctors ordered her to stay there until her injuries had healed and she had completely recovered from the feverish chill. Marguerite had known she was not fit to make the long train journey alone so she was overjoyed by this arrangement and she said a silent prayer for the care and love of her family.

While Marguerite was recovering at Bonnybrae her mother's old friend and nursing colleague, Melissa MacQuade, came to visit. She was now the wife of Dr Frank Meadows and had children of her own but she was also busy with volunteer work. The two old friends exchanged letters regularly so Melissa understood how anxious Marguerite's parents had been when she had insisted on working in France. She also knew they dreaded her returning there, especially now the Germans were bombarding London daily with a hundred or more of their lethal V1 flying bombs, destroying homes and people indiscriminately. Thousands of women and children had been evacuated again and many had already perished or were badly injured. During the frantically busy days in France, working every day with wounded men, Marguerite had been barely aware of the dangers they faced. It was only since she returned home to the relative peace and safety of her beloved countryside that she secretly admitted to her own qualms. She was not looking forward to the tedious journey back to France. When she received an unexpected letter from Dr Meadows she considered it more seriously than she would have done previously. He wrote encouragingly.

> *Your nursing skills would be invaluable to those who have been returned to Britain to recover. You have shared their experiences and you understand many have lost limbs or sight, sometimes both. Others need time and peaceful surroundings to recover from mental scars which are equally severe but cannot be seen. Melissa, my wife, tells me you have inherited your mother's ready smile, bright eyes and cheerful disposition. Apart from your invaluable nursing experience, yours is exactly the sort of personality which would give most help and encouragement to many of our war weary souls.*
>
> *Some large country houses have been opened up as hospitals and convalescent homes for wounded servicemen but*

*they are in need of skilled nurses to supervise the volunteers. Since you have worked with these men in France I know you must have had the courage to deal with some horrific sights without flinching. Such qualities are still needed here. Melissa tells me you are familiar with amputated limbs and helping men on the first steps to rehabilitation. Your help would be greatly appreciated if you would consider living in one of the country houses and probably having to improvise with some of the medicines and nursing equipment.*

*Please write and let me know your thoughts. If you are willing to help with this essential work I will pass on your name and address to one of the organizers.*

Marguerite gave the letter serious consideration for a day and a night before she showed it to her mother and father. Surprisingly it was her father who could not hide his relief at the prospect of his beloved daughter remaining in Scotland. As usual her mother agreed with him and added her support. James and Rina were not the only ones who were relieved to hear Marguerite would not be returning to work in France, nor anywhere in the south east of England where the flying bombs were worst. Rick made his feelings clear.

'*I have been so afraid for your safety, my darling,*' he wrote. '*I can't wait to make you my wife, even though we cannot be together until this cruel war is won.*' As usual he gave little detail regarding his own work but Marguerite knew he often needed to attend meetings in London and she fretted and wondered how safe he was from the dreadful flying bombs.

Although she derived a lot of satisfaction from her work with the wounded servicemen, despite the improvisations necessary in a temporary hospital, she shared Rick's yearning to make their union official, blessed in the eyes of the church and God and their parents, especially now that any meetings they might manage would be in familiar surroundings with either her own family or Rick's. Most women under forty, married or single, had been called up to do war work in some form or other so she knew that being married would not prevent her from continuing her work as a nurse until the war finished and Rick was free to make a home where they could be together.

In November 1944 over a million men and women who were in the Home Guard were disbanded and Rick's friends and family began to believe his prediction that the end of the war was in sight, at least in Europe, although there was still serious conflict in Asia. Consequently Marguerite agreed they should be married at the beginning of December 1944 even though they would be unable to snatch more than a long weekend together. They were young and optimistic; they dreamed of a future with the rest of their lives to catch up on their happiness. Marguerite wrote to tell her parents they planned to marry.

> *I am sorry if this will put a terrible strain on you but we only need a very small wedding and I know now how badly the food supplies have been affected. I am growing attached to many of my patients. Most of them are long term and we get to know them as individual personalities and share their hopes and fears. Since Rick and I cannot be together I would like to spend Christmas with them and help them celebrate as much as possible.*

*'Don't worry about anything, my dearest girl,'* Rina replied.

> *Your father and I will be happy to know you and Rick are happily married. As far as the food is concerned we have all been hoarding coupons and supplies of dried fruit whenever we can get them. Granny Sinclair has offered to make a wedding cake and bring it up with her. All the members of your father's family have offered to help in any way they can. Fiona has taken up sewing and, with Granny Sinclair's guidance, she has offered to make some simple white dresses for your young cousins to be bridesmaids. Mark managed to obtain a quantity of silk, from a parachute, I think. She suggests adding a little colour with a velvet sash and bows down the front of the bodice. She will try to get whatever colour you suggest.*

Marguerite was more than due some time off, so she decided to travel home after her afternoon shift ended and have a full day with her family to discuss the wedding preparations. She was relieved that both her parents seemed happy to accept Rick as their son-in-law, even though it meant she would be moving down to Yorkshire to live eventually. She mentioned this to her father when he met her off the train at Strathlinn late in the evening.

'Aye, lassie, I didna like the idea of you going down there to live, nor did I feel happy about you marrying the son of the laird but it seems there are no borders where love is concerned. Anyway war makes us all get things into perspective. Rick is a fine young man and your mother and I have plenty of family down there to visit, so you can be sure you will see plenty of us, especially now your brothers are growing into responsible men and able to share the responsibility of Bonnybrae.'

'Oh Dad, I'm so happy to know you have accepted Rick. Neither he nor his mother ever act or talk like gentry. They are sincere, ordinary people.' James patted her hands where they lay in her lap and gave his familiar smile.

The following morning Marguerite was up early and discussion of wedding preparations began over the breakfast table with both Liam and Reggie rolling their eyes and making a quick exit back to work as soon as they had eaten up.

'Your father has arranged with Lord Tannahill to hold the wedding reception at Stavondale Tower. He is very generous and he and Lord Hanley seem to be friends because he has invited Rick's mother and grandfather to stay with him in his private quarters.'

'Yes, Rick said something about that, but he says he prefers to stay with Marie and Mark and the children for the night before the wedding.'

'Fiona wrote to say she has made a start on the bridesmaid's dresses.'

'That's an awful lot of sewing. Meg, Janet, Lynn, Helen and Marie all have young daughters now.'

'Everyone is ready for a celebration and a little happiness and we all think they will look lovely. The two youngest will be flower girls really but Meg's daughter, Belle, is a lovely girl and very sensible so she will keep an eye on them. Marie is much the same size as you and she still has her wedding dress stored in tissue paper. She says you can have it if you want. Dear Aunt Maggie has offered to alter it to fit you exactly. Or if you want a dress of your own she says she would make one if we can get enough suitable material. Some of the curtain material is quite nice,' Rina added doubtfully. 'You can have my veil. It belonged to my grandmother and it is lovely lace.'

'I hadn't thought of all the preparations,' Marguerite confessed. 'Aunt Maggie's eyesight is not so good now so I don't want to put her to too much bother. I would like to borrow Aunt Marie's dress anyway when she has offered. Everybody is being so kind and generous to me.'

'Yes, they are all lovely. Every one of the Sinclairs put my mother to shame' Rina said. 'She is the only relative I have and I don't even know whether she is alive or dead.'

'Never mind, Mama,' Marguerite said, using her childhood name for her mother. 'At least you and Dad have each other and I know how much he adores you. I hope Rick and I will be as happy all our lives as you two.'

'I'm sure you will, my love. We had a letter from Rick's mother, Thea Whitelea, asking if she could do anything to help with the wedding. She has obtained some pale blue woollen material if you would like it. It is enough to make you a going away dress and three-quarter jacket and she says Granny Sinclair and Fiona have offered to make it between them if you send your measurements. What do you think? She is also sending some ration coupons to buy tinned fruit or any other wee luxuries that are available. I'm sure she would like to help so perhaps you should accept her offer and include her in all our plans, poor lady.'

'I will. She is very nice, Mum. You will like her. Sometimes she looks a little sad but she has not had the happiest of lives herself and I know she will be very relieved when Rick is finished with the war and safely back home.'

'I know exactly how she feels,' Rina said with feeling. 'Your father and I felt the same about you while you were in France. Liam and Reggie were very concerned too, although they bend over backwards to pretend they are tough, uncaring young men.'

* * *

At Moorend David was surprised when he received a letter from Rick asking him to be his best man. It was true the two had been friends since they were at Silverbeck School together and Rick had always come to Moorend whenever he was home but both David and his father thought Lord Hanley's grandson would want some titled young man for his best man.

'I suppose you should be honoured to be asked,' Emma said. 'Rick has always called to see you whenever he is home. He always says this is his second home but I thought that was his way of saying thanks for a good tea.'

'Whatever the reason I don't think I can go when the wedding is in Scotland and you will both be away, although it would have been nice to meet all our Scottish relations. It will cost Jamie a pretty penny but he seems to be doing his best to invite them all in spite of rationing and things.

'I think Jamie and Rina will be inviting the aunts and uncles to please Jim, Maggie and Joe. After all they have been so good to them and they are like grandparents to Marguerite.'

'Alan can't get away either but Lynn is going with Fiona and taking the children. Harry can't get leave at that time.'

The following day Mike Watt called at Moorend and as usual he came in with William, David and Jean for some tea before starting the milking. The subject of the wedding came up.

'I hope Rick and his grandfather will not be offended with me for refusing to be best man,' David sighed, 'but it's not possible for all three of us to be away. That would only leave Steve and Jean to do everything. Steve hasn't got the hang of using the milking machine yet and Jean can't do it all on her own. Anyway December is a busy time with all the cattle inside, needing to be fed, mucked and bedded. That takes a long time without the milking to do as well.'

'I've been wanting an opportunity to have a go at milking with that new-fangled milking machine you've got,' Mike said. 'If you'll let me come and join you four or five mornings to get the hang of it, and if I get on all right, I'd be happy to come and stay two nights here and help with the milking while you are all away.'

'Hey, Mike,' William chuckled, 'have you forgotten we start milking long before it's daylight. You'll never be out of bed at that time.'

'Ah, but I can be up early when I have a reason and it will be good for me to know what is involved with these machines for milking cows. One of the tenants wants us to pay for installing the vacuum lines because he says it is fixed equipment. If we agree to do that Lord Hanley says we shall need to give you and Alan an extra year's rent at the present rate in lieu because you paid for your own installations. Anyway, if I come in the mornings I shall not be missing my own work. Of course I shall tell Lord Hanley and I know he will not mind me taking two days holiday while you are away. He will be in Scotland anyway but I will look in at the estate office to make sure everything is in order every day.'

So it was arranged and David promised to be Rick's best man.

* * *

All of Jamie's uncles and aunts accepted the wedding invitations. Maggie, Joe and Uncle Jim were delighted their own generation would be so well represented. They were all getting older and hadn't seen each other so often since the outbreak of war. Everyone seemed to welcome a celebration to relieve the dreary days of war. All the relatives were farmers so several offered a joint of lamb, ham or chickens towards the meal to eke out rabbits, pheasant and any other game available. They all preserved fruits and jams which they were happy to contribute and they were diligent gardeners so there was no shortage of vegetables. Lord Tannahill had always had a tender spot for Catherina Capel, as she had been before her marriage to Jamie Sinclair, and he instructed McGill, his farm manager, to supply fresh cream for desserts, and some extra butter and take them to Mrs Scott, who had become the chief caterer at Stavondale Tower. Lord Hanley had volunteered to provide a sufficient quantity of wines and other drinks.

Although it was a cold December day the sun shone brilliantly. The path to the small village church was flanked with tenants from the Stavondale Estate, which now belonged to Mark and was efficiently managed by Marie during her husband's absence. They were proud of the erect figure of their landlord in his smart RAF uniform and they were all eager to offer their good wishes to the happy young couple. Most of them had known Marguerite since she was a small girl riding her pony around the estate with her Aunt Marie and they were proud of her courage in volunteering to go to France to nurse the wounded servicemen. The older tenants also remembered her mother when she was Catherina Capel riding round the farms with her grandfather, the old laird. They cheered warmly at the sight of her when she arrived to shepherd the retinue of lovely young bridesmaids into the church vestibule out of the breeze.

Thea had brought a white fur cape for Marguerite to keep her warm before and after the church service. It had been her own when she attended balls. It was beautiful and very cosy. Lord Tannahill was a generous man, especially considering the wedding was not really his concern. He ordered hot mulled wine from the Stavondale kitchens to be served to those waiting outside the church to see the bride and groom before and after the wedding service. In fact, he enjoyed joining in the happiness of the day and refused to take payment for the hire of the Stavondale Tower function facilities, including Mrs Scott and her team's catering services.

There were cheers and sighs of delight, and even a stray tear or two, when the smiling bride and her groom, handsome in his dress uniform, emerged into the winter sunlight after the service.

The reception was a joyous affair with everyone in good spirits. When the various toasts and speeches had been made there was surprise when Robin Sinclair rose to his feet. Jim and Maggie were the eldest of his generation so he had consulted them first about his suggestion to propose an extra toast. They had eagerly agreed. He tapped on the table for a minute more of silence.

'We are all proud and happy to be here today to join in wishing happiness and good health to the courageous young couple but if you will bear with me for one more tribute I would like to offer the sincere congratulations of the Sinclair and Greig families to our youngest brother, William, and his devoted wife, Emma. They have never asked for help and they have both worked hard to make a success of their lives in Yorkshire. They have reared a fine family, a family they can be proud of, as we can see today.' William's eyes widened and Emma blushed, especially when Lord Hanley cheered loudly and called 'Here, here'. Robin smiled then went on. 'It seems to me, with so many fine sons and daughters, and now the marriage of their first delightful granddaughter, there will soon be as much Sinclair blood in Yorkshire as there is here in Scotland.'

Everyone raised their glasses to William and Emma and cheered loudly.

# CHAPTER SEVENTEEN

Marguerite and Rick were supremely happy and had made the most of their brief five-day honeymoon but it was nothing compared to their joy when peace was declared the following May in 1945. Marguerite had said a tearful goodbye to the men she had nursed but she travelled down to Yorkshire with love in her heart to make a home for herself and Rick in the private wing of Silverbeck Hall. Rick had arrived earlier the same day and they met at the railway station. Everyone smiled at his ecstatic embrace as he lifted her off her feet and swung her round until they were both gasping for breath.

Mike Watt had predicted a budding romance between Jean Jackson, the shy young land girl, and David, the only single member of the Sinclair family now remaining. Jean had no relatives as far as she was aware. She had tried to make contact with her uncle but she did not know if he was still alive. Consequently, the pair opted for a quiet wedding. Mike told Lord Hanley this bit of news when he informed him he had arranged for the old farmhouse at Beckside to be improved and a bathroom installed ready for David and Jean to make their home there.

Since the village and his tenants had been deprived of his grandson's wedding Lord Hanley decided a celebration was called for to welcome home Rick and his bride and what better occasion than a wedding to bring joy to the whole community. He called at Moorend to tell David and Jean of his grand plan. He would pay for the celebrations which would be held at Silverbeck Hall. All the tenants were to be invited as well as the village, including the dozen evacuee families who were gradually being accepted by the locals and were now living in the cluster of prefabricated houses which had been erected at the far end of the village in the small paddock behind the church.

Jean was overwhelmed and very nervous about the whole affair but Emma assured her they would all support her. Fiona was deliriously happy to have Harry home for good and she and David had always been close in age and in friendship and she liked Jean. She offered to make her a wedding dress of her very own. Janet offered to lend her veil. Fiona also accepted Jean's request to be her matron of honour. Both David and Jean decided his young nieces should be bridesmaids since all the other arrangements seemed to have been taken out of their hands. The girls already had the dresses they had worn at Marguerite's wedding so they were delighted. Lord Hanley was pleased when he realised David and Jean were entering wholeheartedly into the celebration and he brushed aside their gratitude. Secretly he had done his best to make enquiries regarding Jean's uncle but he had had no success. Many men had died without trace during the war, especially those in the navy or air force. So on Saturday the second of June the whole of Silverbeck and district had a day to remember with joy, from the youngest to the oldest, and even those who had lost loved ones during the dark days of war. Most of them had known David all his life and many knew Jean had suffered more than most before she found a home and family with the Sinclairs at Moorend.

At the small farmhouse belonging to Beckside, which was now part of Mountcliffe Hill Farm Lord Hanley had decided to build on a large kitchen with an extra bedroom, as well as the bathroom Mike Watt had promised but the supply of materials of all kinds were still restricted and likely to remain so for some time, so progress was slow. David and Jean didn't mind. They were happier than either had dared to believe possible and they were content with Jean painting the woodwork and papering or distempering the walls, while David did minor repairs to the doors and windows and erected shelves where they would be most useful whenever he could obtain suitable wood. An elderly couple they barely knew, who had moved into the new prefabs, offered them a large bed with carved solid oak ends, explaining it was too big and clumsy for their small bedroom. The bed ends were heavy but by the time Jean had washed and polished it the wood gleamed beautifully and they managed to buy a new utility mattress to fit on top of the well sprung base. When they told the old couple how pleased they were the old man said the new utility furniture suited them better in their cosy little home and they would be grateful if David could take away the matching wardrobe and dressing table which were presently cluttering their living room. Fiona and Harry contributed two comfortable armchairs because the School House was quite large and fully furnished.

'Harry has agreed I can make that small room into my sewing room if you will take the chairs,' Fiona said. 'There is a small table and bookcase too if you want them.'

'We're grateful for all contributions, aren't we sweetheart?' David responded with a grin. 'We made a big rug last winter at Moorend. Mother showed us how to do it and we all had a go, even Dad sometimes. We thought it was for Moorend kitchen but Mother has donated it to us since we did most of the work. I reckon everybody but us knew we were meant for each other.' He exchanged a happy smile with his young wife.

Both David and Jean still went up to Moorend every morning and evening to help with the milking and feeding of the cows and calves. When David heard of a second-hand bike to sell he borrowed his father's van and drove to the next village to have a look. The frame was for a lady's bike but he bought it anyway and managed to buy two new wheels. It was almost like new by the time he finished and it suited

Jean well because she was small anyway. When Marguerite heard David was looking out for a bicycle for himself she mentioned it to one of the ex-servicemen who was at the convalescent home where she was working part-time as a volunteer nurse. He was very depressed because he had recently had the lower part of his leg amputated.

'Even if they fix me up with a wooden leg I shall never be able to ride my bike again,' he lamented. 'When they let me go home I shall sell it.'

'What will you do with the money?' Marguerite asked by way of making conversation.

'Maybe I shall buy a dog. At least that would be company.'

'Do you like animals?' Marguerite asked curiously.

'Oh yes. I love dogs. We always had a dog when I was young.'

Marguerite lost no time in writing a short letter to David to tell him he and her patient might be able to do a deal and she thought the prospect of having a dog might cheer up her patient and speed up his recovery. She never called David 'Uncle' because he had only been seven when she was born and Fiona had been four.

Again, David borrowed his father's van and he and Jean drove up to Silverbeck Hall to visit Marguerite and Rick. He had with him one of his favourite collies, which he kept for breeding, and also a small bitch with a slight limp.

'She was the runt of the litter and I had difficulty birthing her. She is healthy enough now and she has a lovely nature. She will make a good pet for somebody, but she will never make a first class sheep dog.'

'Then why don't we take her for the patient to see?' Rick asked enthusiastically. 'Now? Tonight I mean.'

'Oh . . . but I don't know what Matron will say,' Marguerite said doubtfully. 'They will soon be getting everyone ready for bed.'

'To hell with that,' Rick said cheerfully. 'Come on David, we'll go. It might be the very thing to cheer the man.' In the end Marguerite smilingly shook her head at her husband and they all drove to the convalescent home several miles away. Matron was indeed doubtful about any of her patients having visitors at that time in the evening but eventually she wheeled the young soldier out to what she called the garden room. David brought in the two collies and the delight on the young man's face was worth twice as much effort and persuasion. Even Matron agreed it was better than a tonic.

'Sister Fortescue told me she had a relative who breeds the best dogs,' Tim Gray said, 'b-but if I can sell my bicycle would I be able to afford a dog from you?' he asked doubtfully.

'Her name is Petal, but we call her Pet,' David said. 'Jean named her because she is born to be a pet rather than a working dog, but she has all the intelligence of her forebears. I'm certain you will be able to train her to do all sorts of things for you, like fetching you the newspaper.'

'She brings David's slippers already,' Jean said. 'I shall miss her terribly.'

'Do you think I could afford her when I sell my bicycle?' Tim looked up at David.

'If I know she is going to a good home where she will be fed and exercised . . .'

'And loved,' Jean added.

'And loved,' David repeated with a smile at his wife and gave her a hug. 'You can have her as a gift in return for the great sacrifices you have made for all of us.'

'Really?' Tim asked incredulously. There was a sheen of tears in his eyes and he bent and hugged the little dog.

'I would still like to buy your bike though. I need one and I will give you a fair price. You will need money to buy feed for Petal if you decide to give her a home.'

'I would love that more than anything else in this bloody awful world,' Tim exclaimed, then, 'I'm sorry Sister. I didn't mean to swear.' Marguerite smiled at him.

'You're forgiven Tim. Do you think you might be keener now to have a new leg fitted and learn to walk on it a bit instead of using your crutches everywhere?'

'Oh yes. I have good reason to try now. And my father loves dogs. He will take her for walks until I get going myself.'

Matron came to collect him then. She nodded at Marguerite. 'It is obviously what he needs,' she said with a smile.

David suggested a price for the bicycle which Tim considered was too much, especially as he was getting Petal too. David got the address where Tim's parents lived so he could collect the bicycle soon and he promised to keep Petal until Tim was well enough to go home.

'That is truly a good deed you have done today, David,' Marguerite told him with a grin. 'No amount of medicine or persuasion or treats could shake Tim out of his despair. I'll bet he'll not be long now before he gets well enough to go home.'

'He was reluctant to let Petal go,' Jean said. 'He couldn't stop fondling her velvety ears and she loved it.'

Three or four times in the weeks that followed Marguerite drove Tim to visit David and Jean and he spent ages getting to know Petal.

'It is good for them both to know each other before Petal goes away from here,' Jean said. 'I'm afraid I have spoiled her a bit with her being weak as a puppy and then her being lame.'

'That doesn't bother Tim. He says they will suit each other when neither of them are perfect.'

One day when David was working all day at Moorend he took Petal with him and Marguerite drove Tim to Moorend to see the little dog there. Although the weather had turned chilly he spent the whole afternoon with her, even using his crutches to go around the garden, teaching her simple tricks and throwing a ball, or hiding a piece of wood.'

'I'm getting better at using my leg now and it's not so sore,' he told Emma. 'Soon I hope I shall manage with a stick and the doc says I can go home for a trial weekend.'

While he was outside Marguerite flopped into a chair beside the fire and tried to smother a yawn. Emma eyed her granddaughter shrewdly.

'Am I right in thinking you and Rick will be making us great-grandparents before long my dear?' she asked with a warm smile.

'Oh Granny! No one else knows yet, except for Rick of course. We have not even told Mother and Dad, or Rick's mother.'

'Are you keeping well, Marguerite?'

'Oh yes. I felt a bit nauseous in the mornings at first but that is passing now. The baby is not due until April. Mother and Father are leaving the boys in charge for once and they're coming down to stay for a few days for our first wedding anniversary so we thought we would wait until then to tell everyone. Will you keep it a secret?'

'Of course I will, lassie, if that is what you want?'

'It is really. My parents are so far away and I don't want them to worry, but it will be lovely to know I can talk to you now you have guessed. I'm so excited. I have learned to knit and I am making wee jackets and bootees in white and yellow. We don't mind whether it is a boy or a girl.'

'In that case I shall crochet some white woollen blankets for a pram, and maybe I could sew a pram cover and matching pillow cover for later. You'll not mind if I tell Grandad will you? William and I have never had secrets from each other and he is sure to ask what I'm making if he sees me crocheting.'

'Oh I'm so glad you've guessed, Granny. I'm so excited. Will you teach me to crochet sometime please? I shall be giving up working at the convalescent home at the end of December. I think Matron is suspicious but she has not said anything.'

'Rick's grandfather will be absolutely delighted when you tell him. There was a period after his wife died when he was quite down in spirits, believing he was the last of his line after losing both his sons in the last war. He didn't know he had a grandson then but he has had a new zest for life since Rick and his mother came to live at Silverbeck.'

'It is not long until December and we shall share our good news then.'

'Yes, and all the tenants of the estate will rejoice with you. The war is over and a new generation is beginning. We can all look forward to a brighter future. I thank God for that.'

**THE END**

## THE JOFFE BOOKS STORY

We began in 2014 when Jasper agreed to publish his mum's much-rejected romance novel and it became a bestseller.

Since then we've grown into the largest independent publisher in the UK. We're extremely proud to publish some of the very best writers in the world, including Joy Ellis, Faith Martin, Caro Ramsay, Helen Forrester, Simon Brett and Robert Goddard. Everyone at Joffe Books loves reading and we never forget that it all begins with the magic of an author telling a story.

We are proud to publish talented first-time authors, as well as established writers whose books we love introducing to a new generation of readers.

We have been shortlisted for Independent Publisher of the Year at the British Book Awards three times, in 2020, 2021 and 2022, and for the Diversity and Inclusivity Award at the Independent Publishing Awards in 2022.

We built this company with your help, and we love to hear from you, so please email us about absolutely anything bookish at feedback@joffebooks.com

If you want to receive free books every Friday and hear about all our new releases, join our mailing list: www.joffebooks.com/contact

And when you tell your friends about us, just remember: it's pronounced Joffe as in coffee or toffee!

**ALSO BY GWEN KIRKWOOD**

**THE MAXWELL FAMILY QUARTET**
Book 1: AN ORPHAN OF SCOTLAND
Book 2: THE SECRETS THAT BIND US
Book 3: DREAMS OF THE VALLEY
Book 4: SOMEWHERE TO CALL HOME

**THE SINCLAIR FAMILY SAGAS**
Book 1: MOORLAND MIST
Book 2: MOOREND FARM
Book 3: RETURN TO BONNYBRAE
Book 4: A SCOTTISH DESTINY
Book 5: LOVE HAS NO BORDERS

Printed in Great Britain
by Amazon

26614783R00142